# THE MOVING STONE

## Jacqueline Beard

The Lawrence Harpham Mysteries are published by Dornica Press

The author can be contacted on her website
https://jacquelinebeardwriter.com/

While there, why not sign up for her FREE newsletter.

ISBN: 1-83-829550-X

ISBN: 978-1-83-829550-9

First Printing 2021

Dornica Press

Also, by this author:

Lawrence Harpham Murder Mysteries:

The Fressingfield Witch
The Ripper Deception
The Scole Confession
The Felsham Affair

Novels:

Vote for Murder

Short Stories:

The Montpellier Mystery

## Morse Family Swaffham

| Name | Date of Birth | Date of Death | |
|------|---------------|---------------|---|
| John | 1787 | August 1830 | |
| Ann | 1792 | July 1830 | (nee Howes) |
| Arthur | 1814 | Sep 1856 | |
| Ella | 1815 | Sep 1852 | |
| Caroline | 1817 | Sep 1835 | |
| Marian | 1818 | Dec 1843 | |
| Jane | 1819 | Jul 1860 | |
| Margaret Anna | 1821 | Dec 1903 | |
| Isabella | 1823 | Oct 1880 | |
| Henry Porston | 1825 | Aug 1853 | |
| Herbert | 1826 | Aug 1858 | |
| Philip | 1828 | Sep 1836 | |
| Anne | 1830 | Nov 1831 | |

## The West Ham Vanishings – Missing/Murdered

| Name | Death Date | Location | Event | Outcome |
|------|-----------|----------|-------|---------|
| Eliza Carter | Jan 1881 | West Ham | Vanished | Not found |
| Mary Seward | Apr 1882 | West Ham | Vanished | Not found |
| Susan Luxton | May 1882 | Stratford | Kidnapped | Survived |
| Amelia Jeffs | Jan 1890 | West Ham | Murdered | Strangled |
| Ms Kerridge | Feb 1890 | Walthamstow | Assaulted | Survived |
| Annie West | Dec 1892 | Walthamstow | Murdered | Unknown |
| Elizabeth Skinner | Jul 1893 | Walthamstow | Assaulted | Survived |
| Florrie Rolph | Jul 1895 | Walthamstow | Murdered | Strangled |
| William Barratt | Sep 1897 | Upton Park | Murdered | Strangled |
| Mary Jane Voller | Jan 1899 | Barking | Murdered | Stabbed |
| Bertha Russ | Mar 1899 | Little Ilford | Murdered | Suffocated |

# PROLOGUE

### Monday, May 15, 1882

"Well, I never." The man leaned forward and peered at the smudged print of the newspaper, which he'd hastily acquired from the newsstand on Stratford Road. He smoothed the pages with calloused hands and looked again as if the words might have changed in the intervening moments. They had not. *Disappearance from West Ham* screamed the headline. They were bold words implying an important story, yet sandwiched between two trivial articles: one, a recommendation to increase the magistrate's clerk's salary and the other about chicken thievery. He had almost overlooked the story. It wasn't as if disappearances in West Ham were uncommon. There had been several, and the situation was getting worse. But it was a matter of knowing what to believe.

Several years previously, two girls had vanished – simply vanished into the ether, as if whisked away by fairies. They had never returned, and after two years of fruitless searching, the chances were that they never would. But the newspaper reporting was getting out of hand. Anyone absent from their workplace or having left home without notifying their kin was in danger of being the subject of rash assumptions by the press. Indeed, a local reporter had written about a certain Miss Sophia Marsh, maiden lady and elderly spinster of the parish who'd gone missing back in April. Recently located, the newsman, no doubt with his tail between his legs, was now writing about her in less hysterical terms. Sergeant Sewell of K division had tracked her down to Wellesley Road, Leytonstone which she had rented, telling no one of her plans. "Eccentric", they had said in the article with an unsubtle reference to an unhinged mind. It was easier to pass comment on her sanity, he supposed, and imply that she was a dotty old lady than backtrack on the initial panicky account. Still, it was entertaining reading, although the article that followed was not.

The man glanced at the wall clock and gulped a cup of tepid tea. He'd better finish the paper quickly as he was due on site soon and had been late the previous day. Old man Riley had no tolerance for poor timekeeping. He had no patience for anything, come to think of it, and had fired Gal Martin the week before for taking home a roll of dog-eared wallpaper. The mice had nibbled it in the storeroom, rendering its condition too poor to use on a new property. Riley had high standards for a builder and would have ripped it off the wall in a heartbeat. But that wasn't a good enough reason for him to tolerate workers removing things without asking. It could have been me, the man thought, remembering when he had 'borrowed' a couple of planks and the dregs of a tin of white paint from the last empty house Riley had built. There but for the grace of God...

He turned again to the second paragraph of the article that had caught his eye. *Another disappearance of a singular kind is also reported from West Ham concerning a little girl named Susan Luxton. The six-year-old girl is the daughter of a railway mechanic living in Victoria Terrace, West Ham Lane.* The man was familiar with the grubby little terrace – slum houses, poorly built and in need of attention that they would never get. He wouldn't board a dog there, much less a child. He didn't know the family and had never heard of the girl, but that wasn't the point. According to the article, little Susan Luxton had gone to Station Street with a friend last Monday afternoon. That would be the eighth of May, he thought, counting on his fingers. Yes, he nodded – definitely Monday the eighth. On reaching Station Street, her playmate's mother had told Susan to go straight home, but she'd never arrived. At six o'clock on Monday evening, Susan had turned up alone in Ludgate Circus, where a police officer found her. The little girl, bewildered and shaken, remembered nothing of her ordeal. Having questioned her, the police concluded she'd been drugged in Stratford and removed to London while insensible. It was a fair assumption. Susan was too young to have walked from Stratford to the city in two hours. She was not a strong child, and it was beyond her capability.

The man smiled and stretched his legs as a feeling of satisfaction enveloped him. He revelled in the article and the subsequent realisation that he knew something nobody else was aware of. He'd been there and now realised that he'd witnessed an act never meant for public consumption. It gratified him sensuously, like the first time his mother had asked him to slaughter a chicken. He'd been dreading wringing its neck, but the sensation was surprisingly pleasant.

The Susan Luxton article had triggered a memory. The man had been working a few streets away from Stratford station on the Monday in question and had seen two little girls strolling together hand in hand. And less than a quarter of an hour later, while walking home, he had seen one of them again. This time she was with a woman – a woman he knew and who lived nearby. He had watched the woman offer the girl a drink and thought nothing of it at the time. He'd assumed the sleepy girl was a grandchild. How was he to know the woman was up to no good? Perhaps it hadn't been Susan Luxton. He might simply have witnessed a kindly act from an old lady to a well-loved child. But the sketch of the girl in the article was identical to the child he had seen. It was too much of a coincidence to ignore. But what was he to do about it? A responsible man would tell the police. He would march up to West Ham Lane police station, demand to see the officer in charge of K division, and perform his civic duty. That's what a responsible man would do. But to what gain? There would be nothing in it for the responsible man, who might even fall under suspicion himself. No. Helping the police was not his way, and neither was surrendering an opportunity for profit. Instead, he decided to mull it over, place the newspaper in a drawer for safe-keeping, and go to work.

# CHAPTER 1

## *A Discovery*

***Thursday, February 2, 1899***

*Dear Michael*

*How should I begin this letter? I have tried to write it three times already, and every page has ended up in the fire. I don't know what to say to you or how to explain myself. As much as I enjoyed seeing you again, I cannot help but think it would have been better had our paths not crossed. Our unexpected meeting has complicated matters, Michael, for there is still so much I cannot tell you. It's not that I don't want to, but circumstances prevent it. A situation arose – several situations if I'm honest, that made it easier for me to close the door on my time in Bury Saint Edmunds. And as much as I miss living there, I do not regret my decision. I cannot, for it has forced me into living a life that I thought was beyond my capabilities and may not have risked left to my own devices. My aunt's illness presented me with an impossible dilemma and fortunately provided the means to overcome it. But I digress.*

*I must once again prevail upon you to keep my secret, at least as much of it as you know, most notably, my whereabouts. It is a lot to ask of you, especially as you don't understand why I must remain anonymous to my former friends, but do not tell anybody that we are in contact. I cannot emphasise how important this is, though I know I do not need to labour the point as you have displayed your discretion time and again. Of all the people I could have encountered, I am glad it was you. I miss your friendship, and I am happy to keep up my end of the bargain by writing to you regularly, as promised.*

*But what were the chances of us meeting, Michael? I only decided to watch the wedding at the last minute. The bride was not a particular acquaintance of mine, though I knew she was getting married that day. I woke up early wondering whether to go. But curiosity got the better of me, and I headed to the church to wait for a while. After all, what woman can walk past a glowing bride without lingering to admire her finery? So, I watched until they left the church, chatted to some friends and was turning to go when lo-and-behold, you appeared from nowhere. I had not realised that Edna was marrying a member of the clergy, let alone a man with whom you were acquainted. I would have thought twice, had I known. Please don't take offence – I'm only teasing you, Michael. Now that I have recovered from the shock of seeing you and had time to gather my thoughts, I am pleased to renew our friendship. I would not undo our chance encounter even if I could.*

*I want to tell you how sorry I am for leaving in such a rush, and I hope you understand my shock at seeing you. If I appeared hostile, then I apologise whole-heartedly. You asked a lot of questions which I failed to answer, and I will do my best to remember what you said and address them in this letter. Be warned – it might go on for several pages. Even though some things must remain in confidence, there is still much to tell.*

*How did I end up in Swaffham? Well, that is a long story. As you know, my aunt was ill. She died, and her death threw my life into turmoil, presenting grave difficulties with which I will not trouble you. I miss her so much. We had grown close during the prolonged periods I stayed with her, and I must admit that her death hit me as hard as any I have known. She always said that I would receive a small legacy when she died. Well, her idea of small differed greatly from mine. I was expecting a trinket or at best a piece of furniture, but Aunt Floss left me everything, including her house. Shocked and distressed by her death, I went first to my mother in Norfolk. But being independent and with a pressing need for stability, I could not stay there long, and started to look for a suitable place to live.*

*I soon discovered a property in Swaffham perfectly suited to my needs which was not dissimilar to my home in Bury. You will see from the address on the reverse of this envelope that it is a cottage – a comfortable flint cottage on the south side of Norwich Road. My home overlooks the churchyard giving a pleasant view and a welcome degree of privacy. Talking of which, I must ask you to destroy the envelope as I cannot risk anyone finding me if they catch sight of my address.*

*Now, back to the description of my cottage. It has two bedrooms and a pretty little garden which I tend when I can. But my time comes at a premium for I have found myself a few hours work each day in a tea room. My new occupation might surprise you given the difference between it and my old life in private investigation. True, I am not exercising my brain in the same way, and I miss the cut and thrust of detecting, but I am content to serve tea to the good folk of Swaffham. They have treated me kindly, and although my work can be a little boring, it brings me into daily contact with people, and I have made friends. My routine rarely changes. I walk from my cottage, across the churchyard and to the cafe. It is a pleasant walk and gives me the chance to call in on Norma twice daily while she cares for something very dear to me. Norma has become a close friend, always offering kindness and support. I am content with my new life and never lonely.*

*I hope you are all keeping well, and I trust your brother continues his work with the Freemasons in Bury St Edmunds. No doubt, he is still enamoured with motor vehicles of all kinds. I expect that he still has the Arnold-Benz unless he has succumbed to the lure of a newer model. And Lawrence – I suppose he is enjoying married life and all the delights of London? No, don't answer that. It is better to let sleeping dogs lie, and I beg you not to mention him in your letters.*

*I am delighted that the church finally gave you a living in a parish close to Bury Saint Edmunds. Your friends and family will be pleased to see you so happily settled and within easy reach. It is so good to be in contact again, Michael, but the night is drawing in, and I must close for now.*

*Your affectionate friend,*

*Violet*

# CHAPTER 2

## *Helping Isobel*

***Wednesday, March 1, 1899***

"Dennington Park Road, please." Lawrence Harpham boarded the hansom carriage nervously. He rarely travelled alone by cab since Valentine Jennings had coshed him over the head three years earlier. Lawrence had spent an unpleasant night in his captor's cellar surrounded by rat traps and a dead body, before finally extricating himself from the situation. It had left him wary of solo trips – not so cautious that he wouldn't take them at all, but enough to keep it to the bare minimum. This carriage ride had already brought a surge of traumatic memories – a likely reaction to his imminent meeting with Jennings' former employer, Isabel Smith. It was to her home in Hampstead that the carriage was currently heading.

Lawrence stared from the window and tried to take his mind off the empty seat beside him. The inner door handle was missing, the window was stiff, and it lacked an obvious escape route. But although the carriage was travelling apace, the driver showed no signs of slowing down to lure Lawrence to his doom. Eventually, he relaxed and watched the world go by as he listened to the comforting clip-clop of hooves. Lawrence was almost asleep by the time the carriage drew to a halt outside number thirty-five, Dennington Park Road.

Isabel was waiting inside and waved to him from the first-floor window as he alighted from the carriage. He paid the driver and loitered by the low wall of the handsome, four-storey red-brick building until she appeared. She must have taken the stairs at speed as she was out of breath when she closed the door and hurried towards him, flashing a broad smile.

"Lovely to see you," she said, offering her hand. "Thank you for coming all this way. I can't tell you how much I appreciate it."

"Your letter was a welcome distraction," said Lawrence. "My housekeeper has decamped to Norwich to spend a fortnight with the family of her intended. The thought of trying to manage the office and my domestic affairs alone was enough to send me running to London."

"Good," said Isabel. "Because it might be a waste of your time and, as I explained in my letter, I can't offer to pay you a fee."

"I don't expect one," said Lawrence. "I only take interesting cases these days."

"But you may find it dull or too improbable to bother with. I don't know if it's worth your while – especially as I haven't told you anything about it yet."

"No need. I have faith in your judgement."

"If only that were true," said Isabel. "I still have nightmares about the harm Jennings could have done if you hadn't overpowered him. He seemed like such a nice man. I had no suspicions about his true character."

"It's not your fault," said Lawrence. "I met Jennings several times, and he struck me as a perfectly normal chap. And in my experience, that is usually the case. I have yet to encounter a madman who looks like he belongs in an asylum. They hide it well."

"I thought we could take a walk as it's such a nice day," said Isabel, changing the subject. "There's a pretty little park nearby."

"Of course," said Lawrence. "Being cooped up on a train all day is tiring. I'll be glad to stretch my legs."

"Where are you staying?"

"Nowhere yet," said Lawrence. "I've left my bags at the station. I thought I'd decide once we'd spoken."

They reached the end of the road, walking in silence as they crossed over the railway tracks. "There it is," said Isabel. "I come here when I need to escape. My lodgings are very comfortable, but it's nice to get away from people sometimes."

"I'm not surprised, with your job," said Lawrence. "You see the worst of humanity. Is this case something to do with the council?"

"Partly," said Isabel. "Although it doesn't concern my department. Shall we sit while we talk?" She pointed to a wooden bench beside a large pond.

"That looks like a nice peaceful spot," said Lawrence. "I can imagine you relaxing here and trying to cast off the day's woes."

Isabel nodded. "How well you know me. I come here often. I was sitting here when I first contemplated contacting you."

"About the disappearances you mentioned?"

"Yes. It's troubling. Lots of girls are missing, but very little is being done about it."

"By the police, you mean?"

"Yes. The constabulary has spent years trying to get answers. They say they have followed every clue, but without success. And I can't help feeling that there are more missing girls than the newspapers have reported."

"Start at the beginning," said Lawrence. "Who is missing?"

"It's not that simple," said Isabel. "Two girls disappeared over a decade ago, and I doubt their parents will ever see them again. But it's not only the vanishings but the murders that worry me most. Many girls have died, and I fear poor Bertha may be one of them."

"Who is Bertha?"

"A poor little child recently snatched from the streets."

"Can't Richard help?" asked Lawrence, remembering the charismatic police sergeant from North Woolwich.

"No," said Isabel, sadly. "They transferred him to another department two years ago."

"That's a pity. Tell me what you can about the vanishings."

"As I said, it happened a long time ago," said Isabel. "In the early eighties. Two girls went missing from West Ham never to appear again. Then eight years later, it happened again. This time they found the girl, stuffed into a cupboard in the bedroom of a locked, newly-built property. Someone had strangled her."

Lawrence stroked his chin. "Two different crimes and two different methods. Are you sure they're connected?" he asked, doubtfully.

"I don't know," said Isabel. "But that's not the only problem. There have been other murders around the area, most recently in Walthamstow. And I am concerned because the girls are getting younger. Little Bertha is only six years old, and I fear there will be an unhappy outcome for her parents."

"Undoubtedly," said Lawrence. "I wish I could reassure you otherwise, but it is a fair bet that she's in harm's way. Did Bertha go missing from Walthamstow? It's quite a distance from West Ham."

"I know and I understand your doubts about the location, but my department is well connected. Though West Ham is outside my jurisdiction, we still see the reports and they show distinct similarities. Yes, there are some differences, and that is why the Metropolitan Police are looking at the crimes individually. But in doing so, they are overlooking vital clues. I'd rather not say too much more. Part of the reason I asked you here is to set my mind at rest. If you investigate and don't see a connection between the crimes, then I will accept them as a series of unfortunate coincidences. But I fear somebody is preying on young girls and that all these disappearances are linked."

"I don't know where to start if you've nothing more to tell me," said Lawrence. "I need some information about the girls. Where they lived or went to school at the very least. Better still, a name."

"Samuel Higgins," said Isabel.

"That's not a girl's name."

"It's a reporter's name," said Isabel. "Samuel works for the *Barking Advertiser* and has accumulated a considerable amount of information on the case. I first met him when I visited the police station in West Ham Lane. I'd seen the reports by then and was starting to worry, so I approached K division. I don't know why I bothered. Honestly, Lawrence, they wouldn't give me the time of day. The police usually treat me respectfully given my work with the council, but not this time. They dismissed my concerns out of hand and told me not to interfere. I left feeling angry and on the verge of complaining. But then I met Samuel outside the police station. He was there on a different matter – a news story, I suppose. But he'd heard me speak about the girls and followed me outside. He introduced himself and told me he'd been following the story of the missing and murdered girls for some time. We spoke at length and have kept in touch ever since. Samuel is a resourceful man and an excellent acquirer of information. But he faces certain challenges and can't proceed any further alone. He considered employing the services of a private detective, and after ruminating on it for a while, I thought of you."

"I see," said Lawrence. "I've never colluded with the press before, and frankly I'd rather work alone."

"Samuel is not your average reporter," said Isabel. "He's quietly spoken and highly intelligent. And he has principles. You'll know what I mean when you meet him."

"Well, it can't do any harm to see what he has to say," said Lawrence.

"Then you'll try it?"

"I will."

"You can find him here," said Isabel, passing a slip of paper to Lawrence. "Please let me know what you think. I'll accept your judgement, whatever it may be."

Lawrence opened the paper and read the address. "I'll be off to Barking, then," he said.

# CHAPTER 3

## *Samuel Higgins*

The journey from Hampstead to Barking involved several changes, and an extra stop to collect his luggage from Liverpool Street station where he'd left it earlier. But the press office was due to shut at five o'clock, and Lawrence saw no reason to delay his visit. Isabel had assured him that Samuel Higgins would be there until the end of the day and she had already warned Higgins that Lawrence might make contact.

Once seated in the train, Lawrence reclined in the seat. Ignoring a passenger who opened his mouth as if to strike up a conversation, Lawrence spread open his newspaper and pretended to read it. As his eyes settled over the international news, he considered Isabel's words. The case she had presented seemed disjointed to say the least and the perceived connections made little sense. Frankly, the crimes did not excite him and were it not for his regard for Isabel he would have refused to act. But Isabel Smith was a perceptive woman who had been professionally involved with children for a long time. She knew when to trust her instincts, and if she felt something was awry, then he ought to take her concerns seriously. Isabel had been cooperative when Lawrence needed help, and they had stayed in touch by letter ever since. Though he had not shared his most intimate problems with Isabel, her presence in his life mattered. Being able to tell her a little about Violet had helped him through one of the darkest times in his life. Not the blackest – that had been when he'd lost Catherine and Lily, but recent years without Violet had proved almost as challenging. Meeting Isabel Smith again had dredged up a surge of uncomfortable memories of his time in captivity with Valentine Jennings. But that wasn't the only effect. Deep and powerful recollections of Violet's part in the case had given way to unbearable grief, the like of which he hadn't felt in a long time.

Over three years had passed since Lawrence had last seen Violet Smith, but it seemed like yesterday. He often thought of their last investigation together; still recalled the moment she had walked into their office while he was at his wit's end wondering how to deal with Loveday. Above all, Lawrence remembered her last letter gifting him their business. He'd folded the tear-stained paper in half and put in his wallet. It was still there. Violet had been generous to the end, giving up her stake in their partnership which she had thoroughly earned. The business had a monetary value, yet it didn't stop her walking away. And Violet must have needed the money. She wouldn't have had much in the way of savings, yet she was so desperate to end their acquaintance that she'd left it. Where had Violet gone? Why hadn't she been in touch? He knew he had treated her abominably, but it hadn't felt that way at the time. Not for one moment had Lawrence considered that he might lose Violet altogether, but that's what had happened. Not a word, not a whisper of her whereabouts had emerged since the day she left. He had tried to find her, pestering Michael and Francis relentlessly until they had to be firm. As hard as it was to believe, Violet had abandoned everyone. Annie didn't know where she was, and she'd only given the land agent her solicitor's address. The solicitor refused point-blank to see Lawrence, let alone answer his many letters. In the end, Lawrence had ventured to Cornwall, thinking it would be easy to track Violet down. He knew the village in which her aunt dwelled and after asking around, had found her address. But the aunt was dead, and the house already occupied by new buyers. Finally, in desperation, Lawrence broke into Violet's cottage in Bury, which for some unfathomable reason, had neither sold nor let. Only a few pieces of furniture remained and barely any personal effects. A large vase painted with daisies and a coal scuttle were the only moveable items in the parlour, and a wall clock lay haphazardly in the kitchen window. Upstairs, a picture of a ship hung against daisy patterned wallpaper that Lawrence could not remember seeing before. Violet must have had it freshly papered before she left, suggesting that she went in a hurry. But her rushed exit was the only clue, and it wasn't enough to find her.

There were no leads and probably never would be. He had lost Violet and been careless of her feelings, all for the sake of Loveday Graham who was now Loveday Melcham. Despite their betrothal, she had never become Loveday Harpham. By the time Violet vanished, their affair was almost over. Lawrence had already torpedoed Loveday's expectations of buying a property in Gloucestershire. He had nothing against the Cotswolds – Gloucestershire was a fair county and Cheltenham was one of his favourite towns. But it was too far away from family, friends and his business. Loveday's compromise of settling in London was even worse. Lawrence couldn't bear the thought of taking up permanent residence in the busy metropolis. He'd prevaricated, twisted, turned and railed against it without actually saying no. Then Loveday had discovered his trip to Cornwall looking for Violet. Incandescent with rage, she had written a scathing letter, telling him to buy a property in London by the end of the following month or it was over. Lawrence had ignored the letter, disregarded her instruction and thrown himself into a fresh case. Six weeks later, the postman delivered Loveday's ring in a brown envelope with no covering letter. And the following month, he had opened a copy of *The Times* to see the formal announcement of Loveday's engagement to his old friend Tom Melcham.

It ought to have troubled him. He should have felt at least a pang of regret, but the wave of sadness that he'd expected never materialised. Instead, he felt a profound sense of relief. Loveday's loss did not compare to Violet's absence. Dazzling, beautiful, graceful though she was, Loveday had shared none of Violet's values. Not her loyalty, her wisdom nor her intelligence, and especially not her regard for Lawrence. For like every kind of fool easily swayed by a pretty face, Lawrence realised that Loveday was as selfish as Violet was faithful. He had tossed away diamonds for fool's gold, but that was of no consequence now. Lawrence's recent life lacked a woman's presence. The only exception was his postal friendship with Isabel Smith. He valued her more than she would ever know, and that was why he was willing to throw himself into an investigation for which he cared little. Her goodwill was worth so much more than an inconvenient journey to Essex.

Lawrence arrived at Barking lost in a sea of nostalgic memories, but the sight of the station banished all other thoughts apart from the case at hand. He exited the platform and asked a friendly barrow boy to point him towards The Broadway. Striding out, despite his heavy suitcase, Lawrence located number fifty-seven with relative ease. The press office door had been propped open but not far enough for smooth access. A man in tattered trousers and rolled-up shirtsleeves lugged two heavy packages of newspapers as he forced himself through the door.

"Watch out," spat the man as Lawrence nearly careered into him in his haste to hold the door open to its fullest extent.

"I'm sorry," said Lawrence, "I was only trying to help."

The man sighed and dropped the bundles. "It's too late," he said, massaging deep grooves in his fingers where the string had bitten into his flesh. "Once you pick them up, you've got to keep going. I've told them not to bind so many together, but will they listen? No.

Of course not. But then I'm only a working man and not a la-di-dah writer."

"I'm sorry," repeated Lawrence.

"Where are you going, anyway?" asked the man. "Mr Taylor is out."

"I was hoping to see Mr Higgins," said Lawrence.

"He's here," said the man. "He's always here. He might as well move his bed into that office."

"Well, thank you," said Lawrence.

The man grunted and picked up the bundles again before staggering towards a nearby cart.

The door opened into a dark hallway with two other doors leading off and a large, wooden noticeboard which took up most of the back wall. Inscribed at the top, in large, tiled letters, were the words *Barking, East Ham & Ilford Advertiser, Upton Park & Dagenham Gazette*. Lawrence stared at the two lines of text.

"It's a bit of a mouthful, isn't it?" said a friendly voice.

Lawrence spun around to see a man who appeared on the surface to be too old for employment. A pair of bottle-lensed spectacles incongruously strapped to his head by a belted device, dominated his pinched face. On closer inspection, Lawrence could see why. Most of the man's right ear was missing, and one of the spectacle lenses was black.

"How can I help?" asked the man.

"I'm looking for Samuel Higgins," said Lawrence uncertainly."

"And you have found him." The man smiled and held out his hand.

Lawrence shook it and introduced himself. "I was expecting…" he said, then stopped for fear of offending.

"You were expecting a younger man," said Samuel Higgins, helpfully.

Lawrence nodded. It was a more palatable version of what he had been about to say. No wonder Higgins needed help, ageing and damaged as he was.

"You came after all," Higgins continued. "Isabel wasn't sure, and neither was I."

"I cannot refuse Isabel," said Lawrence.

"What has she told you?"

"Very little and not enough to know whether I can be of practical help."

"I'm sure you can," said Higgins. "Come this way, and we'll talk."

#

The dull, nondescript beige wall in Samuel Higgins' office was no reflection of his character. The ageing reporter was outwardly ebullient, and despite his unusual looks, was not without charisma. His office, on the other hand, was an undisciplined mess. Someone had squashed two desks together and forced another into the impossibly small space below the only window. Bookcases and shelves covered two walls with an array of overflowing pigeonholes crafted expertly around the door recess. In one corner several stacks of newspapers, writing paper, pens and various items of stationery leaned carelessly against the side of a desk. The office looked frantic and disorderly.

This does not bode well, thought Lawrence as he surveyed the scene.

"It's a bit of a mess," said Samuel, perceptively. "I share this office with young Malcolm. He's as keen as mustard and an able reporter, but not so concerned with the discipline of office life. He's untidy, but I gave up that battle a year ago and have accepted his shortcomings. He is first class in all other ways."

"I don't know how you bear it," said Lawrence, thinking of his own tidy office, pristine now that Violet was no longer there to leave muddles.

"As I said, it's not worth the fight. And you will see what I mean when you go through there."

Samuel Higgins pointed to the recessed door hiding in the nest of pigeonholes. "Go ahead," he said, nodding to Lawrence.

Lawrence crossed the office and gingerly opened the door. "Ah," he said, smiling.

"You approve?"

"Oh, yes."

The room into which Lawrence had stepped had once been the press office stationery cupboard. At some stage in the recent past, Samuel Higgins had commandeered it. Daylight struggled through a solitary window at the back of the small room. But Samuel had fitted a pair of gas wall lights in addition to the formerly solitary ceiling lamp, and he ignited them with a spill. As Lawrence's eyes adjusted to the light, he saw a wooden noticeboard peppered with newspaper clippings. The articles, affixed with drawing pins, filled the space above a dark wooden desk and chair. Likenesses of young girls occupied the remaining wall space. A piece of string linked each picture with a written description containing relevant dates and locations.

"This looks like a police incident room," said Lawrence, admiringly.

"As well it might." Samuel crossed his arms and regarded his work with an air of satisfaction. "It took a long time and a lot of research to get this far."

"But why?" asked Lawrence.

"Because, like Isabel, I am gravely concerned about these girls. A series of crimes have dominated the papers over the last twenty years. You would think by now that the police would have done something. But no. Not a sign of the missing girls and not a decent suspect for the murdered ones."

"Why do you think that is?" asked Lawrence, leaning against the wall as he tried to read the intricately looped writing next to a picture marked 'Amelia Jeffs'.

"I don't know," said Higgins. "I mean he's clever – the murderer, that is. He changes his modus operandi often, not to mention the location of the crimes."

"Which would suggest that he wasn't responsible for all of them."

"That is what the police believe, and it is why they cannot find him."

"Him?"

"Oh, yes. The monster violated several of the girls."

Lawrence grimaced. "Isabel said some of the victims were very young. I hope they were not outraged."

"I wish I could give you that assurance," said Higgins, shaking his head. "The man is ruthless, organised and without conscience."

"I'm going to need details," said Lawrence. "Isabel didn't tell me much. She wanted me to judge any connection between the crimes without being prejudiced by her thoughts."

"Very sensible and an example I intend to follow," said Higgins, gesturing to a chair in front of the desk. As Lawrence took a seat, Higgins reached down the side of a wooden cabinet and withdrew a folding stool which he opened and placed next to Lawrence. He sat down heavily, wincing in pain.

"It's my back," he said. "Now, Mr Harpham. I fear I have already told you too much. Isabel is right to be cautious. To avoid influencing your investigation, we must stick to the facts, at least to begin with. I am quite sure that you will form an opinion very soon."

"But you'll start me off with the salient points?" asked Lawrence, removing a notebook from his jacket pocket.

"I'll do more than that," said Higgins. "He reached past Lawrence and heaved open the bottom drawer of the sturdy desk. "This is for you," he said, pointing to a brown paper parcel tied with string.

"What is it?"

"Any spare press cuttings I've acquired about the missing and murdered girls," said Higgins. "It's not comprehensive, but the collection will help you understand what's been happening around here."

"Hmmm. Some light bedtime reading," said Lawrence, placing the large package beneath the chair.

"It will give you nightmares," said Higgins. "Those poor girls..."

"How many crimes are we talking about?"

"At least seven."

"That many?"

"I said at least. There may be more."

"But on reflection, seven deaths in twenty years isn't excessive."

"No. But the manner of their demise and the geography is troubling."

"Tell me about it."

"I'll tell you the bare facts. That will have to do for now."

Lawrence looked at his pocket watch. "I see what you mean. Time is running away with me, and I need to find lodgings."

"Remind me about that before you leave. I'll be able to help." Samuel Higgins slowly inched himself off the stool and got to his feet before placing his index finger on a black and white line drawing of a young girl. "This is Eliza Carter," he said. She was twelve years old when she vanished. She left home to run an errand never to return. And one year later, the same thing happened to Mary Seward." His hand moved towards another drawing.

Lawrence licked his pencil and took notes. "How old was she?"

"Fourteen."

"Was she running errands?"

Higgins nodded.

"Then what happened?"

"Nothing," said Higgins. "It went quiet. The girls vanished never to appear again, and life went on until January 1890, almost nine years to the day that Eliza Carter disappeared."

Lawrence twirled his pencil, waiting for Higgins to continue, but the reporter stared into the distance, lost in thought. Lawrence coughed, and Higgins snapped back to the present.

"Sorry. But it still affects me. I'll never stop wondering how two healthy girls can vanish into the blue. There were no witnesses, no clues, nothing. Those poor parents – endlessly waiting for news that will never come."

"I can only imagine how they felt," said Lawrence. "Losing a child is bad enough, but not to know how or if you will ever see her again..."

"Anyway. Nine years passed, and another girl vanished, but this time they found her. Amelia Jeffs was fourteen years old. Her parents raised the alarm as soon as they missed her. They contacted the police and searched the streets but did not locate her for another two weeks."

"Where was she?"

"Strangled and violated in the upstairs cupboard of a newly-built property close to where she lived."

"I see," said Lawrence, lowering his notepad. "So, the first two girls vanished, and nine years later somebody strangled Amelia Jeffs. There is a logical connection between the first two incidents but no link whatsoever to the third girl. The circumstances are dissimilar and the timing highly unlikely. What man leaves almost a decade between crimes?"

"Indeed," said Higgins. "The timing is a significant flaw in my theory. But there is an important connection between the three events of which you should be aware. Amelia Jeffs was living at number thirty-eight West Road when she died, and Mary Seward dwelled at number ninety-eight West Road. Eliza Carter lived in Church Street, which is not far away and would ruin the connection, but for one thing. Eliza had a married sister who lived at number twenty-five West Road and Eliza slept at her sister's house the night before she died. The last sighting of Eliza Carter was as she delivered laundry to number seventy West Road. Nobody ever saw her again after that."

Lawrence whistled. "Then they all went missing from West Road. I don't believe in coincidences," he said.

"Neither do I," agreed Higgins, scratching the skin beneath the band holding his glasses to his head.

"Were the other girls connected to West Road?"

"Not as far as I know. Apart from the child who vanished from East Ham, the remaining three lived in Walthamstow."

Lawrence opened his mouth to speak.

"I know what you're going to say. Walthamstow is a long way from West Ham."

"Exactly."

"I'll tell you what happened in chronological order. In December 1892, they found Annie West, aged ten, dead in a ditch at Low Hall sewage farm, Walthamstow. Six months later, a man went off with Elizabeth Skinner in full sight of her brother and friends, leaving her for dead in Paddy's Field. That's also in Walthamstow if you are wondering. Her attacker attempted to violate her, and she survived against all the odds. Then, on the last day of December in 1898, they removed the body of poor little Mary Jane Voller, a child of only five, from Loxford Brook."

"Where is that?"

"Not far from Upton Park."

"So closer to West Ham than Walthamstow."

"Indeed." Samuel Higgins nodded enthusiastically.

"It bridges the geographical gap," said Lawrence. "But if not for that murder, it would look like the work of two distinct killers."

"Yes. And only time will tell where the next corpse will turn up."

"I hope you don't mean Bertha Russ?"

"I'm afraid so."

"You don't think they'll find her alive?"

"I'm certain of it. Bertha is already dead. They just haven't found her body yet."

"How can you be sure?"

"This is where I must stop talking," said Higgins. "Inside the envelope on top of the papers is a timeline of the crimes – names, dates, ages, addresses. Everything you need is there. Take your time and see what conclusions you come to and be sure to let me know. Isabel values your opinion, and that is good enough for me."

"But you have discovered so much already," said Lawrence. "I can't see how I can improve on your research."

"My research hasn't got us anywhere," said Higgins. "And if we don't put a stop to it now, how many other girls will die?"

"It sounds like you need more than an opinion," said Lawrence.

"Exactly." Higgins uncrossed his legs and gestured to the right-hand desk drawer. "In there, are all the newspaper reports I haven't had the time to check. It's quite a number, and there could be more unconnected crimes than those we have discussed. That's my task for the next week. As for you, please read everything you can. If you

25

come to the same conclusion, then start investigating the crimes as you would have done if you'd taken the case at the outset. The police have missed too many clues already. And that is not only my opinion. The inquest reports contain detailed accounts of the inadequacy of the investigations to date."

"But why me?" asked Lawrence. "I've only a cursory knowledge of West Ham and I didn't know the girls. There must be much better qualified local private detectives who could pursue the investigation."

"I don't think so. The crimes have been going on for so long that the police have become jaded. They have forgotten the parents' grief and the pitifully brief lives of the victims. And even though they acknowledge their mistakes, the Metropolitan Police won't collaborate. In short, they don't listen. And I fear private investigators would be the same. You know what it's like when you visit somewhere for the first time. You don't have to look hard to see the surrounding beauty. But the grand buildings and exquisite gardens in the town in which you live, don't warrant a second thought. In other words, everyone here is too close to the killings now. We need a fresh pair of eyes."

"Except you," said Lawrence. "You haven't become complacent."

"No. But I am not getting any younger, and I lack the physical strength to deal with this myself. If you choose to help us, you will need to visit the murder scenes, talk to witnesses and make a nuisance of yourself. Those days are behind me now if I was ever capable of such things."

Lawrence took the envelope and removed the paper summarising the deaths. He scrutinised the page and after a few moments, looked at Samuel Higgins. "I wouldn't agree to this case but for Isabel," he said. "Yet parts of it are compelling, and a particular fact bothers me enough to make an immediate start. I will find lodgings tonight and read through your notes. If I agree that there is something worthy of pursuit, then I will begin in earnest tomorrow."

"Excellent," said Samuel beaming. "And what is it about the case that bothers you, if I may ask?"

"The seven-and-a-half-year gap between Mary Seward's disappearance and Amelia Jeffs' murder."

"Exactly." Samuel crossed his arms and regarded Lawrence with a Cheshire cat-like expression. "In that case, I am sure I will see you again soon."

# CHAPTER 4

## *Introducing Ella Morse*

*Thursday, February 9, 1899*

*Dear Michael*

*Thank you for your letter, and I am sorry to hear that you have been suffering from influenza. All week in bed without fresh air or company must be lonely and made tolerable only by the amount of reading you say you have managed while confined. I too have read stories by Charles Dickens, but I find his tales rather depressing and cannot think they will help your mood. I am pleased you are feeling better. You must eat plenty now that food is palatable again. You can ill afford to lose weight.*

*I have had a strange week, Michael, reminiscent of my last month in Fressingfield. But I will start at the beginning and tell you all about it. You will have plenty of time to indulge me in reading what will probably turn into something of an epistle.*

*As you know, my little cottage is on one side of the churchyard which I cross every morning on my way to the tea room where I work. Well, yesterday was Monday. I don't work at the weekend and left for the tea room with a spring in my step, eager to spend time in adult company after a few days at home. On the way, I popped in to see Norma as usual, but as I closed her gate and walked away from her cottage, I had the strangest feeling that someone was following me. I held my umbrella firmly in my hand for the greying sky was a mass of dark clouds, and rain threatened at any moment. But even though I wanted to rush onwards, I could not. The feeling of eyes upon me, boring into my back, caused me to seek an excuse to stop and turn around without it being obvious. I surreptitiously dropped my umbrella, and as I knelt to recover it, I peered behind. Nobody was there, Michael. Nobody. So, I proceeded up the path and towards the church, my senses still alive to the possibility of a presence that I could feel but not see. I cannot adequately describe how keenly I sensed it. My imagination must have been running riot. I felt as if the hidden stranger was about to plunge a knife straight into my spine at any moment. I don't know what has got into me, Michael. I have never been fanciful, not even as a child.*

*As I reached the side of the church, my eye fell upon a stone cross, set askew from the other gravestones in that row. But it was not so much the stone itself as the item that had fallen upon it. At first, I wasn't sure what it was, but as I advanced towards it, the dreadful truth caused me to gasp out loud. The unwanted visitor was a dead bird – a crow. Can you believe it? My thoughts naturally turned to that awful day in Fressingfield when you and Lawrence found the trunk full of decomposing crows. For a fleeting moment, I wondered if Hannah Roper had escaped from gaol. But she is now in an asylum and will never see the light of day again. I can only suppose that the position of the crow was a random act of nature. But I don't like coincidences and, as Lawrence often said, I don't believe in them.*

*I hastened to work and tried to put the matter from my mind to no avail. I could not concentrate at all that day and dropped a large china basin on the floor. But I rallied, and when I returned home later, I made a point of examining the cross on the way through the churchyard. The sexton must have tidied the stone for the crow had vanished, and not a mark remained, not even a feather. But the inscription on the grave was fresh and clear. It read, 'Ella Morse, September 8, 1852, aged 37, By thy Cross and Passion, By thy precious death, God deliver us.' Thirty-seven is no age to be in the ground. I have already lived longer than she ever did.*

*I can't say why, but her stone intrigues me. It stands out, being a cross among tombstones and out of kilter in the row. I have little with which to occupy myself in the late evenings and will try to find out something about Miss Morse if anyone remembers her after all this time. The local brewery bears the name of Morse, so that might be a good place to begin.*

*A day has passed since I started this letter, and it is now eight o'clock on Tuesday evening. I avoided the churchyard on the way to the tea room this morning, but not on the way back. It is too foolish. I will not deviate from my daily routine because of a dead crow and a strange feeling of fogginess in my head as if I were dreaming.*

*But I have wittered on enough and have selfishly failed to ask your news. Who is preaching sermons in your absence? And who is looking after your domestic affairs? Is there a servant to prepare your food while you are unwell? I am sure there must be someone to minister to your needs, but you have never mentioned it – hardly surprising after all these years with no contact. Please tell me everything about your situation in your next letter to make up for my self-indulgence in this one. I must close now and will post this on my way to work tomorrow.*

*Yours ever*

*Violet*

# CHAPTER 5

## *Digs in Buxton Road*

*Thursday, March 2, 1899*

Lawrence woke to the sound of a door slamming, then peered at his pocket watch and curled into the warmth of his blanket. His bedroom was colder than usual, and six o'clock was too early to be rising if it wasn't strictly necessary. He slid back into a peaceful slumber, and the next time he checked his timepiece, a chink of light heralded mid-morning. He cocked his head and listened as an unfamiliar noise intruded from outside, hearing the chatter of children's voices followed by a hissed reprimand from a woman pleading for quiet.

Children? Why were children in his house? Lawrence sat up and rubbed his eyes, then stared at his hands. They were filthy with newsprint, and he was lying in an unfamiliar bed next to a copy of

*The Illustrated Police News*. His notebook lay crushed beneath his elbow, and something was jabbing into his back. Lawrence reached behind and recovered a pencil as recollections of the previous evening flooded back.

He had left Barking with a bundle of newspapers and his suitcase, then caught a cab to fifty-five Buxton Road. Samuel Higgins had obligingly given him a shortlist of lodging houses ranging from small hotels to room shares. Lawrence had settled on a home at the edge of Forest Gate occupied by a family, no doubt trying to eke an extra income by letting out a bedroom. Though the room was far from comfortable, the location was ideal for his needs, being close to a railway station, and only a short walk from West Ham. Lawrence could have stayed in a grander location, but decided he was more likely to gain the trust of the local people if he lived among them.

He had knocked on the door while the family were eating their evening meal. The room was still available, and a man with a northern accent had welcomed him inside and introduced himself as James Aslin Ward. His wife had insisted that Lawrence must join them for dinner and had served him with a hearty bowl of stew while Mr Ward took his bags upstairs. Agnes Ward had asked his trade just as her husband returned to the dining room. Having also carried the bundle of newspapers upstairs, James Ward immediately assumed that Lawrence was in the newspaper trade, guessing his occupation as a printer's compositor. Lawrence smiled, pleased at the notion. A connection to the newspaper industry suited him well, and he didn't want to lie to the pleasant young couple but Lawrence would have to ask questions in the course of his investigation. With this in mind, he guided the conversation towards a more active role in the print office. Without Lawrence misleading them, the Wards concluded he was a reporter. Lawrence studied them as they speculated about his employment. Hearing no objection to a pressman in their home, he allowed them to accept it as a matter of fact. Being a reporter was the perfect way to amass information without suspicion. The easy subterfuge left him eager to begin the case.

Three of the Ward children played nearby during the evening meal while Agnes Ward balanced her one-year-old on her lap while they ate. For young children, they were tolerably well behaved. And although Lawrence might have thought twice about taking the room if he'd known there were so many youngsters in the house, their presence was not disruptive. The children were as quiet as was reasonably possible and he could talk to the Wards without interruption.

Loathe as he was to engage in excessive small talk after a long day, Lawrence politely enquired about his hosts. James Aslin Ward was an iron moulder at the local foundry in Canning Town. The work, he said, was hard and laborious but it provided a steady wage for the young family. The arrival of their fourth child, little Mabel, had stretched the family's finances. Reluctantly they had rented out the back bedroom. So far, their lodgers had proved amiable, and it was a small price to pay for a more comfortable existence.

Lawrence had mopped the rest of his stew from the bowl with a large slice of bread and butter, then politely took his leave. He'd retired to the bedroom and looked through the papers. But after a day of travelling, a meeting with Isabel and another with Samuel, his concentration had lapsed. His eyes had grown heavy and his head lolled back. He'd forced himself to get up and undressed intending to continue reading in bed in his pyjamas, but it was not to be. Lawrence fell asleep without completing his ablutions with a newspaper still clutched in his hands. It had been a long day.

All this flashed through Lawrence's mind as he orientated himself ready for the day ahead. As he rose from the bed, his stomach growled. No wonder. It was after nine o'clock and well past breakfast time. Lawrence inwardly groaned with embarrassment as he contemplated presenting himself at the table at this late hour. He rose, washed and dressed, then having neglected to do so the previous evening, he unpacked. After scribbling a quick letter to Michael, he finally made his way downstairs, well after nine thirty.

Lawrence peered into the dining room, expecting to find it cleared. To his relief, the table still contained a single knife and fork and a glass of water. He turned as a voice greeted him.

"Good morning, Mr Harpham. What would you like for breakfast?"

Agnes Ward stood in the doorway with the baby on her hip and her little boy toddling beside her.

"Anything," said Lawrence. "I hope my late start hasn't been inconvenient," he continued.

"Not at all," said Agnes. "The baby's sleepy. If you give me a moment to put her down, I'll bring you something."

"Before I forget, can you point me towards the nearest post box?"

"I can, but I'm going past it later. Leave your letter on the table, and I'll take it for you."

Agnes left the room, and Lawrence read through his notes as he waited. They were scant and barely legible, reflecting his fatigue when settling down the previous night.

A heavy rap at the front door roused him from his thoughts, and he waited for Agnes or James Ward to appear. Neither answered the door, and the knocking began again. Ward must be at work, thought Lawrence as he realised Agnes was upstairs settling the baby. Sighing, he decided that the least he could do for this hard-working couple was to help by opening the door. He ventured down the hallway as the third series of raps began. Then Lawrence wrenched open the door to find a wiry man with a greying moustache and a bucket under his arm. The handle of the bucket had come away on one side.

"Who are you?" asked the man.

"A lodger," said Lawrence. "I've taken the back bedroom. And you are?"

"Gilbert Cooper, from number forty-three," he said, waving vaguely down the road. "My bucket's broken."

"Mr Ward is at work," said Lawrence, and I'm not sure his wife can help you."

"Oh, but she can. I borrowed their bucket last time it happened."

"I see. Well, Agnes is busy."

"Hello, Gil," said Agnes cheerily as she descended the stairs. It was the first time Lawrence had seen her child-free. "I see you've met our neighbour," she continued. "And thank you for answering the door. Mabel's asleep and your namesake has joined her," she continued, smiling towards her visitor.

"Dear little chap," said Cooper. "And young James and Agnes?"

"Both at school. Anyway, how can I help?"

"It's broken again." Gil Cooper held the bucket aloft as Lawrence watched, wondering whether to stay put or retreat to the dining room. He was standing uncomfortably between Gilbert Cooper and his host.

"You'll be wanting to borrow ours again, I daresay?" Agnes replied. "Come inside. You're letting all the warm air out. I'm brewing a pot of tea for Mr Harpham. Come and join us while I fetch the bucket."

She stood back, and Lawrence followed her as Gil Cooper squeezed through the door, still carrying the pail.

"Put it down there and go inside." Agnes directed him towards the dining table, took the bucket and proceeded to the kitchen.

Lawrence resumed his seat, and Gil slid into the opposite chair.

"Nice couple," he said, lounging back against the chair with his legs splayed. "Very accommodating, the pair of them. Always ready to help. Hannah and I aren't getting any younger."

"You don't look that old," said Lawrence, struggling to find the correct response.

"Well, we're not old, old," said Gil. "But I'm nearly fifty and no spring chicken, as you'll know yourself."

"I'm still in my forties," spluttered Lawrence, affronted.

"Keep your hair on. I'm only joking." Gil Cooper grinned as pulled a handkerchief from his paint-spattered overalls and loudly blew his nose. "What's your game, anyway?"

"My game?"

"Your occupation. What do you do?"

"I see," said Lawrence. "I'm a reporter."

"What? Fleet Street?"

"No. Nothing so grand. I'm from Suffolk."

"What are you doing down here? Are you lost?"

"No," said Lawrence, searching for a suitable story. "I'm doing a piece on local crime."

"Well, there's plenty of that," said Gilbert. "Why here, though? Doesn't Suffolk have criminals?"

"Many," said Lawrence. "But my editor wants a historical piece set in or near London."

"About gangland crime?"

"Yes, some of that," said Lawrence, feeling out of his depth. He didn't know of any criminal gangs who operated near West Ham although London had plenty. "Gangs like the Wild Boys," said Lawrence, snatching a name he'd once heard from deep in his memory. "That sort of thing, though any murder and mayhem would be of interest, particularly crimes that have happened over the last few decades."

"The Wild Boys were fictional," said Cooper, suspiciously. "Though I know what you mean. There's plenty like them in the East End. But you've come to the right place if you're looking for unsolved crimes."

"So, I believe," said Lawrence "I hear you've had more than a few people go missing in West Ham."

Gilbert nodded. "Quite a number," he said. "Though your pals in the local press have done themselves no favours exaggerating the numbers. Several missing people have turned up never having gone anywhere. Reporters make it up as they go along. Anyway, where do you go to track down old crimes then? Are you going to rub shoulders with the police? Don't get too friendly. They're not trustworthy."

"I won't," said Lawrence. "I've got a lot of information from newspapers already. "But first, I must get to know the area. I'm not familiar with West Ham."

"Tea," said Agnes Ward, as she bustled in with a large tray containing three cups and a plate of toast and bacon.

"That looks good," said Gilbert, eyeing the meal.

"It's not for you," said Agnes. "I'll pour you a cup of tea. I've put the bucket in the hallway, and you can take it with you when you go. James will take yours to the foundry tomorrow and have it welded."

"Appreciated," said Gilbert. "Anyway, how does it feel to have a spy in your midst?" He winked at Lawrence.

"Spy? What do you mean?"

"He's a reporter," said Gilbert.

"He is our paying guest," said Agnes, pursing her lips. "Mind your manners."

"I'm used to it," said Lawrence. "Nobody loves a pressman."

"At least you're not a bluebottle. It could be worse." Gilbert chuckled at his joke, then leaned forward. "Where are you going first?"

Lawrence set his knife and fork down and consulted his notebook. "I'll go to Walthamstow tomorrow," he said. "I daresay I will pay a visit to the police station, for all the good it will do. But first, I'll take a walk to West Road."

"West Road?" Gilbert raised an eyebrow. "Why there?"

"Several of the missing and murdered girls lived there. It seems like a good place to start."

"So, you're more interested in the girls than the gangs?" asked Gilbert. "I should have thought knife crime and larceny would be more interesting to your readers than a couple of missing children. They left the house, and that was that. It doesn't make much of a story."

"I'll take notes anyway," said Lawrence, trying to divert attention away from his real purpose. "My editor will make the final decision."

"Well, if that's your choice, I'll take you there myself," said Cooper. "I can introduce you to one or two of the residents."

"Of course. You used to live near there, didn't you, Gil?" said Agnes, draining the last of her tea.

"Yes – a while ago now and before Hannah got the shop. I pass through often and still see many of the old faces. You wouldn't think

37

so with the number of houses they've built around here. There's a lot of property to rent, and it's cheap too. It's having the park nearby that does it."

"I'll want to see that too," said Lawrence.

"Finish your tea then. I don't have to be at work until midday. I'll take you there now."

# CHAPTER 6

## *The Moving Stone*

*Sunday, February 12, 1899*

*Dear Michael*

*I hope this letter is not an unwelcome surprise, following on so soon from the last. After all these years with no contact, you must be getting fed up with me. But you expressed such kindness in your reply and acknowledged my letter with such haste, that I hope you will not mind. Please don't feel any obligation to reply straight away.*

*I am glad to hear that your illness has passed and that you are back in the pulpit on Sunday, and I am pleased you enjoyed your trip to Netherwood. What a fortunate coincidence that Flora Johns was visiting her uncle when you arrived. Young Bertie must be quite the little boy now. Did you see him? It is a pity that you missed Francis. You said he was abroad, but you didn't mention where. I hope he appreciates your vigilance in keeping an eye on the house. Not that it's essential as his butler is so reliable, but Albert is getting on a bit, and you are not. I am surprised that Albert hasn't retired by now, but he seems happy enough, and with a servant to rely upon, his duties are not onerous. Anyway, I am rambling, Michael, and torn between seeking your advice on a particular matter and embarrassment at mentioning it at all. But I have decided upon the former as I appreciate both your wisdom and discretion.*

*You will remember that I mentioned the gravestone of Ella Morse in my last correspondence. Well, I have enquired into the family and have learned more about her. Ella was the eldest daughter of John and Ann Morse, and her father was a local brewer who operated out of White Hart Lane in Swaffham. Well, his son took over the brewery and ran it for several years and on his untimely death, it passed to his business partner who traded as Morse & Woods. A company in Norwich has only recently acquired the brewery. So, that is the background, and I am sure you will agree that it is not especially exciting.*

*I have continued my twice-daily walk through the churchyard despite my earlier concerns. But some days I have to force myself, Michael, and on one or two occasions have been, quite literally, sick with dread. I cannot account for it. The walk is pleasant, and the church structure easy on the eye. There are no strange gothic features and nothing untoward, at least on the outside. I am rarely wholly alone, and people are usually within sight. But I cannot shake off that feeling that someone is watching me. From the moment I leave Norma's home until I reach the tea room, I am in a constant state of nerves. So much so, that I wonder whether I ought to see the doctor. And what I have learned this week has unnerved me further still.*

*The place in which I work is called The Singing Kettle. It is a small establishment with few employees kept busy serving tea and cakes with little time for anything else. So, the administration and* upkeep of the business fall to Olive, the owner, including all the cleaning. But in January, Olive fell victim to the weather when she slipped on the icy pavements and broke her wrist. She couldn't manage any physical work afterwards. The doctor strapped up her wrist, but it didn't offer enough pain relief to keep up with the chores. The solution presented itself in the form of a charlady by the name of Mrs Brett. Mathilda Brett is my age, but recently widowed and dependent upon the paltry income she earns from her toils. With two young children to support, her life is hard, yet she is of a cheery disposition and eager to share the local gossip. I hope my behaviour won't shock you, Michael. I don't normally encourage hearsay since retiring from private detective work. But I wanted to find out about the Morse family, so I engaged her in conversation and led it towards the Morse brewery. That might seem like an odd place to start an investigation, but I did not want to draw attention to my interest in the family. Finding out about a long-standing Swaffham industry seemed like a sensible and casual starting point. My approach immediately paid dividends. Though resident in the village only since the early eighties, Mathilda knows everything about everyone, inclined as she is, to talk. But unlike most village gossips, she is not only a talker but a listener too and what she told me chilled me to the marrow.

The people of Swaffham speak of a legend – a tale often told about the churchyard, directly concerning the Morse gravestone. You may remember that I said the cross is out of kilter. That is to say, it is more or less lying at a forty-five-degree angle compared to the other stones in the row. But it was not always the case. The stone has moved and not only once, but several times before. The stone began turning several decades ago, and travelled over time, inching around every year until it reached a difference of ninety degrees. The vicar remained unperturbed, assuming that tree roots or subsidence had caused the movement. He couldn't be sure, of course, but he never wavered from thinking it was an act of nature. But the travelling stone caused great upset among the townsfolk. They were superstitious and refused to accept his rational explanation. In the *end, he deemed it wise to reposition the stone, which was not a straightforward task.*

*The base of the monument is square and heavy with a large cross set above. It took several men to complete the job. But finish it they did it, and the cross settled back in line among the other headstones. A few years passed by and nobody thought any more about it, then the vicar appointed a new sexton who was particularly vigilant in his duties. One day, while carrying out his daily tasks, he noticed the stone seemed crooked, and he mentioned it to the vicar. They watched the grave for several months until they were confident that it was on the move again. Not only did they regularly check the stone, but they surveyed the movement to prove it was not a figment of their imagination. And it was not. Their carefully recorded measurements proved it. Under cover of darkness, they repositioned the stone again and kept its travel secret. Except that there is no such thing as a secret in a small town. It so happened that Mathilda's husband Peter was a licenced victualler. One night a labourer who had helped move the stone started talking about it while in his cups. He had consumed a great deal of ale, and the first time he spoke of it, Peter assumed he was telling a tall tale. But when the labourer repeated the story while sober, Peter told Mathilda and it didn't take long for the account to get around town. Since then, they've moved the stone and repositioned it on at least one other occasion, and now it is moving again.*

*Hearing this tale has not diminished my fears of walking through the graveyard. But as I still consider them wholly irrational, I refuse to give in and take the long way around. Yesterday, I returned to Ella's stone and examined it again. Flattened grass at the base of the cross bore evidence of a twisting motion, but when it happened and how long it took, is impossible to deduce.*

*So here is my dilemma, Michael. I was already fearful of the graveyard before learning of this local legend, and there is no doubt that it has preyed upon my mind. Yet, I long to learn more about the tragic Morse family, especially why so many of the Morse children died young. I know there is a mystery here, and for the first time in a long while, I find myself missing the thrill of the chase. My life here is quiet, and I occupy myself only with work and domestic matters. You know me well, Michael – sometimes better than I know myself. What do you think I should do? Walk away or immerse myself in something that does not concern me, for which there is no financial reward, and which could challenge my sanity? But then, abandoning the matter could have an equally detrimental effect.*

*Do you still have easy access to parish records, Michael? I could ask the vicar here, but I have made Swaffham my home and do not wish to involve myself openly in matters that don't concern me. The townsfolk might tolerate nosiness from a long-time resident, but I am a newcomer. Can you find out how many children were born to John and Ann Morse, and whether any of them are still alive? That information would give me a starting point to understand the family better without asking too many questions. Their descendants may still live in Swaffham, and I am sure they would not appreciate indelicate enquiries.*

*I must close now, but before I go, I have not asked you about your sister Ann or young Sidney. Though I have not been in touch these last three years, I still think of them often and would like to know that they are safe and well. Much as it grieves me, please do not send my regards or wishes as I must preserve my anonymity here and it is all too easy to slip up.*

*With best wishes*

*Violet*

# CHAPTER 7

## *West Road*

Lawrence got his wish to see West Ham Park about twenty-five minutes after leaving Buxton Road when Gil Cooper used it as a shortcut to Portway. The park was pleasant as parks go but Lawrence couldn't visit the area he wanted to see for fear of alerting Cooper to his intentions. He would rather have walked to West Road alone but Gilbert Cooper insisted on showing him the route. No doubt the man was trying to be friendly. Lawrence didn't want to offend his hosts' neighbour and tolerated the endless stream of gossip as they walked without comment. Gil Cooper was a jocular man, with a story for every circumstance. His ability to indulge in small talk without requiring a reply left Lawrence almost impressed. Almost, but not entirely. Despite barely having to take part in the conversation, Lawrence would rather have done without it.

Having left the green lawns of the park, they crossed over Portway and soon arrived in West Road. Lawrence was about to thank Cooper and say his goodbyes when the man unexpectedly strode to the front door of number one and hammered loudly.

"What are you doing?" asked Lawrence alarmed.

"Introducing you to William Donaldson," said Gil. "He's lived here for twenty years."

"Right," Lawrence said, feeling uncomfortable. He hadn't planned to speak to anyone unless it happened spontaneously and he was ill-prepared. He half hoped that Donaldson was out, but within moments the door opened, and a bearded man in his late fifties appeared.

"Gilbert. How are you?" he asked, thrusting his hand forward. Lawrence detected a faint Scottish accent.

"Well, my back is still giving me gip, but it could be worse." Gil Cooper smiled ruefully.

"Get that woman of yours to make up a poultice," said Donaldson.

"She has, and it didn't work. Now, I want to introduce you to Mr Harpham. He is a Suffolk reporter and has come here to write a piece on some of our crimes."

"Pleased to meet you." Donaldson offered his hand, and Lawrence shook it firmly. "Why West Ham?"

"I don't know. My editor particularly asked for an article on historical crimes. Perhaps he didn't think ours were interesting enough," quipped Lawrence disingenuously. It seemed to satisfy Donaldson.

"I thought you could help," said Gil Cooper, "as you've lived here for a long time. I've told Mr Harpham about the local happenings, and he's expressed an interest in the missing girls. I expect you can recall the details."

"I suppose so," said Donaldson reluctantly. "What do you want to know?"

"Whatever you can remember at this stage," said Lawrence. "its early days."

"You won't write about me?"

"Of course not. It's the crimes themselves that are important."

"You know the police never solved them?"

"Hence my brief," said Lawrence, "unsolved crimes."

"Come through," said Donaldson. "You too, Gil."

"No. I must go to work later. I'll wander back now."

Donaldson waved a hand in acknowledgement, then directed Lawrence through a door which he expected to lead into a parlour. But as Lawrence entered, he realised its function was utilitarian. A large, mahogany wooden desk dominated the room while wooden cabinets surrounded each side. Several dozen hooks peppered a noticeboard hanging from the wall, most of which contained keys.

"Oh," said Lawrence.

"It's my office," said Donaldson. "I'm a house agent."

"I see. You operate from home?"

"I do. I am fortunate to have ample space to run both my domestic and business affairs."

"I'm sorry to intrude on you," said Lawrence. "I came to look at the area with no intention of troubling anyone. Mr Cooper took the decision out of my hands."

"I'm free at the moment," said William Donaldson. "And Gilbert is an impulsive man. I'm sure he was only trying to help. He's right, you know. I've lived here for a long time, and I can tell you a certain amount about the girls, though I am sure you would get more from the police."

"They have no reason to cooperate with me," said Lawrence, ruefully. "Though the same applies to you, and I am grateful for your willingness to talk."

"What have you heard so far?"

"I know of seven unsolved deaths or disappearances," said Lawrence. "All female – three in West Ham, three in Walthamstow and one in Barking."

Donaldson nodded. "I suspect that there are more than that," he said. "And I am not alone in my thinking. Now, I am not prepared to discuss the Walthamstow crimes. I don't know enough about them. But I'll talk about what happened here. Take a seat."

Lawrence sat, opened his notebook and began to write.

#

"She was a slip of a thing," said William Donaldson. "Eliza Carter, I mean. She was twelve years old when she disappeared, but a pale and underweight girl who could have passed for a child two years her junior. Eliza lived with her parents in Church Street. I never met them, but we all knew the girl because her sister lived in West Road. Number twenty-five, I think it was. Now, who was she married to?"

Donaldson sighed and clicked his fingers as if trying to jog his memory. "Slaughter," he said triumphantly. "John Slaughter. He was a bricklayer and moved away a long time ago. Anyway, young Eliza was staying with the Slaughters the night before she disappeared, as she had so often before. That morning, she took some washing up the road to Mrs Sayer at number seventy, dropped it off and went on her way. Eliza usually took the back way across the common ground. But when they questioned Eliza's sister after the disappearance, she said she didn't see her going that way, so Eliza must have walked up West Road and along Portway near to West Ham Park instead."

"I walked that route today," said Lawrence.

"It's the only way you can go now. The strip of common land is long gone. They've built on it like every other piece of spare ground. I'm only surprised that they haven't demolished the park."

"Isn't that to your advantage?"

"Very much so from a business point of view," said Donaldson, "but I still remember my homeland and the fields and moors of Bannockburn. Sure, I have prospered here, but it is so dense with buildings that I will never acclimatise."

Lawrence nodded sagely, knowing how much he would have regretted following Loveday to London. He had done the right thing in standing his ground.

"But I digress. The last person who saw Eliza spotted her with a woman in a long Ulster and a black bonnet."

"Did they name the woman?" asked Lawrence.

"I couldn't say. The papers were full of rumours and speculation, but I didn't read every article, and it might have passed me by. Anyway, that was that. No more Eliza, although there was some excitement when they found her jacket."

"Why?"

"Well, it was a normal jacket, much like any other. But whoever took Eliza left her coat by the fence close to the corner of West Road. Inside the pocket, were a few crumbs from an arrowroot biscuit."

"There's nothing unusual about that."

"No, but whoever discarded the jacket didn't want it, yet they took the time and trouble to cut off all the buttons."

"Strange," said Lawrence.

"Isn't it? And they never found her, poor little mite. That was the last we heard of her."

"And the other girl?"

"Mary Seward? Yes. An almost identical story so full of coincidences that you won't believe your ears."

"Try me."

"Well, Mary was the youngest daughter of Lewis Seward. They lived at the top of West Road at number ninety-eight and had a married daughter. Guess where she lived?"

"West Road?"

"That's right. Both missing girls had married sisters in West Road. Mary's sister was Sarah Collier, and she married a baker. Surly looking chap if I remember. They lived at number fifty, which is slap bang in the middle of this road. Once again, the girl visited her sister to fetch some linen."

"When?"

"Good lord – my memory isn't that good. About a year later, I would say. But a decade has passed since then, and I can't remember the finer details. Anyway, Mary Seward left home never to be seen again."

"There are too many coincidences creating confusion," said Lawrence "It explains why this crime remains unsolved."

"That's not the half of it," said Donaldson. "The best part of a decade passed. Both the Carters and the Sewards moved away, and we tried to forget all about it. Not easy when every mother and father was fearful of their child leaving the house. But after a few years, it seemed safe again, and life went on as before. Then, one day in January 1890, Millie Jeffs vanished from number thirty-eight."

"West Road?"

Donaldson nodded. "The Jeffs had lived here for about a decade in another house further up the road. They knew both of the missing girls, and when Amelia went out and did not return, Charles Jeffs suspected the worst."

"You're not going to tell me she was visiting a married sister?"

William Donaldson pursed his lips. "Not in this case and try not to be flippant. Millie grew up in this street. She was a quiet, unassuming girl, and we were fond of her."

"I meant no offence," said Lawrence. "But I don't like coincidences, and there are too many here."

"Yes, I can see your concern by the heavily underlined sentences in your notebook – more like a police officer than a reporter."

Lawrence squirmed uncomfortably and changed the subject. "How old was Amelia?"

"Fourteen, going on fifteen," said Donaldson. "She'd left the house to go to the fish shop in Church Street," he continued. "So, I expect she took the same route as the other girls – down West Road and along Portway."

"What makes you so sure?"

"Because she never got as far as the fish shop. She was missing for the best part of two weeks. Then they found her lying dead on the floor in a newly built house at 126 Portway – a house, I might add, that is currently available to rent."

Lawrence shook his head. "It's almost unbelievable," he said.

"And tragic. Someone had strangled the girl with a piece of rope. She was foully outraged and thrust into the cupboard of the main bedroom. Her devastated parents, like the Carters and Sewards before them, moved out of West Road as soon as they could secure another property."

"Were there any suspects?" asked Lawrence.

"Several, notably the watchman and the builder at the property, both of whom were related. Joseph Roberts built the houses, and his father Samuel watched over them. The local children called Samuel 'Old Daddy Watchman,' and it was not a term of endearment, let me tell you. Samuel wasn't unkind, at least not as far as I know, but those houses were still and quiet, the roads incomplete and there was an extreme want of gas lighting. I disliked walking down Portway after dusk, and I'm a grown man. For a child, it must have been terrifying, pitch black and cold and made worse by candlelight shadows. Then, from nowhere, Old Daddy would shuffle past, lantern raised high, barking at them to stay away from the buildings. He must have put the fear of God into those young children. It's a mystery how someone lured Millie into that place under those circumstances, but they did, and the rest is a mystery."

"Lured by whom? Not by Old Daddy Watchman?"

"No. That's not what I meant. The coroner questioned Samuel Roberts at the inquest and found the Roberts family to be a tricky bunch, evasive and contradictory. They closed ranks, that's for sure. I won't try to tell you what subsequently happened to the key belonging to the house where they found Millie. It is almost impossible to recount with any level of accuracy, and the story is so wildly improbable that you would suspect me of making it up. But if you can lay your hands on an old newspaper report, you'd gain a lot from reading it."

"I've got several newspapers," said Lawrence. "I haven't read them yet, but one will inevitably cover the story."

"Make sure you do. Your readers will love it if you can simplify the account."

"And that was the end of the killings as far as a connection to West Road was concerned?"

Donaldson nodded. "Yes. No other crimes have touched us as closely as those three, although the Walthamstow outrages are too similar for comfort. And with Millie ill-used as she was, any comparable crime is of great concern. I've read about so many terrible crimes against children that these days, I avoid newspapers altogether."

"What do you think happened to the missing girls?"

William Donaldson rose from his seat and plucked a key from the hook. "I don't know," he said. "I can't offer you much of an opinion at all. Amelia Jeffs was the object of savage desire, but whether that was the case with the other two girls, I cannot say. But whoever murdered Millie, successfully gained access to a locked building. And if I were the police, I would have looked for people with a legitimate reason to be in an empty property."

"Builders, carpenters, watchmen?"

Donaldson nodded. "Anyone who might have known how to get his hands on the house key. Now, I don't wish to be rude, but I must press on."

Lawrence rose and offered his hand. "Of course. I have taken up far too much of your time. But before I go, did you say that the house on Portway was available to rent?"

"I did."

"Through yourself?"

"Sadly not. Manisier's got it."

"Who?"

"John Manisier. Number twenty-seven. But then, he's cheap, so what do you expect?"

The question was clearly rhetorical, and Lawrence did not reply. Instead, he thanked William Donaldson and made his way back towards Portway.

# CHAPTER 8

## *The Morse Family*

***Thursday, February 16, 1899***

*Dear Michael*

*How can I begin to thank you for your prompt reply and all the useful information that you have sent me? It is so much more than I could have acquired myself. And yes, if it's easy to get copies of the last will and testaments of Ella and Arthur Morse, then please do so. This family intrigue me.*

*I have added your information to my notebook. John and Anne Morse, whose former name is Howes which I now know thanks to your detective work, had eleven children. All but one has passed away. The eldest child was born in 1814 and the youngest arrived in 1830, so it is reasonable to assume that by 1899 most of them would be dead. But I no longer need to make guesses with the benefit of this week's progress. Your notes are invaluable, and together with my visit to the churchyard, I now have more information than I ever thought possible.*

*At the start of the week, I knew nothing about their resting place. But I gave in to my inquisitive nature on Monday and made discreet inquiries about the Morse family to a lady in the tea shop. Elsie is a regular and has lived in Swaffham all her life. She is in her seventies, but sharp as a tack and interested in the church and all its doings. So, I asked her about the graveyard and casually dropped the Morse name into our conversation. I thought she would tell me about Ella's headstone. Instead, she started talking about another part of the church where they'd laid other Morse relatives to rest. Elsie was about to give me more details when the door opened, and a steady stream of customers kept me too busy for further discussion.*

*I did not work on Tuesday and bumped into Elsie again while out shopping. Remembering my interest in the Morse family, she suggested we went for refreshments. Over coffee and cakes, she mentioned a glass window at the east end of the church where I could find a plaque dedicated to Ella Morse. Well, Ella must have held some influence within the town to have a window dedication, not to mention the funds with which to buy it. Had you not told me that her parents both died in 1830, I would have assumed that they were behind the acquisition of the window, but that cannot be the case. Anyway, that is not all that Elsie told me and what she said chilled me to the marrow. She says a manifestation haunts Swaffham churchyard and reports of it are plentiful. The apparition appears in the back garden of a cottage near Northwell Poll and walks towards the churchyard, searching in vain for a headstone. They say the grey figure is that of a woman. Some say it is Ella Morse.*

*Michael, I don't believe in ghosts. I never have, and I never will. And though we could never account for the strange events at Chelmondiston Rectory, I did not consider them the work of the dead. To my mind, it was merely an unresolved investigation that we could have explained in scientific terms if we'd had more time. Yet an irrational part of me is irresistibly drawn to the notion of Ella Morse wandering the churchyard. I can see her in my mind's eye twisting and wrenching her stone trying to draw attention to some undiscovered ill. Giving voice to these thoughts is so unlike me. My rational mind is fighting fanciful ideas, but why? I wonder if I am having a nervous breakdown. Lawrence battled with depression, and I don't suppose he is the only one. Can a nervous complaint come from nowhere for no apparent reason? Or is it my sixth sense warning me to stay away? But I will not.*

*Fear not, Michael. I have broken from this letter to make a pot of tea, and my reason has returned. I will carry on my story and do not pay any attention to my outpourings. Anyway, the next time I crossed the churchyard was yesterday. I heeded Elsie's words and located the graves to which she had directed me. The inscriptions on the stone lay crisp and clear, unmarred by the ravages of time. And having now seen all the Morse children's death dates, either from your research, or my own, I know that the last to die was Isabella in 1880.*

*How clever of you to find her burial record and to have located clergy records relevant to several of the other children. I knew Jane Morse was Ella's sister but had not realised that she married a rector until your letter arrived. As you say, Jane died in 1860 and her brother Herbert, a curate in Emsworth, drowned in 1858. But you may not know that all but one child had already passed on by then. The eldest died aged forty-one and the youngest at not quite a year old. That's ten out of eleven children who died young with both their parents expiring unnaturally early. Only one member of the family still lives, and that is Margaret Ann Morse, who was born in 1821. I would like to seek her out, but I don't know on what pretext to approach her. Perhaps I could feign an interest in the glass window dedicated to her sister. Or tell her I would like to make a history of the brewery. I shall give it some thought. Or if you can think of a better way, then let me know.*

*Your sincere friend*

*Violet*

# CHAPTER 9

## *Amelia Jeffs*

John Manisier had not yet arrived home when Lawrence called by, but Lydia, his well-informed wife, kept a tight diary. Her husband, she said, was already conducting a viewing at 126 Portway later that evening. Lydia appended Lawrence's name into her day journal, saying she felt confident that her husband would show Lawrence the property after. He should present while John was conducting the appointment and make himself known. Lawrence wasn't sure whether it was worth the time or trouble. Visiting a crime scene so long after the event had occurred was unlikely to reveal anything of interest. But it would give him some idea of the visibility from the house, particularly over the park. Though not much to gain, Lawrence had nothing better to do and decided he'd go along anyway. The five-hour gap until the appointment was a long time to kill so he purchased a meat pie from a shop in Church Street and ate it in West Ham Park while he decided his next move. His hands shook as he unwrapped the warm pie. There was a distinct frostiness in the air and Lawrence wished he'd remembered his gloves. But his greatcoat kept him well protected from the elements, and despite chilly hands, Lawrence passed a pleasant half-hour outside. After eating, Lawrence rose and made his way to the corner of the park where he examined the area where they'd found Eliza Carter's coat. He was none the wiser by the time he had finished and left for Buxton Road, having run out of things to do.

On arriving back at number fifty-five, Lawrence slunk upstairs trying not to disturb the Ward family as he was going out again. He shed his coat and spread all the newspapers on the bed before sorting them into date order. Two hours later and having read accounts of the disappearances of Eliza and Mary from several sources, Lawrence finished. He examined his notebook and nodded, pleased with the salient points he had pulled from the reports then closed his notebook and sifted through the papers for 1890. 'Make sure you read about the keys,' William Donaldson had said when he'd told Lawrence about Amelia Jeffs. 'It's too complicated for me to explain.' Well, if Donaldson was right, and the key situation was challenging, it might be worth planning ahead. Lawrence decided to take the newspaper cuttings with him to keep about his person while seeing the house. Samuel Higgins had given Lawrence four individual newspapers relating to Eliza and Mary which were too bulky to stow. Lawrence thought about the practicalities as he checked his timepiece. He hadn't left enough time to examine the reports with any level of accuracy. So, he opened the papers, tore out the relevant articles and shoved them in his jacket pocket. Pausing only to pour a drink from the jug by his bed, Lawrence left the house once again to retrace his steps from earlier.

The lighting outside 126 Portway must have improved considerably in the nine years since Millie Jeff's death. While far from well lit, the gentle glow of a gas lamp close to the house was reassuring. The front room curtains were open, revealing a dim but partially lit interior. Lawrence couldn't see anyone, but he heard the murmur of voices inside and knew he wouldn't have long to wait. Reluctant to intrude, Lawrence loitered on the doorstep for five minutes. When nobody emerged, he retreated to a low wall where he sat for another five. The temperature had dropped by several degrees, and Lawrence shivered as he waited in front of the tall, three-storey house. Though Portway was a major thoroughfare, it was quiet for the time of day and Lawrence shut his eyes and tried to imagine it without gaslighting. The image was unappealing, and he opened his eyes just as the front door swung open, and three people emerged. Lawrence jumped to his feet and extended his hand before announcing himself.

"Wait a moment," said the estate agent curtly before concluding his business with his married clients. All three turned their backs on Lawrence, and he stood uncomfortably listening to a conversation that seemed likely to end in a deal. Fortunately, the male party baulked at the price and though his wife was enthusiastic, said he would need to go away and think about it. After shaking hands, they proceeded up the street, and John Manisier turned to face Lawrence with a sigh.

"Sorry to keep you," he said, without sincerity or warmth. "How can I help?"

"Can I see the house?" asked Lawrence, pointing towards the building. "Your wife said you would be willing to show me around."

"She did, did she? Well, that's good of her when I'm supposed to be conducting a viewing in Geere Road in five minutes. Not possible, I'm afraid."

"Are you sure? I'm very keen to rent, and I can pay you six months in advance."

Manisier bit his lip. "Oh. I see. Can't you wait until tomorrow?"

"No, I can't. Don't worry then. I saw another property with Mr Donaldson earlier. It will have to do."

John Manisier snorted. "If you mean that thing on Stratford Road, then don't. It's damp and full of woodworm."

"It doesn't sound like I have any choice," said Lawrence. "I'm in a hurry."

The land agent bit his lip. "Look. I don't normally do this, but as there's no furniture in the house and I've got to pass it on my way home, I'll let you in and lock up later. Will that do?"

"Perfect," said Lawrence.

"Here are the details," said Manisier, as he handed Lawrence a typewritten document. "If you want it, you must secure it with a deposit. Come and see me tomorrow."

"I will," said Lawrence disingenuously, hoping that he wouldn't have to return to West Road. Any further encounter with the agent would prove awkward.

"Right. I'll be about half an hour."

"Thank you," said Lawrence as he pushed the door open.

#

John Manisier had extinguished the lights making it necessary for Lawrence to resort to his trusty tin. He ignited a candle before locating the gas mantle in the living room where he also found a glass of spills in the hearth. He took one and walked to the gas mantle where he pulled the chain and ignited it. The lamp spluttered into life, revealing a smartly decorated house with a wooden floor and good quality doors and architraves. The composition of the building would usually have been of interest to Lawrence, who was fond of architecture. But not today. His sole reason for being inside the property was to familiarise himself with the scene of Amelia's murder. He reached into his jacket pocket, extracted the clippings and sorted them into date order. Then he sat on the bottom of the stairs and began assimilating the noteworthy points from *The Essex Standard* of 22nd February 1890.

Lawrence shivered as he read the chilling reports about the discovery of Amelia's body. They had found Amelia in the empty house – a house guarded by a watchman, with closed doors and windows and having lain empty for at least three months. Constable Cross had entered the property through an unlocked window at the rear when his approach to the caretaker yielded little assistance. The watchman denied having a key which seemed odd to Lawrence considering it was his raison d'être. Cross had opened the front door and admitted his colleague Detective Sergeant Forth, and together they'd searched the house. They found a penny piece at the foot of the stairs and a brooch on the top landing. Then, filled with trepidation, they'd proceeded to the front bedroom, finding the floor thick with dust and covered in footprints. They immediately noticed marks from the door leading to the window where someone had dragged a large object towards a cupboard. Lawrence lowered the article and imagined how the policemen would have felt as they walked towards the cupboard door. They must have known, must have feared what was inside. Yet they did it anyway. He read on. The men had approached the door, opened it and found Amelia's remains inside. She was lying on the floor with a scarf tied tightly around her neck, her skin marble cold. Lawrence licked his pencil and wrote in his notebook. 'Check patterned flannel scarf, eighteen inches long by four and a half broad belonging to the victim'. Lawrence continued reading the article. Someone had disturbed Amelia's clothing, exposing her left knee and her body showed clear evidence of a violation. The poor young girl had died of suffocation arising from strangulation.

Lawrence shifted his weight, and the stair creaked. It was dark upstairs, the only light coming from the living room mantle and his candle. The house, shrouded in blackness and deathly quiet, was too oppressive for him to read any more about Amelia's savage death with any degree of comfort. The hairs on his neck stood on end as he contemplated her last hours. Lawrence folded the clippings, knowing he must enter the bedroom where Amelia died. But when he thought about moving, his imagination ran riot. The dark void loomed ominously ahead, and his legs would not carry him forward. Pulling himself together, he looked for another candle, something better than the worn-out stub he kept in his tin. A cursory search of the hallway yielded a long beeswax candle which he lit and held aloft as he mounted the stairs. Once on the landing, he headed straight for a pair of wall-mounted candle sconces and lit the conveniently placed tapers. He repeated the same actions on the second floor. Then, taking a deep breath, he entered the top floor bedroom.

Shadows played across the walls as Lawrence proceeded towards the window. He drew the curtains and looked below, relieved at the comforting glow from the outside lamp. Beyond it lay West Ham Park, shadowed and ominous in the distance. Anyone could have lurked there, waiting in the darkness for an opportunity to strike. Had that happened to Amelia? Did a faceless predator hide in the gloom? Was he waiting for Millie or would any young girl have done? Lawrence turned to face the cupboard where the body had lain all those years before. He opened it gingerly, but there was nothing to see. It was only a cupboard, a cold empty space large enough to accommodate the body of a girl, but with no other redeeming features. Leaving the cupboard door ajar, and igniting the wall candle, Lawrence settled on the floor and removed the sheaf of clippings again.

Lawrence had been careless when separating the articles from the rest of the newspaper, and the extract from *Lloyd's Weekly* was now in two pieces. He held them together and squinted, trying to line up the sentences. The house, it appeared, had been accessible without a key only because of an unlocked rear window. In the coroner's opinion, someone had admitted the deceased through the front door. Dr De Grogono, the divisional police surgeon, had autopsied Amelia's body and found her face and tongue swollen and her eyes dilated. Particles of wool from her scarf lay in the constriction wound, and death took place on or near 31st January. But Lawrence was more interested in the excerpt relating to Samuel Roberts, the nightwatchman. If the reports were anything to go by, there was something deeply suspicious in his conduct. Amelia's father had approached Roberts on the night she disappeared and asked if a young girl could have entered number 126 Portway. Robert said no – only two properties were accessible without keys, and number 126 was not one of them. Two weeks later, having decided to search every empty property in the area, the police tried again. They consulted Roberts who repeated his claim that he could not let them into 126 because he didn't have the key. Yet Constable Cross had accessed the property through the open rear window. It was inconceivable that the watchman hadn't thought to do the same.

Lawrence lowered the pieces of paper and scowled in concentration. Samuel 'Daddy Watchman's' behaviour had been far from helpful. The newspaper article implied he was a prime suspect in Amelia's disappearance, but they didn't arrest him, much less gain a conviction. And the assumption of guilt made little sense. If Roberts had killed Amelia, he'd had two full weeks in which to dispose of her body. Given that the rear of the property was on common land, he could have done so without fear of prying eyes. But what was it that William Donaldson had said about keys? A story so complicated and unlikely that he could not explain it himself. The Lloyd's article was relatively straightforward, so it must be in a different report.

#

Lawrence turned to the final clippings, read one then the other, squinted and read them both again. William Donaldson was right. What had happened in the Portway house was difficult to fathom. The builder, Joseph Roberts, had kept the keys at home, but not the key for number 126. Roberts explained that his father Samuel, the watchman, had slept at the house on the night of the murder. Not only had his father slept there, but his son, Joseph Roberts junior, also claimed to have been in the house that same evening. Neither man saw Amelia's body and to complicate matters still further, their stories about the keys flew in the face of the evidence. A few months earlier, there had been a theft of iron and lead in the local area. Police Inspector James Harvey had approached several builders during his investigation. Joseph Roberts allowed him access to every one of the empty properties, including number 126. And he'd got inside using keys held by Samuel Roberts affixed together on a large chain. So, the key was available a mere two months earlier, and someone was likely lying.

The events described in the last newspaper article written in May 1890 were stranger still. Lawrence bit his lip while he concentrated, trying to work out the facts from the reporter's embellishments. By May, the rental agent had let out the house, now occupied by two families, the Hewitts and the Rittens. One night, footsteps, followed by a loud crash, woke both couples in the early hours of the morning. Mr Hewitt and Mr Ritten rose and started investigating, eventually tracking the sounds to the attic window. Someone had forced it open. The noises attracted their attention to a trapdoor in the attic ceiling which they accessed using a bench. They climbed into the void and noticed that someone had removed several bricks from the wall adjoining number 125. Inside the aperture, were two keys each tagged with pieces of brown cardboard and marked with number 126. One key fitted the front bedroom door where Constable Cross found Amelia and the other might have been the front door key. Unfortunately, they couldn't check as the lock was changed when the original key went missing.

Lawrence held his forehead as he focused on the pages. The print was small, the wall lamps not terribly effective, and his eyes were blurry from tiredness. The complicated nature of what he was reading was giving him a splitting headache. According to the newspaper, a house painter by the name of Warren said he placed the keys in the aperture a few weeks earlier. He'd been papering the house, and when he had finished, he left them there. But his story seemed unlikely, and Warren never explained why he hid the keys instead of giving them back. The coroner had asked Joseph Roberts why this should be, and the builder refused to say anything further on the subject. He told the inquest that Warren had gone and his whereabouts were now unknown, so how could he know what the man was thinking? But it was a well-known fact that Amelia's father thought she knew her killer and Charles Jeffs treated Warren's story with considerable scepticism.

Lawrence shoved the papers in his breast pocket and heaved himself from the floor, right leg tingling with cramp. He left the front room, pausing only to close the cupboard door and located the trapdoor to the attic. It was too high to reach, and with the house unfurnished, there was nothing available to use as steps. This came as something of a relief. Had they been there, Lawrence would have felt compelled to look inside and see where the keys had lain. In the half-hour Lawrence had been in the house, the temperature had dropped still further, and the thought of Amelia lying broken on the floor was giving him palpitations. The floorboards creaked and groaned with his every step, echoing through the empty property and reminding him he was here alone. Lawrence rarely left lights on in a vacant property. But Manisier was due to return at any moment, and he couldn't face descending two sets of unlit stairs. He was not often frightened, but there was something sinister about the house. The unnerving atmosphere usually occurred in far older properties and didn't belong in a home completed only nine years before. Something evil had happened in the house, a crime for which there could be no excuse or explanation – an act of wanton cruelty Lawrence shuddered as he shut the front door and made his way back to Buxton Road. Though it made his journey fractionally longer, he kept well clear of the sinister shadows of West Ham Park.

# CHAPTER 10

## *A Grave Disturbance*

**Monday, February 20, 1899**

*Dear Michael*

*I doubt if you've had time to read my previous letter much less respond, but I wanted to share some news with you. I am embarrassed to mention the first item concerning an impulsive action on my part. Against my better judgement, I asked Elsie at the tea shop for an address for Margaret Morse. Elsie knew her well – I believe they were school friends – and Elsie was more than willing to provide her address without asking why I wanted it. I wrote a letter to Miss Morse as soon as I finished my last one to you. Having no real purpose for corresponding with her, I asked her outright about her family, and particularly Ella's headstone. Well, I must have greatly offended her for she wrote back by return. And I do not use that word lightly. She must have penned her reply the moment she received my letter, and it was not pleasant reading. Margaret Morse told me in no uncertain terms, to mind my own business and never to contact her again. Well, I lost no time in confessing my unwise behaviour to Elsie as I did not want her to hear it from Miss Morse. The indiscretion was mine alone, and Elsie should not pay the price for giving me information in good faith. I need not have worried. Elsie accepted my apology with good grace and told me not to worry and pay no heed to Margaret. Although fond of Miss Morse, she is the first to admit that her friend is plain-speaking and intolerant. I was not the first, nor would I be the last to fall foul of her short temper. I asked Elsie to send my apologies next time she writes. Elsie says that there is no need, but she will pass them on if it makes me feel better. I don't, of course. I feel foolish and impetuous, and the old me would have done nothing so ill-considered. But I have learned my lesson and will give more consideration to my actions in future.*

*Anyway, I have changed my daily routine, Michael, for reasons which will soon become apparent. As you know, I visit Norma's house every working day, and I have been making myself walk through the graveyard. I know my fears are irrational, and I have tried to conquer them, but in doing so, I realise that I have been negligent of my responsibilities. With that in mind, I now allow myself to walk the long way to work some of the time, and during the rest, I continue to run the gauntlet past the gravestones. But when I take this route, my heart beats so fast that I fear it will stop one day at the sheer terror that stalks me without real form or purpose. Or that is what I thought until yesterday when my fear took physical shape.*

*I cannot help but walk past Ella's grave. It sits there like a malevolent will-o'-the-wisp, luring me, daring me to approach. And even if I did not feel drawn to it, I would make myself go there because I will not give in to this irrational dread. So, yesterday, I passed it as I always do, but even from a distance, I could see it had changed. The grass had disappeared as if pulled from below. Not a blade remained. And in its place was a mound of earth piled high on one side, the stone now listing towards the church more angularly than before. The soil lay churned and disturbed in such a way that it seemed as if the grave's occupant was trying to escape – almost as if Ella herself was on the move. I stopped dead in my tracks, Michael, nearly faint with horror. And then I caught sight of something glinting in the soil. I reached towards it, half expecting a skeletal hand to shoot from the grave, circle my wrist and haul me in. But it did not. Instead, I found myself pulling out a length of chain on the end of which was a key with a skull fashioned into the design. I could hardly believe my eyes and stood there for a few moments, hoping I was dreaming.*

*Then I heard a loud voice bellowing behind me. I turned toward the shouting and saw an old man bent over a walking stick. He wore a dog collar around his neck, below which hung an ornate cross. I stood, open-mouthed, as he hobbled towards me, expecting him to sympathise. Instead, he began berating me for the condition of the grave. But the fear in my eyes must have been apparent, and after a few moments, he stopped, surveyed the damaged cross, and apologised. He said he had made a mistake and I evidently could not have caused the damage, at least not without a strong man and a spade. Then he stopped talking and stared at the ground for a long time.*

*I did not know what to do or say, so I waited, and eventually, he spoke. "Last time the stone moved naturally," he said. "This is a new development." I asked him what he meant, and he told me that when he first arrived at the church, he heard rumours of the moving stone. He disregarded them until early in eighty-one when it began to twist again. "But never," he said, "has the earth spewed forth like this. The stone has travelled, and the grass has shown signs of disturbance, but these mounds of soil are a different matter." He stroked his chin as he contemplated the damage and then asked me if I had seen anything unusual in the preceding days. I said I had not and only happened upon the scene moments before he arrived. I did not mention the key. I know I should have done, but I could not help myself. I kept it, and it is currently in my purse where it will remain for the time being.*

*My fear vanished with the arrival of the elderly priest. You might know him, Michael. His name is George Winter, and he is long retired though you may have seen him when you visited recently. Anyway, he suspects the movement might be man-made rather than supernatural, which has left me feeling better, of course. Yet, if so, why was a key left lying in the earth as if thrust up from below? But isn't that a silly thought? Whoever damaged the grave must have dropped it. It's by far the most rational explanation, though why anyone would disturb the remains of a long-dead woman, is a mystery. Ella Morse was a God-fearing woman and a loyal and well-loved sister. She cannot have had enemies in her lifetime, much less forty years after her death.*

*I have pondered on these matters all day. Now that we've finished supper and completed our ablutions I find myself unable to sleep for the thoughts streaming through my head. Writing this letter is cathartic, and I am glad to have your sage counsel to call upon if required. Recalling the day's events and the sensible conclusion of the clergyman has put my mind at rest, at least for now. So, I will close and wish you a peaceful and productive week.*

*With my fondest regards*

*Violet*

# CHAPTER 11

## *The Press Office Calls*

*Monday, March 6, 1899*

"Hold on. I'm on my way."

Lawrence awoke to the sound of shouting coming from the direction of the hallway at his lodging house in Buxton Road.

"I said, hold on."

Lawrence kneaded his eyes and opened his pocket watch. It was too dark to see, so he fumbled on his bedside table and lit a candle before checking again. It was a little after five in the morning, and someone was urgently hammering on the front door. He rose, donned his dressing gown and peered downstairs to see a half-dressed James Ward yanking open the door.

"What the devil do you mean creating all this noise at this time of the morning. Stop it at once before you wake up the children." But it was too late. A high-pitched wail came from the back bedroom where the baby was sleeping.

"You'd better have a damn good reason for this," hissed Ward.

Lawrence craned his neck to see a young boy waving an envelope in the air. "I've got an urgent message for Mr Harpham," said the boy. "And I'm not to leave until he's read it."

Lawrence descended the stairs and approached Ward sheepishly. "I don't know what this is about," he said, "but I apologise for the disturbance."

"I was getting dressed anyway," snapped Ward. "I start at the foundry at six thirty, and Aggie will see to my breakfast, but they don't need to be up yet." He gestured towards the room where the children slept."

"I really am sorry."

James Ward shook his head and retreated upstairs.

"Who are you?" asked Lawrence, regarding the boy with an air of resignation.

"I'm the *Barking Advertiser* messenger," said the boy. "Mr Higgins told me to bring you this note and make it snappy. So here I am, and here I'll stay until you've read it and given your answer."

Lawrence tore open the envelope and squinted at the page, but it was still too dark to see.

"Use this," said the boy holding a bull's eye lamp aloft that looked suspiciously like the police issue version.

"Where did you get that?" asked Lawrence

"Ask no questions, tell no lies," said the boy, winking. "Now, are you going to read your message or not?"

Lawrence held the note beneath the light.

*Dear Mr Harpham*

*Little Bertha Russ is dead as I predicted. They found her in the early hours of this morning. I am at the press office now working on the morning edition. Please come as soon as you can."*

*Samuel Higgins*

Lawrence folded the letter and shoved it in his dressing gown pocket.
"Are you coming?" asked the boy.
"Yes."
"When?"
"I'll be there by eight o'clock," said Lawrence.
"Right you are." The boy took his lamp, turned, and scurried up the road.

#

Lawrence was as good as his word. After a hurried breakfast served by Agnes Ward while she tried to pacify two tired and fractious children, he left for the press office. Lawrence was growing fond of Agnes and her offspring, but today he was glad to be going. James had left in a foul mood, and Agnes was quiet and subdued. Lawrence suspected they'd had words.

The door to fifty-five The Broadway was closed when Lawrence arrived. His mood darkened, irritated at the impediment to quick access having been hauled halfway across town for an urgent meeting. But after a few seconds, the door opened, and he came face to face with the boy he had last seen only a few hours before.

"Good. I thought it must be you," said the boy. "I've been waiting for your knock. Mr Higgins won't have the door open unless there are plenty of people around."

"Where is he?"

"In his office," said the boy, jabbing at the air.

Lawrence entered, and Higgins jumped to his feet. "Oh, good. Thank you for coming," he said, holding out his hand. "Take a seat. Shall I ask Stanley to rustle up a cup of tea?"

"No need," said Lawrence. He had already eaten a perfectly adequate breakfast. Besides, there was something about the messenger boy that suggested his tea making would be a slapdash affair. His hands, and particularly his nails, were not in a state of cleanliness that inspired confidence.

"So, they've found the girl," said Lawrence.

Higgins nodded. "Yes. It was only a matter of time, but even I could not have predicted the circumstance of her death."

"Tell me about it," said Lawrence. "And how did you come to hear about it?"

"The other fellow at my digs works at the mortuary in Wakefield Street," said Higgins. "I suffer from extreme insomnia and was still awake reading into the small hours last night when I heard my neighbour come home. Gustav dropped something as he came up the stairs after finishing at the mortuary. I opened my door to check all was well, and it wasn't. The poor chap looked dreadful, and when I asked him what was wrong, he blurted it out. I took him inside, and we talked at length over a glass of port."

"Is he the mortician?"

"No. Nothing so grand. Gustav prepares the corpses for burial or hands them over to the surgeon if they require an autopsy. And he sees young children all the time, of course. But not like this. Someone had murdered Bertha Russ and squashed her body into a cupboard."

"How did she die?"

"From suffocation. The police called James Shimeld, the divisional surgeon as soon as they found her. He ordered the removal of her body to the mortuary then conducted an immediate autopsy. It is my good fortune that Gustav was there throughout. Seldom is there such a felicitous opportunity to learn so much about a crime so quickly."

Samuel Higgins flipped open a notebook. "I didn't like to make notes in front of Gustav, but I did it the moment he left, my memory not being what it once was. Now, there's a lot to get through".

"First, there was a great deal of post-mortem staining on the body. Bertha's hair came out easily, indicating that she had been dead for some time. She probably met her end on the day that she went missing. Her body was normal in all other ways, and Shimeld concluded that somebody had placed an object over her face causing suffocation. They stuffed her into the cupboard and later rigor mortis set in."

"Just like Amelia Jeffs," said Lawrence. "But that was nine years ago."

"I haven't told you where they found her yet," said Higgins, pushing his glasses up his nose. The threadbare strap securing them to his head looked as if it was about to snap. Lawrence averted his eyes, not wanting to know what lay beneath the blacked-out lens. But not before he noticed the scarred, inverted dent on Higgins temple between his absent ear and his eyebrow. Whatever had happened to the man, had caused substantial damage.

"Did you hear me?" Higgins had cocked his head and was peering at Lawrence.

"Yes. You said Bertha was in a cupboard."

"More to the point, she was in a cupboard in an empty house in Ilford," said Higgins. "Seventy Lawrence Avenue, to be precise, assuming Gustav has remembered correctly."

"Ah," said Lawrence. "No doubt they set out to search all the empty houses. Perhaps they have learned something from the Jeffs murder, after all."

"You would think so," said Higgins. "But I'm told that the prospective tenants found her when they viewed the property?"

"Surely not?" Lawrence gazed at the pressman, open-mouthed. "It shouldn't be possible. The police would have searched all the empty houses as soon as Bertha went missing."

"Well, if they did, they made a poor job of it."

"Could she have wandered in and shut herself in the cupboard?"

"One police officer asked that, and Shimeld said not."

Lawrence leaned back in his chair and looked outside, deep in thought. "Was a house agent involved in showing the property?" he asked.

"I couldn't say."

"It's important. All the articles I've read about Amelia Jeffs suggest the involvement of a workman in her murder. The killer definitely had easy access to the property, but wouldn't that be equally true of a house agent?"

Higgins considered the matter. "Well, of course, it could," he said. "But who and why?"

"I don't know, but two agents are living and working in West Road," said Lawrence. "And both had dwelled there long enough to have been around when Millie Jeffs died."

"It's worth considering," said Samuel Higgins. "But I'm certain of this. Whoever killed Amelia Jeffs also killed Bertha Russ, however unlikely the timescale suggests."

"If that's true, it would imply that the same person has been killing young girls for at least ten years, and possibly longer."

"Quite – which is why I asked you to come straight away. The police refuse to understand that this is the work of one person."

"But why?"

"Their objection is mainly geographical. The constabulary can't grasp that the distance between West Ham and Walthamstow does not rule out the same killer. At least now, there can be no doubt. Even an idiot can see that the deaths of Amelia Jeffs and Mary Jane Voller bear too many similarities with Bertha's to disregard. They have run out of excuses."

"I haven't read about Mary Voller yet," said Lawrence.

"Well, you need to get on with it then. Or you won't understand what I mean."

Lawrence scowled. He had read what felt like dozens of papers from cover to cover. It would have helped if Higgins had marked the relevant articles rather than present him with the whole thing.

"Are you going to help me, Harpham?"

"Yes. Of course. Don't worry that I'm not quite up to speed. Even with a little knowledge, I can see the connection. I'll do anything to assist. I had a daughter once." Lawrence's voice broke as he tried to say her name, but he could not bring himself to do it.

Higgins's voice softened, and his lip trembled momentarily. "Then you must do your research. Finish reading everything tonight. Get your notebook and come with me."

Lawrence followed Higgins into the hidden room containing his files.

"Write this down," Higgins commanded, before reeling off a list of names and dates. When Lawrence had finished, he examined the page.

"There's still an eight-year gap before Amelia Jeffs and a five-year gap after Elizabeth Skinner," said Lawrence.

"There isn't," said Higgins. "There's more to come, and I'm yet to complete my research. Go home and read everything you can find. Let this murder be the last."

# CHAPTER 12

## *Dead in a Ditch*

The loan of a Rover safety bicycle from the press office aided Lawrence's journey back to Buxton Road considerably. Higgins had initially purchased the bike for young Stanley who refused point-blank to use it. It surprised Lawrence to hear this. The boy had presented an unusually confident demeanour and should have been a perfect candidate for a cycle given his role as a runner. But he viewed it with wary suspicion and insisted on walking.

"It's rusting in the workshop," Higgins had said. "If you don't use it, it will end up with the totter." And Lawrence had acquiesced. It wasn't because he cared less whether the cycle went to the rag and bone man, but because he could take a direct route back and save time.

Higgins lingered outside after handing the bicycle over. Lawrence waited for him to leave, having no intention of mounting the beast with an audience. Eventually, Samuel Higgins took the hint, closed the door, and went inside. Lawrence gritted his teeth and put his weight on the pedal, before heaving himself into the saddle. It had been a long time since he'd last ridden a cycle and he wobbled through the abbey grounds as he tried to get his balance and his bearings. Half an hour later, Lawrence found to his relief, that the streets were recognisable and within a few brief minutes, he was back in Buxton Road. Lawrence was cycling towards his lodgings, thoughts elsewhere, when a shout momentarily startled him. He braked hard, then saw a man crouching on the other side of a wooden fence by the side of the road. As the man stood, Lawrence recognised him at once. The shouting man was Gilbert Cooper.

"I can give you something for that," said Gilbert, waving a paintbrush in his hand.

"I beg your pardon?"

"That squeaky wheel. I could hear you coming a mile off."

"I hadn't noticed. I expect it needs oiling."

"You can say that again. I'll bring you some round in a bit."

"No need," said Lawrence. "I'm sure I can find a tin."

Gil Cooper ignored him and continued painting the gate. Lawrence dismounted the cycle and pushed it the short distance to number fifty-five where he left it propped against the wall. Then he tried the door and finding it locked, located the key under the flowerpot Agnes Ward said she would use if she went out. Relishing the unusually empty house, Lawrence boiled a pan of water and made himself a cup of tea. He took it upstairs, then settled down to make notes on the conversation he'd had with Higgins that morning. "Read everything," Higgins had said before providing him with a list of names, three of which were unfamiliar. Lawrence sighed. He was a practical man and preferred questioning witnesses to poring through press reports. Lawrence didn't wholly trust reporters and had grave doubts about the accuracy of their stories. But he couldn't expect any help from the police, and there was little choice in the matter.

The news about Bertha Russ had been upsetting, and Lawrence could feel the black dog nudging in the background. Having the life snuffed out of your child at only six years old, was too much for a parent to bear. If his daughter Lily had lived, she would be twelve years old by now – the same age as Eliza Carter when she had disappeared. What if Lily had vanished? Would it have been easier, or would he have suffered more? Yes, undoubtedly, it would have been worse. At least he knew what had happened to Lily. The torment of waiting daily, hourly even, for news of a missing child was a torture with no end. Thoughts of Lily snaked through his mind, worming into the deepest recesses and proving a feeding ground for the black dog. A wave of despair coursed through his body.

Lawrence knew nothing about the case, was unfamiliar with the area and doubted his ability to bring a resolution. Why had Isabel asked for his help? What was the point? Lawrence put his head in his hands and blinked his eyes open as Violet's face swam into view. Violet. What would she say if he was with her now? He smiled as he remembered the way she used to sit with her hands in her lap, regarding him patiently. Violet never interrupted, never spoke until he had got everything off his chest. Then she would tilt her head to one side as she considered whatever problem was uppermost in his mind. Violet would gently offer kindly meant advice, never reacting if he ignored it. What would she say now? She would say, of course, he was the right person to catch the killer, that he should rely on his instincts and listen to his sixth sense.

"But, Violet, you were the rational one, it was your ability to analyse that won through in the end."

Then do as I would, he almost heard her say. And he did. Lawrence pulled the bundle of papers towards him, devoting a page of his notebook to each of the girls. He read through, extracting any information that gave him pause for thought and worked systematically until seven pages were full.

#

Reading about Annie West, Elizabeth Skinner and Mary Jane Voller, was exhausting. Images of Lily lingered as he analysed every terrible word. It was as if Lily was the victim and he the grieving parent. Lawrence felt a deep and visceral pain at the loss of innocent lives and the agony of their families. And thoughts of Lily always provoked memories of Catherine. Especially as two of the girls died in a ditch. It reminded Lawrence of an old nursery rhyme that Catherine used to sing when coaxing Lily to sleep. He remembered it now as if no time had passed and he could almost see Catherine, kneeling by Lily's bed singing in a low whisper about Moss's missing mare. 'Dead in a ditch he found her, and glad to find her

77

there.' Lawrence wondered in hindsight whether it was a fitting rhyme to sing to a young child, but Lily did not suffer from nightmares about dead horses or anything else.

Memories of the song distracted him from his work. It was hard enough to remember all the names and connections of the dead girls without nursery rhymes grinding in his head. At least the police had conceded that the same man was likely responsible for the Walthamstow murders. Each girl met her end in water. Two had died, and against the odds, one child survived.

Annie West was the first of the three to die. Her death almost passed unnoticed because of the judgemental coroner. Annie's mother was far from maternal and had thrown the child out in late December with no boots or hat. They'd argued and not for the first time. Rather than blame the killer, the coroner chastised Annie's mother, saying she had no proper feeling for her child. If the newspaper reports were accurate, Lawrence could see why. No matter what the justification, he could not imagine turning his child outside with no proper clothing. Tired and hungry, Annie had sought refuge from a friend who offered her room in the shed where they kept the dog, but Annie declined. The inquest could not determine how she found her way into the ditch, and she died of exposure, not drowning. That would have been the end of it but for an unexpected confession from a man recently released from a local lunatic asylum. Nobody believed him, and they forgot all about Annie West until the next crime occurred six months later. This time, it happened to Eliza Skinner.

Lawrence shifted position on the bed as he re-read the articles, comparing them to his notes. He was going to have to use the dressing table as a writing desk. Lounging on the bed was giving him back pain and cramp. He rubbed his eyes and read on.

Eliza Skinner's parents had left their house one night at about nine o'clock. Their elder son Thomas, a responsible fourteen-year-old, had charge of the baby. Having no duties of her own, Eliza went out to play in the street while her brother minded the child. Later, Thomas went outside to check on his sister and found her in the company of a stranger. The man had asked her for directions and rather than explain, Eliza showed him the way. Thomas dutifully watched as they walked across the fields, suspecting nothing untoward. But when Mr and Mrs Skinner returned to their house and Thomas told them what happened, they immediately feared the worst. They set off in swift pursuit, but it was too late. Neighbours had already found Eliza in Paddy's field, legs bound, and her mouth stuffed with weeds and mud. The man had foully outraged Eliza, and after he had his way, tossed her into a dirty ditch and left her to die. But Eliza was a fighter. Barely alive, rescuers carried her to an aunt's house, and the doctor attended her, holding out no hope for recovery. Though Eliza was too unwell to talk, her brother remembered every detail of the man's appearance. He wore a cheese cutter cap, blue serge suit and black whiskers. Lawrence sighed as he underlined the word 'whiskers'. If the description was accurate, the assault could be a random act by a disturbed man. But if Higgins was right, and the killer was prolific, and had operated for a long time, then he was probably in disguise. The black whiskers were a ploy, and the man could be clean-shaven. Lawrence had used a false beard and moustache many times, and nobody had ever guessed. No, he could not set any stock by this description. More worrying was the audacity of a man who attacked in broad daylight in front of witnesses. His reckless disregard for anonymity implied he would take any risk to get what he wanted. No girl was safe from such depravity. Eliza was a much-loved daughter, unlike poor Annie West. But not content to defile the poor girl, the stranger had tossed her aside as if her life meant nothing.

The report was hard reading, and Lawrence paused for a moment, trying to put thoughts of the child, bound and despairing in the ditch, from his mind. His only consolation from the grim report was the comparison with Amelia Jeffs' murder. Both girls were violated, which, together with other similarities highlighted by the press, gave ammunition to support the single killer theory. If Lawrence failed to do anything else, he would hand this information to the police and insist that they listened. They had seen it all before, and it hadn't resulted in any meaningful action. But that was no reason to stop trying.

By the time Lawrence finished reading the account of Mary Jane Voller's death in January 1899, he felt sickened by man's inhumanity. The little girl, only five and a half years old, had taken a thrupenny piece to the grocer's shop to buy some linseed oil for her father. When she didn't return, Henry Voller went straight to the shop and asked if they had seen his daughter. He raised the alarm as soon as the manager said she had not arrived. Voller went straight to the police station but couldn't stand idly by waiting for them to act. He borrowed a lantern and started searching empty houses in the district accompanied by his father. They walked into nearby Barking Lane and noticed a shed by a ditch. A split second before their lantern blew out, Voller saw something floating on the water. With no more oil or matches, the men worked in darkness. Henry Voller felt around in the freezing pond before his hands settled on the cold dead corpse of his daughter. Wounds covered little Mary's body, and an autopsy later showed that she died from asphyxia. She was probably dead before entering the water, but she hadn't been violated. There being no clues or suspects, the inquest returned a verdict against a person or persons unknown.

Lawrence shook his head as he pencilled the details into his notebook, and regarded his handiwork. At the end of the book, he'd written a list containing the names of seven girls beginning with Eliza Carter in 1881 and ending with little Bertha Russ. Each entry contained the dates and locations of their deaths and how they expired. But two names stood out. Bertha Russ and Amelia Jeffs. Bertha's death troubled him enormously, but she was so young that his feelings were inevitable. He wasn't sure what bothered him about Amelia. Perhaps seeing the place where she'd died made her death more personal. Either way, Lawrence felt they mattered. He snapped his notebook shut. No. He knew why. It was because they'd found the girls in cupboards in empty houses – an unlikely and statistically improbable event. Lawrence glanced at his fob watch on the side table and raised an eyebrow as he noticed the time. He had been reading for hours, and it must be close to suppertime. His stomach growled as if on cue and Lawrence opened the door listening for sounds of the family. A delicious aroma wafted across the landing, and Lawrence heard Agnes singing quietly to herself while the children played. Lawrence must have been concentrating so hard that he hadn't heard them return. He was hungry now and eager to eat. A little nutrition might fortify him for later. He put his notebook away and took his coat and hat downstairs to prepare for what he intended to do after supper.

# CHAPTER 13

## *A Gypsy Curse*

*Thursday, February 23, 1899*

*Dear Michael*

*I have made some progress at last in my quest to discover more about the Morse family. It is good to have a purpose again though it does not bring the same satisfaction as successful detective work. Everything concerning Ella is tainted with the supernatural and things that cannot be real on this earth. Even moving from my home to my place of work has become a trial, and I grow ever more fearful of a sinister force that I cannot name. But I must put these thoughts aside so I can tell you about the unexpected letter I received today.*

*Elsie was as good as her word and wrote to Margaret Morse, as she had promised. I don't know what she said, but it elucidated a response from Miss Morse, who wrote a second letter apologising for the first. The letter offered useful information about the family, and Margaret told me a little about herself. I can't remember if I mentioned it, but she lives in a small cottage in the Lake District, which she shares with a close friend called Hannah. They have lived together for over forty years and Hannah, some ten years older than Margaret, is a calming influence upon her friend. Elsie thinks Hannah might have caused this change of heart. Whether it was Elsie's letter or Hannah's kindness is immaterial, the result is the same. But it leaves me uneasy, for it has produced yet another set of unlikely circumstances.*

*Not only did Margaret send a list of her siblings, their birth and death dates, all of which match our findings, but she told me something else. It turns out that the information she gave is common knowledge around the town, and I am only surprised that I did not learn of it sooner. It is a verse, a piece of doggerel directly relating to the Morse family and arising from an incident that happened to Ann Morse many years ago. Ann, you will remember, was the matriarch of the Morse family. One day, in the summer of 1830, Ann was walking through Swaffham with some of her children, one of whom was Philip Morse, a child of tender years. The boy escaped from Ann and ran into the path of a pony and trap driven by an elderly gipsy. Philip bumped into the horse which reared up, but the gipsy woman kept firm control, and neither child nor horse came to harm. The little boy lay crying on the floor, and the gipsy paused her journey to check on him. She left the cart and approached him holding something behind her back. Ann Morse, in a state of panic and confusion, thought the gipsy was about to strike Philip. Ann raised her hand intending to stop the gipsy in her tracks, but the gesture frightened the pony who took flight. It bolted across town trailing the cart in its wake and causing untold damage. Eventually, the poor thing tried to jump across a ditch, broke its leg, and a local farmer destroyed it.*

*Well, the gipsy was furious. Not only was the horse valuable, but she had formed a sentimental attachment to the beast. Ann Morse tried to offer compensation for the animal, but it wasn't enough. She asked her husband for more money, but he refused, and the gipsy retaliated with a curse.*

*I can see you now, Michael, rolling your eyes heavenward as you read my words. The idea of a gipsy curse is nonsense, of course. Yet if you consider the words of the rhyme, that they sing in the schoolyard to this day, they are curiously apposite considering the family's fate.*

*You will meet your God within a week,*
*And then your husband's death, I'll seek,*
*Beware the summer when I'll come,*
*And take your children one by one,*
*The first of these will die next year,*
*I'll take the youngest and most dear,*
*And none will ever reach fourscore,*
*Or lay in peace forevermore.*

*Ann died on the third of July 1830 and her husband John followed her to the grave within a few short weeks. The next year little Ann, her youngest child and namesake expired followed by Caroline and Philip. The longest-lived child died before sixty leaving Margaret the sole survivor of a family of thirteen. Margaret alone has beaten the curse. Or has she? Margaret will be eighty in 1901, only two years from now – if she lives that long. You would think that Margaret would live in fear, but she does not. Despite all that has come to pass, she says that she doesn't believe in the curse and the deaths of her siblings were part of God's plan. The Morse family were all religious, and none of them gave credence to the curse, yet many in the village believed it. The idea of a curse flies in the face of logic. It should not be possible, yet the sequence of events that followed lends weight to the gipsy's threat. Curiously, Margaret made a further comment which she failed to develop in any meaningful way. Her remark suggested that there was a discrepancy in Ella's will. Have you made any progress locating it? I would like to see a copy and have something tangible to distract my attention from moving stones and gipsy curses. Really, it is like one of my gothic horror stories.*

*Talking of which, I am not the only one who has become fanciful lately. Poor Elsie sees strange things too. It started when a man came into the tea shop last week. Elsie was alone – it must have been my day off, and he seemed a pleasant enough chap. He sat down and ordered a cup of tea, then stayed for several hours, as if he were waiting. She offered to fetch him another drink, but the stranger kept refusing. After two hours staring out of the window and twitching like a cat on hot bricks, he spied something outside. The man leapt from his chair as if he'd been scalded, spilling a salt cellar in his haste. He did not stop to pick it up, and Elsie wouldn't have thought further about it except that she has seen him twice since although he hasn't come in. I asked her to point him out to me, but so far, he hasn't been near the tea rooms when I am there. I teased Elsie and said that she must have imagined him, and she became quite cross. Then I suggested that he might be an admirer and when I said it, Elsie blushed to her roots so it must have crossed her mind too. At least we have found some levity in the events of the week.*

*As for the graveyard, I have avoided it since I last wrote and haven't passed through once since encountering Reverend Winter. I am not giving in to fear, nor will I refrain from crossing the churchyard indefinitely, but it is provoking irrational thoughts. I have, therefore, been kind to myself and avoided the unpleasantness. Since then, the nightmares have stopped, and I can concentrate again.*

*I have rattled on long enough. I hope you are safe and well, Michael, and I will write again soon.*

*Your friend*

*Violet*

# CHAPTER 14

## *Under Attack*

Streams of unlikely coincidences flooded through Lawrence's mind, as he donned his greatcoat and set out into the wintry night. Though early March, the weather was far from springlike. He mounted the bike, tempted to return indoors and spend the rest of the evening reading a book. But the coincidences spurred him on. There were too many similarities between the deaths, ages, and locations of the murders, not to mention the methods. Now, to top it all, he, Lawrence Harpham, was heading towards number seventy Lawrence Avenue when most people were settling down for the night.

From the moment Lawrence mounted the bicycle, an embarrassing squeak screeched through the night air. Lawrence grimaced, wishing he had taken Gil Cooper up on his suggestion to oil the gears. The noise hadn't been so noticeable when travelling in daylight. But in the still evening, he might as well announce his arrival with a foghorn, so obtrusive was his chosen means of travel. And given that Lawrence intended to break into a property within the next half hour, he was going to have to do something about it.

Lawrence ploughed on down Buxton Road and into Forest Lane, taking an almost straight route onto Church Road. He stopped and dismounted, hoping that the noise would lessen if he pushed the cycle instead. To his relief, the absence of his weight all but eliminated the annoying sound, and he could finally hear himself think.

Though only eight o'clock, Church Road was empty and unsettlingly quiet. Stars dotted the cloudless sky, and the hedges bore traces of a delicate frost. Now that he was pushing the cycle, Lawrence could hear the smallest sound – a rustle of leaves, the low whistle of the wind. A dog barked a few roads beyond before the gruff bark turned into a shrieking howl, then a whimper, and silence. As Lawrence pushed his cycle towards Lawrence Avenue, his footsteps echoed in the empty street. But the echo had an echo of its own, and he felt a hidden presence nearby. Lawrence stopped and turned, but the road was empty. He took a few more steps and turned again – still nothing. He felt foolish. How could anyone be following? He hadn't said a word about where he was going or what he was doing. Not to the Wards, not even to Samuel Higgins. His imagination was running riot, and he steeled himself to get on with it. Lawrence gritted his teeth and proceeded silently up the avenue, searching for number seventy. But as he came close to his destination, he saw an immediate impediment to his plan. Pacing up and down the pathway was a disgruntled-looking policeman.

Lawrence was already too close to risk doubling back. It would look more suspicious than continuing. He elected instead to cycle past the policeman while eyeing the property to check for rear access and soon found it was too dark to see clearly. Lawrence continued to the other end of the street and turned, hoping to find an alleyway to the rear. But the properties directly backed onto those in the next road. The best he could hope for was to go through the opposite garden and hop over the fence. On closer scrutiny, even that wouldn't work. There was no easy access to the rear gardens in the neighbouring road, and it was impossible to tell which property adjoined number seventy. The whole idea had been a complete waste of time. Lawrence remounted his bike and returned up the road, almost running into the police constable he had just passed. The policeman strode purposefully across the street towards a fellow constable walking his beat on the other side. Lawrence grinned, feeling sure that the man was breaking the boredom of his duty by indulging in some gossip. It would distract him for a little while.

Lawrence lost no time in taking advantage of the opportunity, leapt from his bike, and steered it into the front of the house. He unlatched a wooden gate to the side which he hadn't seen from the road. There was no lock and Lawrence pushed the cycle through and lay it on the ground at the rear. Though the sky was clear, the bike was well-hidden, and only the sharpest eyes would notice the glint of metal in the moonlight. Lawrence tried the side door, but it wouldn't budge. The side window was another matter. Although open, it was too small to climb through. But the rear window to the dining room was on the latch and easily big enough to enter. Lawrence opened it using a pocketknife and climbed through closing it behind him. With a police officer close at hand, he could not risk using the gas mantle. Darkness cloaked the cold, draughty house, and he fought his fears as he felt his way through. He took the stairs two at a time, safe in the knowledge that he had a few moments before anyone would hear him, and soon arrived on the landing. Lawrence removed the tin from his pocket and lit a candle, before holding it low to the floor. The landing doors led to three bedrooms, and he glimpsed a blue bow covered in dust and hair, lying on the ground by the entrance to the middle room. Lawrence shook his head in disgust. The bow must have belonged to Bertha and out of respect, if not good policing, someone should have moved it. "Slapdash," he muttered aloud.

The bedroom doors were ajar, but it wasn't hard to identify the one in which Bertha had recently expired. The smell of death permeated the landing but was most objectionable by the middle room. Lawrence pushed the door open and went inside. The freshly painted bedroom was empty and clean though dust coated the windowsill and skirting boards. There was no rug or carpet, and white paint speckled the floorboards. A cupboard hung open by the window, its position identical to the one in the Portway house. Though not surprised that this should be the case, Lawrence still shuddered at the sight of it. He approached the cupboard. There was no door furniture, and if closed properly, it would not be possible to open it again. He used his boot to push it to its widest extent, moving his head as the worst of the odour assailed him. Lawrence set the candle on the floor and reached for a handkerchief, holding it over his nose as he surveyed the scene. Bertha's body was safely in the morgue, but a mess of her dried blood and hair still coated the rough floorboards. Nobody had attempted to clean it, and there was a clear impression of a footprint nearby. Lawrence raised the candle and tried to estimate the size of the print. Whoever made it wore boots roughly the same size as his own. He pushed the cupboard too and followed the faint outline of the footprints across the room, expecting them to lead to the door. One set did, but a second trail unexpectedly led to the far corner of the room. Lawrence put the candle on the floor then ran a hand over the walls and the skirting boards. Something wasn't right, and there was no obvious reason for someone to walk to the corner of an empty room. None the wiser when he finished, Lawrence crouched down and examined the floorboards to find a hole the size of a penny piece caused by a knot in the wood where the board met the wall. Lawrence pushed his fingers inside and touched something soft. He pulled it out and held to the light, interest turning to disgust as he opened it. The paint-spattered cloth contained the remains of a half-eaten meat pie. Lawrence returned the cloth to its hiding place and wiped his hands on his suit before extinguishing the candle. He stood in the darkness for a few minutes, visualising Bertha's last moments while his eyes grew accustomed to the dark. Then he returned to the landing before descending the stairs to find a shadow looming through the door light. The policeman had returned to his post, preventing an exit through the front of the house. Lawrence shook his head. He had half expected this, but it was still inconvenient. He returned to the back of the house and climbed through the rear window, regretting his decision to examine the property. He had given little thought to what he might find in the house but had hoped for a clue. A footprint and a half-eaten pie fell short of his worst expectations. And now he needed to find a way out of the rear garden without drawing attention to himself – a hard enough feat under normal circumstances but next to impossible carrying a cycle. For a fleeting moment, he considered leaving the bicycle behind. But it had been useful so far and was quicker than walking or using public transport, and he dismissed the idea. He located the bike and wheeled it to the bottom of the garden searching for an exit route. To his relief, the rudimentary fence only comprised two lengths of wire. He manoeuvred the bicycle through, but the neighbouring garden was more established, and he fought through a thick hedge to get to the other side. Lawrence slid the cycle under the bottom of the hedge, emerging with a stained coat and twigs in his hair. Picking his way past rows of winter cabbages, he found himself at the rear of an unlit house with an unlocked iron side gate. A moment later he was clear of the house and making his way on foot to Church Road. Lawrence glanced at his fob watch. It wasn't too late, and he shouldn't disturb the household. It was time to get on his bike and make his way back. After a shaky start, he was almost level with the junction, cursing the squeaking cycle when he heard the whir of wheels behind him. Someone was travelling at speed. Lawrence vaguely wondered what the urgency was at that time of night. Then a sickening thud came from nowhere, accompanied by a searing pain on the side of his head. Lawrence reeled in shock, fell from the cycle and clutched his skull. Half dazed, he examined his palm. It was wet he couldn't see the colour of the substance dripping from his skin in the dark. He held it to his nose and smelled a familiar metallic odour. Trembling, Lawrence reached for the cycle, and his fingers brushed a heavy object wet with blood. His blood. Someone had cycled past at speed and thrown half a brick. It could have killed him. Lawrence's head was throbbing. He pressed two fingers against his temple, checking for fragments of bone, but somehow his head was still intact. He staggered to his feet and recovered the cycle before considering his next move. But as he glanced behind, a shadowy figure moved along the road. He looked again. The man was speeding forwards and coming straight towards him. Adrenaline coursed through his body as Lawrence realised that his assailant had circled the road and was coming back for another try. Ignoring the pain and blood streaming from his head, Lawrence leapt onto the cycle, weaving and dodging through the roads of East Ham until he reached the safety of Buxton Road.

# CHAPTER 15

## *Tampered Will*

*Saturday, February 25, 1899*

*Dear Michael*

*Well, our letters must have crossed. No sooner do I write to you asking if you have found Ella's will than you send me a transcript. I dread to think how much time you have taken in duplicating the document, and in your best handwriting. I can see from the gaps in the text, and the question marks how difficult it must have been to read. I am not surprised you almost gave up, and I cannot thank you enough for persevering. Please don't apologise for the missing words and paragraphs. I am all too familiar with the inconsistencies in legal writing. For every solicitor who wields a fountain pen like a calligrapher, there is another as unskilled as a spider. You have had the bad luck to happen upon the latter. But what you have transcribed, upon closer inspection, tells an interesting story. And not one that I have chanced upon before during this kind of investigation. The anomaly is in the codicil to the will, which I can see because I have filled in some gaps despite not having seen the original document. But having pondered the paragraphs overnight, I have made reasonable guesses at the missing words based on the use of language. I believe the writer intended the last section to read as follows:*

*"Shortly after the death of the said deceased which took place on the eighth day of September eighteen hundred and fifty-one, the said Herbert Morse discovered the will in a writing table among the private papers of the deceased. The word 'Ann' had been added after 'Elizabeth', and the name 'Edward' was inscribed in pencil before the surname 'Halls' after the original will was written. The said Arthur Morse and Herbert Morse jointly made oath that they verily believe the special writing is similar to the handwriting of the said deceased. But after diligent enquiry, they cannot ascertain when and where this alteration took place."*

*According to your notes, they proved the will and distributed Ella's legacies in the usual manner. So, the brothers cannot have been unduly concerned with the pencilled entries. Ella must have been a generous woman for she left many gifts upon her death, including substantial donations to the vicar. I have seen the handsome glass window at the east end of the church which she paid for from the will. And now we find out that Ella funded the relocation of the organ and donated to the parish poor. She even left gifts to several religious societies for spreading the word of the Lord abroad, of which I am sure, you approve. Yet is it not curious that somebody inked the will save for two names written in pencil? Why would that happen? The obvious answer is that Ella was unsure of the beneficiary's names – but who leaves money to someone with whom they are not intimately acquainted? Yet, if someone other than*

*Ella made the entries, then why were they written differently to the original document?*

*Do you see where this is leading, Michael? I cannot help myself. I see mysteries everywhere, but there is some justification in pursuing this one. Ella's brothers were content to see her will enacted and would not have done so if troubled by the contents. Her family knew her well, particularly Arthur, with whom she lived. He must have met her friends, but curiously didn't state this in the codicil. The brothers seem more concerned with the date of the pencil marks rather than the content. Ella also left bequests to her family who, thanks to your records, are easily identifiable.*

*I have made a list of all the beneficiaries, but particularly the names on the corrected entry, that is to say, Elizabeth Ann, the wife of Edward Halls. She is not family as far as I can tell, nor am I convinced that she is a servant. Perhaps she was Ella's friend, and if I am fortunate, she may still be alive. There are missing facts in the will, and I mean to track them down. It is good to be back on the trail again, and this work is distracting me from darker thoughts.*

*I remain your friend always.*

*Violet*

# CHAPTER 16

## *A Sore Head*

*Tuesday, March 7, 1899*

Lawrence sat at the table, clutching his bandaged head and trying to ignore the throbbing in his temple. He had returned late the previous night, put a towel on his pillow and gone straight to bed without examining his injured head. When he'd awoken fully clothed, he'd moistened a flannel and dabbed nervously at the dried blood. The wound was deep but not bad enough to send for a doctor. Lawrence had changed his shirt and gone downstairs, dreading the inevitable reaction from the Wards. James Ward had already left for the foundry, but Agnes had stared at him in horror. "What on earth have you done to yourself?" she had demanded. Lawrence had already rehearsed his story.

"I fell off the bicycle," he'd said ruefully.

"I'm not surprised riding around late at night. It's a shame that whatever it was couldn't wait until morning."

Lawrence hadn't replied.

"You'll need to get that bandaged," Agnes had continued.

"Please don't trouble yourself. It's unnecessary."

"I don't want blood all over my tablecloth."

Lawrence had checked his wound to find it open and oozing again. Agnes had sighed and passed the baby to Lawrence. She turned tail and reappeared a few moments later carrying a bandage which she wound tightly around his head.

That was an hour ago, and the mild headache he had woken up with had escalated into a pulsing fury. Lawrence forced himself to drink a cup of tea and was working up the enthusiasm for a cold slice of toast when a loud knocking set off another wave of nausea. Lawrence closed his eyes as Agnes tiptoed from the room and answered the door.

"I've brought some oil for the lodger." Gilbert Cooper's voice boomed through the hallway, and Lawrence lowered his head, hoping to God that Agnes would send him away.

"I'll take that, Gil," said Agnes. "He's not too good today."

Lawrence didn't hear a reply and assumed that Gilbert had gone, but his heart sank when Agnes returned with her neighbour in tow.

"Blimey, you've come a cropper," said Cooper jocularly. "I've brought you some oil."

"Thank you," said Lawrence, pointedly ignoring the rusty tin on the table. Agnes glared at Gil and swiped it away, but it was too late. An orange stain leeched into the tablecloth. If Gilbert noticed, he didn't acknowledge it and turned to Lawrence.

"How did you get on with Bill Donaldson?"

"He was helpful," said Lawrence, trying not to encourage further conversation. His head was swimming, and he needed to lie down.

"Yes, but did he tell you about the girls?"

"Which one?"

"Any of them. Or did you settle for stories about the local criminals?"

"Mr Donaldson told me about the girls," said Lawrence. "I've spoken to my editor, and he wants me to concentrate on the murders and disappearances."

"Does he now?" Gil Cooper picked at a jagged piece of his fingernail and flicked it under the table. Agnes glared but said nothing.

"Yes. He thinks our readers will be more interested in them. Mr Donaldson knew the missing girls. I didn't ask him about Amelia Jeffs, but I got inside the house in Portway."

"How?"

"Mr Manisier is trying to let it out."

"You've met Manisier? How is the old rogue?"

"I couldn't say," said Lawrence. "We weren't together for very long. But he didn't strike me as a rogue, and he wasn't that old."

"You don't know him, though. A bit too slippery for my tastes," said Gilbert, "and very fond of the ladies."

"Which ladies?"

"Any. He's not choosy."

"Mr Manisier seemed perfectly respectable to me," said Lawrence.

"I'm glad you think so." Gilbert Cooper appeared affronted by Lawrence's confidence in the house agent's character. He glowered at Lawrence with his arms crossed.

"I suppose you've heard about young Bertha Russ?" said Lawrence, changing the subject.

Cooper nodded. "Yes. I've read the paper. It looks like your mob spared no time in getting the gory details."

"My mob?"

"The local reporters."

"Oh, yes. Of course. They found Bertha in a cupboard, you know."

"Poor little mite. I hadn't heard." Agnes Ward scooped her infant from the floor and cuddled her tight. "How could anybody be so cruel?"

"It's hard to fathom," said Lawrence opening his mouth to change the subject again, but Gil Cooper beat him to it.

"Anyway, you didn't tell me how you did that?" He pointed at Lawrence's temple with dirty nails.

"I fell off the bike," said Lawrence, trotting out the same excuse he'd successfully used on Agnes.

"You should stick to the train. I've seen four-year-olds with a better sense of balance."

"Charming," said Lawrence. "I'm getting the hang of it now. It's been a few years."

"Are you finished then?"

"Cycling?"

"No." Gilbert snorted. "Reporting. Have you got your story?"

"More or less," said Lawrence. "I've accumulated quite a lot of useful information though I suppose I ought to go to Walthamstow and write a brief account of what happened there. I don't suppose it will take very long."

"Are you leaving us so soon?" Agnes Ward started to clear the cups away in an attempt to get on with her chores. Gil Cooper was reclining in his chair looking as if he had all day to spare.

"In a week or so," said Lawrence, trying not to give too much away. Two days would be more than enough in his guise as a reporter, but solving a series of murders, if it were possible, would take far longer.

"And you, Gil?" Agnes was getting impatient now.

"What time is it?"

"Ten thirty," said Lawrence looking at his watch.

"Yes. I've got a job in Barking. I suppose I'd better get on. See you around, Mr Harpham. And Agnes – give my regards to James." Cooper winked as Agnes showed him to the door.

"How are you feeling?" she asked when she returned.

"Better," said Lawrence, thankful that the pounding in his temples had tailed off.

"Sorry about Mr Cooper," she continued. "A nice man, but he can talk the hind leg off a donkey."

"I don't mind. He's been helpful."

"You're not really going to Walthamstow looking like that?"

Lawrence turned and looked in the mirror. "I must," he said. "It's either that or go back to bed. I may as well make the most of the day."

"But you'll be back for tea?"

Lawrence nodded. "Barring another accident," he said.

# CHAPTER 17

## *Haunted*

*Monday, February 27, 1899*

*Dear Michael*

*Forgive the absence of a chatty opening to this letter. I write in haste to request your wise counsel on two matters that have happened in the brief time since I last wrote to you. The first of these occurred last night, or was it in the early hours of the morning? It could have been any time for I did not consult a clock, although I can say with certainty that it was dark. Though restless, I must have fallen asleep. I dreamed that I was back at school, sitting at my little desk. I remember watching Miss Laycock reach for the globe she kept in the corner. "Where is that?" she asked, tapping her ruler on the top of the globe. I tried to remember the name of the landmass by the north pole, but try as I might, it would not come. "Well, Miss Mills?" she said. "Try harder." She tapped again and again as she waited for my response. Suddenly, she lunged towards me, and the tapping of the ruler turned into a crescendo of noise. Louder and louder, quicker and quicker it went until her face was almost touching mine. Then she opened her mouth, and her teeth turned into spikes, and I screamed and woke up.*

*I lay there, shivering in fright, hardly daring to wipe the perspiration from my brow. It took a few moments to realise I'd been dreaming, but then something happened that made me wonder if I was still asleep. I heard the tapping sound again. It had not stopped, and a regular pulse of noise drummed against my window pane matching the rhythm of my racing heart, beat for beat. I clutched the bedspread to my chest and thought of rational reasons for the noise at my window. The regularity of the sound was unnatural, and I tricked myself into thinking that someone was trying to gain my attention. Perhaps they needed to deliver an important message that could not wait until morning.*

*I fumbled on my nightstand, located a match and lit my night light. Then, taking a deep breath and with considerable trepidation, I threw back the curtains and peered into the inky blackness. It took a few moments for my eyes to adjust to the dark, and when they did, I saw nothing untoward. The sound had stopped, and nobody was outside – not a person or even a cat. It took a long time for sleep to come again. I lay awake until the small hours shivering and alone, trying to decide whether I had imagined the noise. Could I have thought I had woken when I was still in the dream? A kind of false consciousness. But much as I would like to, I don't believe it. Too much time had elapsed between my waking and opening the curtains. Enough time for rational thought and close consideration of circumstance which wouldn't occur in a dream state. Which only leaves one alternative – that someone or something was knocking at my window. And if so, who and why?*

*Which brings me to the second matter – I left for work today intending to ask Elsie about the beneficiaries of the will, specifically the Halls. But my restless night chased this thought from my mind until now. I was still reeling from lack of sleep when I entered the tea shop. I had taken the long route from Norma's again. I will go through the graveyard soon, to prove I still can, but today was not the day for it. Olive took one look at my pale face and sat me down with a cup of strong tea and a bun. I could not have felt less like eating, but she insisted. I offered her no explanation for my condition but implied that I suffered from insomnia. I don't like misleading people, but I did not want to appear foolish in front of Olive, kind though she is. The constant state of turmoil in which I live is embarrassing enough without it becoming public knowledge. Groundless fear dogs my every thought, and if I am losing my mind, then my employer will be the last to know.*

*Olive was right to make me eat. I could not face breakfast before leaving home and felt much better with something in my stomach. As it was Monday and Mildred was coming to work, Olive said she didn't need me to wait tables and would prefer me off my feet. Instead, she asked me to sit at the table in the corner of the room then she gave me a pot of boiling water and a napkin so I could give the cutlery a thorough polish.*

*After half an hour, the pile of clean cutlery was growing, and I was feeling calmer having accomplished something practical. But not as calm as I thought. When the door next opened, I wasn't paying attention. The bell jingled, and I jumped out of my skin, tipping the pot of water over the table. I jumped to my feet and mopped up the watery mess with the tablecloth, then I took it away and fetched another. I shook the creases out, and as I spread it across the table, I glimpsed a scratch – a series of scratches. And the series of scratches formed two distinct words. ELLA MORSE.*

*I sat back in the chair, gazing at the words in horror, then rubbed my eyes and looked again. They were still there. Olive was out the back, attending to some cleaning chores. Two customers were in the shop, both served and satisfied. Thankfully, they did not see my expression, for they might have come to my aid, and I did not want them to acknowledge the words because the repercussions were dreadful whether or not they were there. Either I was imagining things, in which case I was losing my mind, or the words actually existed, in which case – what? What would it mean? That a dead woman was haunting me? Not possible. There was only one thing to do, and I steeled myself for it. I waited until the tea room was empty, a series of hours that ticked past second by painful second. As fast as customers left, new ones arrived eager for conversation and a smile. Today I could provide neither. When the last person finally left the building, I could wait no longer and summoned Olive over. I pointed to the table with my heart in my mouth as I waited for the verdict. She frowned and regarded me with disappointment.*

*"Did you do this?"*

*And now you know. The words were there, gouged into the tabletop, but not by me, as I hastily explained to Olive. Her puzzled expression revealed concern about the truth of my response. After all, Elsie and I had discussed the Morse family in her presence a few times by then. And, as she said, "Why would anyone carve the name of dead woman onto my table?" I could not answer her for I do not know. I have only spoken of Ella to Elsie and Mathilda Brett, and I am as sure as I can be that Mathilda hasn't entered the tea rooms since I last saw her. In any case, there is no reason for her to frighten me.*

*So, tell me, Michael, what do I do? What is happening to me? Or am I making too much of this? Some might see these events as trivial, but they are terrifying to me. I hope you will tell me not to worry and say that I am being silly. You will do that, won't you?*

*Your friend*

*Violet*

# CHAPTER 18

## *Trip to Walthamstow*

Lawrence regretted his continued use of the bicycle more than once during the long and arduous trip to Walthamstow. It was a relatively short distance to travel and shouldn't have involved much more than half an hour of his time on a slow day. But during the journey, a speeding cart had almost knocked him flying. Moments later a dog had chased him, and he'd narrowly missed running over a child who stepped out in front of the bike. How he had stayed upright, was a mystery. Not only had his headache returned, but he had a bruise on his behind that made cycling a feat of nightmarish proportions. Still, he was here now, and keen to familiarise himself with the area and particularly the ditches in which the girls had died.

Lawrence knew it wouldn't be a covert operation. He was unfamiliar with the area and stood no chance of orientating himself without help. Lawrence stopped outside the only address he knew, and only because he had passed the road quite by accident on the way. Then he propped his cycle against the lamppost near fifty-one Markhouse Place, the former home of Annie West.

The miserable terraced property bore more than a passing resemblance to those he'd already seen in West Ham. Almost every street and house were carbon copies of their neighbours, and necessarily so. Never had there been such demand for new homes, but they were soulless shells without craftsmanship or character. Lawrence sighed as he studied the house, caught unexpectedly by an overwhelming sense of homesickness for his beloved Suffolk with its pretty painted cottages and bountiful greens. He was adrift in this unfamiliar world, close to London but so distant from Violet. Violet – where had that thought sprung from? It had been years since he had seen her, and he didn't know how far apart they lived now. For all he knew, Violet could have a home here in Markhouse Place, unlikely though it was. But of course, the last time he had seen Violet was in Silvertown, which was only a short train ride away. Being this close would inevitably provoke memories, and it shouldn't come as a surprise. If only Violet were here now, she could tell him whether he was on the right track. Or indeed on any track. Lawrence knew he was blundering around with no logical plan in place. And even his instinct had absented itself from this investigation. Were it not for the enthusiasm of Samuel Higgins he would give it up as a bad job and go home to Suffolk. But even as the thought entered his head, Lawrence knew he wouldn't do it. He could not abandon all those missing and murdered girls to the indifference of the Metropolitan Police.

Lawrence removed his notebook and reminded himself of the places he wanted to visit. Though Annie West had lived in Markhouse Place, the last sighting of her was in Collingwood Road, and she had died in a ditch at Low Hall sewage farm. Elizabeth Skinner had lived in Beaconsfield Road before being pulled half-dead from Paddy's Field wherever that was. Lawrence stared at his list. Yes. Paddy's Field was going to be the biggest problem. He had no chance of locating it alone and no explanation to offer about why he might want to know where it was, other than for ghoulish, voyeuristic purposes. Lawrence would need to rely on his reporter persona and hope that enough time had passed for people not to take offence at his interest.

Brandishing a pencil and his notebook, he strode into the nearest shop, which was a greengrocer. Ten minutes later, and several coins lighter, Lawrence emerged with a bag of carrots which he thrust into his coat pocket. The shop owner had also given detailed directions to each of the locations of interest. Lawrence never set foot in a shop to procure information without having the courtesy to spend money first. Experience had taught him it yielded far better results. But the shop was small, his needs non-existent and carrots seemed like the least worst option. He climbed on the bicycle again, paper bag rustling in his pocket as he cycled, then made his way to Beaconsfield Road only a few streets away.

As Lawrence cycled past the door of number five, a woman emerged with a young child, and he wondered whether she could be Elizabeth Skinner's mother. Could they still live in the same house? It seemed unlikely, and he was reluctant to stop and speak. There was little to gain from the family at this stage.

Lawrence needed to connect locations rather than look for information. And it was turning out to be much easier than he'd anticipated. Annie West's last known sighting in Collingwood Road was on the same estate and close to Beaconsfield Road. The girls' paths must have crossed, and they would have known each other, at least by sight. And if the information from the shopkeeper about Paddy's Field was correct, then it wasn't far from Annie West's final resting place. It was to the latter location that Lawrence was now pedalling.

Five minutes later, he arrived and pushed the cycle up a narrow lane running alongside an untidy area of scrubland. Lawrence held his breath as he parked his bike, trying not to inhale the putrid odour of the sewage farm. He picked his way across the grass alongside the ditch which ran almost the length of Low Hall Lane. The ditch was not only overflowing with rainwater and sediment but halfway along, Lawrence saw, then smelled the bloated body of a pig. No part of the ditch was clean, and weeds and long-abandoned detritus lurked in its watery depths. Lawrence shuddered, imagining Annie's last moments, submerged in this hellhole of decay, terrified and struggling to breathe. She must have known what would happen to her. But her short, unhappy life left her vulnerable to a predator, and she may have viewed the end of it with relief. It was not a thought to dwell upon, and Lawrence turned away to retrieve his bicycle, glad that he had found the place. One thing was sure. Only someone with an intimate knowledge of the area would know where to take a young girl and attack her mercilessly without fear of exposure.

Lawrence had almost reached his cycle when he tripped over a stray tree root and staggered forwards. He recovered himself instantly, but not before the root dragged his boot off. He automatically planted his foot in the damp ground, leaning towards the boot with the intention of re-tying it but the lace had snapped clean in half. Sighing, Lawrence removed his soggy sock and stuffed it into his pocket. The boot would stay on his foot while riding, but he would need to get another lace before trying to walk anywhere. Abandoning his plans to find Paddy's Field, Lawrence hastened towards the row of shops he had passed earlier.

There was no sign of life in the hardware store, and Lawrence checked the time to see if he was encroaching on the storekeeper's lunch hour. On closer inspection, he could see someone inside. As Lawrence tried the door a second time, a shape moved into view, and the sound of a key rattled in the lock. "Hold on," came a voice from the inside.

Moments later, the door opened, and a shopkeeper fastening a leather apron across his midriff strode forward. "Sorry about that," the man said. "I'm just back from Alf's."

Who or what Alf was, Lawrence failed to ask. He was only interested in acquiring shoelaces at the earliest opportunity. He offered the broken lace towards the shopkeeper who examined it, opened a drawer and put what could have been its twin on the counter.

"Perfect," said Lawrence reaching in his breast pocket for his wallet and finding nothing there. He patted his chest, found no familiar bump, then panicking, he emptied his pockets. A moment later, the candle tin joined the rest of Lawrence's moveable possessions on the counter. He cringed at the sight of the bag of carrots and the damp sock, knowing that no amount of small talk would explain his reasons for carrying them. Then, to his relief, he found his wallet in his trouser pocket where he had inadvertently put it earlier. Lawrence opened it, extracted a few coins and handed them to the shopkeeper.

"There's a name missing," said the man, pointing to the notebook which lay open beside the carrots. Lawrence peered at the page containing the names and addresses of the two Walthamstow girls. "I'm sorry?" he asked.

"You've only written two names, but there were three murders."

"Yes, I know. Mary Jane Voller's not on the list because she didn't live in Walthamstow."

"I didn't mean her."

"They found her dead body in the water though," said Lawrence, losing concentration.

"I daresay. But I'm talking about Florrie Rolph."

"Florrie Rolph? Who on earth is she?"


#

"Florrie was George and Martha's girl," said the shopkeeper, assuming a familiarity with the locals that Lawrence did not possess.

"George and Martha?"

"You must know George. He's a cabman. Works for Mr Reaves."

"I don't know George, Martha or Mr Reaves, but I would like to hear about Florrie."

"You're not a copper, are you?"

"No. I'm a reporter."

"That's not much better," said the shopkeeper warily. "And if you're a reporter, then why don't you know about Florrie?"

"I'm from Suffolk," said Lawrence.

"I see. Then I'll tell you about Florrie if you like, but if it gets busy, you must come back another time."

Lawrence nodded. "I will if there's no other way but tell me what you can for now. When did Florrie die?"

"In the summer of 1895," said the man. "And I know a lot about what happened because my missus is friendly with Martha Rolph. Best friends, you could say. Now, what's your name?" he asked abruptly.

"Alistair Blatworthy," said Lawrence caught off guard and resorting to his nom de plume.

"Dennis Parkes," said the shopkeeper, offering a scaly hand. Lawrence shook it half-heartedly, deterred by the man's obvious skin complaint.

"Yes. Heartbroken, Martha was," said Parkes, resuming his story. "Poor woman. Wracked with guilt, you see."

"Why?"

"Because she sent young Florrie for beer, and if she hadn't done it, the girl would have been safe at home."

"Where was home?"

"Brown's Road, north of here. George liked a pint for his supper, so Martha gave the girl a can and sent her to The Rose and Crown."

"Did she get there?"

"Oh, yes. Florrie purchased the beer and must have been coming back when someone took her." Dennis Parkes shook his head. "Dear little thing she was too. Only six years old with her life ahead of her. Well, they missed her straight away. They loved young Florrie, and when she didn't come back, George went straight to the pub and asked if they'd seen her. Aggie Butcher served that night. She'd taken a shine to Florrie's checked pinafore dress and knew who George meant when he asked about her. Florrie looked like a proper little lady, she said. And she told George that she'd served her and sent her on her way."

"And just to be clear, someone murdered Florrie Rolph."

"Oh, yes. But not before he knocked her about."

"Was she found in a ditch?"

"No. Why would she be?"

"Because Elizabeth Skinner and Annie West were both found in ditches."

"Not Florrie. They found her under a pile of leaves in the rectory gardens."

"When?"

"The day after she went missing. The gardener found her with marks over her face and blood on her clothes. Your mates in the press reported it so graphically that I had to hide the newspaper from Mrs Parkes for the rest of the week. A man had used her, you see. Only six years old and subjected to that. Not the sort of thing for a woman to read, especially one who was fond of the girl."

"I understand," said Lawrence. "And when you say used...?"

"I mean he violated her," said Parkes. "Then he killed her to stop her from screaming."

"How close is the rectory from The Rose and Crown?"

"It's not on the way if that's what you mean. He decoyed her a fair distance from home."

"Do you think that's what happened?"

"Yes. Florrie must have gone willingly. Someone would have noticed if he'd tucked her under his arm and carried her off screaming. Besides, there was a can of ale next to her body in the rectory garden. I daresay he got it from Florrie when she left the public house and took it with him."

Lawrence shook his head. "It doesn't bear thinking about."

"Here, don't write a report about it, will you? George won't want it dredged up again, and I don't want my name in the newspapers."

"I won't mention you," said Lawrence, "and my readers are in Suffolk."

"Good," said Parkes, looking relieved. "Odd that you didn't know about Florrie though. Who else is on your list?"

Lawrence took his notebook and turned a few pages to find the names he had written in date order before he knew about Florrie Rolph.

"Here," he said, pushing the notebook over.

Dennis Parkes squinted as he examined the writing. "Yes, these look familiar," he said. "It's been like a ruddy epidemic since those two went missing in West Ham. Do you think it was the same man?"

"Do you?" asked Lawrence.

"I don't know," said Parkes. "I'm not a copper, but then again, I could probably do a better job."

"There are too many gaps to be sure," said Lawrence. "Anyway, thank you for your time. You've been very helpful."

"Hang on," said the shopkeeper. "Do boys count?"

"I'm not sure what you mean."

"Murdered boys. Do they count?"

"Are you suggesting there has been another murdered child?"

"Not suggesting. I'm telling you."

"Was he found in a ditch?"

"No."

"Or in West Ham or Walthamstow?"

"Neither."

"Then, I doubt it."

"Someone strangled the boy and left him near Upton Park Station."

Lawrence whistled. "That's in the right area, and the method of killing is consistent with Florrie and Amelia Jeffs. When did it happen?"

"I can't remember. I'd have to say late 1897 if you pressed me, but I can't be sure."

"What was his name?"

"Barratt. William Barratt. I can't give you any more detail than that."

"You've given me more than enough," said Lawrence. "Thank you."

He doffed his hat and left the shop, then considered the matter as he threaded the new lace into his shoe. The further information neatly plugged the gap in time between the death of Elizabeth Skinner in 1893 and Mary Jane Voller in 1898. But why hadn't Samuel told him about their murders? It was inconceivable that

Higgins didn't know. He was a reporter, after all. Lawrence checked his watch. It was mid-afternoon, and he still had enough time to get to Barking before the press office closed. He mounted the bicycle and ignoring the pain in his rear, pedalled swiftly southwards.

# CHAPTER 19

## *Ill-gotten Gains*

**Wednesday, March 1, 1899**

*Dear Michael*

*Ella's will has turned out to be a damp squib. The big mystery behind it was nothing more exciting than trivial thievery. A few days ago, I visited Mathilda Brett to check whether she had been in the tea shop recently. That way, I'd know if she could have been responsible for the table marks. I took her a small posy to say thank you for her previous help, and she asked me in for a cup of tea. We chatted for a while, and she mentioned a recent visit to her sister in Kings Lynn. So, without asking, I immediately knew that she couldn't have damaged the table and somebody else must have carved Ella's name.*

*While at Mathilda's house, I threw caution to the wind and asked other questions about the Morse family. I didn't hold back and talked openly about the will. Unusually, for Mathilda, she couldn't add any more to the subject, but when I asked if she knew Edward and Anna Halls, her face lit up. 'Yes, I do,' she said and what did I want to know about them? I didn't need to lead the conversation any further, as once she started talking, she couldn't stop. She said Edward Halls had sold all his personal effects not long before Ella Morse died. The poor chap went bankrupt owing to some unsuccessful business venture. Since then, Edward Halls had passed away, and Anna is now a widow, still living here in Swaffham and not far from my cottage. I thanked Mathilda and having half an hour free before going to Norma's, I hastened straight there.*

*Anna answered the door, listened to my questions, and was not interested and refused to speak to me. But I was firm with her, and put my foot in the door, preventing her from slamming it and sending me away. Seeing the determination in my face, she capitulated. Her shoulders slumped, and her head bowed as she waved me through. Her cottage, if I could call it that, stood on one level. The front room was bare with only a mattress and a wooden chair in front of an unlit grate. A door led to another even smaller back room where she slept. I stood, for there was nowhere else to sit apart from a chair. But I couldn't use that because she'd left her supper on it. And a poor meal it was too of a crust of bread and a small bowl of dripping.*

*"Don't let me stop you from eating," I said, and she grunted, put her hands on her hips and asked me what I wanted.*

*So, I told her, Michael. Just like that, with no softness in my manner. Tiredness had overwhelmed me, both physically and mentally, and I grew fearful that the Morse mystery would cost me my sanity. I inwardly cringe when I remember how I spoke to that poor woman, hectoring her in her own home. "Did you tamper with Ella's will?" I asked.*

*She was equally succinct. "Yes, I did," she said. "And what of it?"*

*I told her in no uncertain terms what I thought of her subterfuge, and she countered it by telling me not to make so much of it. Her attitude towards the deception surprised me, and I asked where she kept her conscience. At first, she laughed, and then her forehead scrunched into a frown. "I am not a wicked woman," she said. "And the sum of money involved was nothing to Miss Morse and everything to me. It kept me from the workhouse." Her words left me feeling distinctly uncharitable, and I asked her to elaborate, feeling it my Christian duty to give her the benefit of the doubt. And she told me her story.*

*Anna Hall, it transpired, was a domestic servant, employed by Arthur and Ella Morse, not long before Ella died. One day, she saw one of the other servants witness a copy of Ella Morse's last will and was curious about what it contained. Anna found the document laid out on the desk and noticed that Miss Morse had left legacies to the other servants. Even though she had only lately joined the household, Anna was jealous and resentful. For reasons Anna didn't understand, Miss Morse had written parts of the will in pencil although the majority was in ink. Over the following weeks, Anna kept a close eye on the will, hoping that Ella Morse would include her name, but it never appeared. And, in due course, she noticed that Ella had overwritten some pencilled sections using her pen. By the time of Ella's death, only a few uninked words remained. And by happy coincidence one referred to Elizabeth wife of William Balls.*

*While the other servants mourned the passing of their mistress, Anna hastened straight to the desk to check the condition of her will. To her relief, the pencilled words were still there. Knowing that her husband's business was in dire straits, and they were about to lose everything, Anna altered the names. She changed them to read Elizabeth Ann wife of Edward Halls and, deciding not to risk a mismatch of ink, she re-wrote it in pencil. Although Ella's brothers challenged the timing of the alteration, it never occurred to them to question the content. Anna presented herself as Elizabeth Anna Halls and claimed the money intended for Elizabeth Balls. I can only presume that Elizabeth didn't challenge it, because she didn't realise, she was due a legacy.*

*Nobody knows about this, and I'm not going to tell them. The legacy only amounted to a mere five pounds. While this was enough to stave off grievous hardship for Anna Halls, it is a paltry sum in the scheme of things. And it doesn't explain Ella's unwillingness to lie silently in her grave. Not that I am suggesting for one moment that she is the phantom seen in the churchyard. But had the fraud been substantial and spirits existed, it might have been a reason. What am I saying, Michael? I don't believe in ghosts and speculation about churchyard phantoms is ridiculous. But so many disturbing events have happened to me in recent weeks, that Ella Morse seeking her revenge from beyond the grave would come as a relief. So, the mystery is over, and hopefully, these disquieting feelings of dread will disappear too. Next time I write, it will be with jolly news, I promise.*

*In the meantime, take care.*

*Yours most sincerely*

*Violet*

# CHAPTER 20

## *More Victims*

Lawrence hurled the bicycle against the red brick press office and stormed inside, not waiting to see if it stayed upright. It did not, and the bike slid down the wall, before settling on the path with its wheels spinning. Marching into the lobby, Lawrence strode towards the press room door, hand outstretched.

"Oi, don't go in there," yelled Stanley, from his position behind the counter. "Come back."

But it was too late. Lawrence had already flung the door open and stepped inside, coming face to face with a sight that left him squirming with embarrassment. An elderly woman was sitting next to Samuel Higgin's desk; her eyes screwed tight in concentration as she sewed a pair of trousers. Stanley Higgins stood beside her dressed in long cotton drawers.

"Dear God," said Lawrence, putting his hand over his eyes. "Forgive me."

Higgins sighed. "Meet my aunt," he said awkwardly. "Aunt Lavinia, this is Mr Lawrence Harpham."

Lawrence opened his eyes, extended his hand and shook it. "Pleased to meet you," he mumbled. "I'll wait outside."

Back in the hallway, Stanley greeted him with a knowing smile. "I told you," he crowed. "You should have listened."

Lawrence resisted the urge to clip him round the ear and paced the lobby waiting for Samuel to finish. Ten minutes later, the door opened, and Lavinia emerged.

"You can go in now," she said haughtily.

Lawrence flashed a weak smile before returning to the press room where Samuel was standing with his back to the door, gazing out of the window.

"What's got your dander up?" he asked amiably.

Lawrence, whose original intention had been to confront Higgins and demand an explanation, was wrong-footed again.

"I don't know what you mean," he said.

"Yes, you do. I know a spot of unbridled rage when I see it. What's the problem?"

Lawrence opened his notebook, turned to the list and placed it firmly on the desk.

"They are," he said.

"Ah," said Higgins, turning the page to face him. "Good. Tell me all about it."

"Do you recognise those names?"

"Yes, I do."

"Then why didn't you tell me about them?"

"Why should I?"

"Because they were both murdered."

"Should I have told you about every murder that has taken place in the last decade?"

"Obviously not all of them," said Lawrence, scowling in frustration.

"Then, why these two?"

"You don't think they're relevant?"

"I didn't say that," Higgins replied. "Tell me why you think I should have mentioned them. You must have noticed that one victim is male."

"Of course," said Lawrence. "Surely you can see how Florrie Rolph's death fits into the pattern. She died in Walthamstow, and someone lured her to the rectory gardens where they outraged and murdered her. The circumstances of her death were almost the same as Amelia Jeffs, including dying from strangulation."

Higgins nodded. "And the boy?"

"I must confess that I know little about him, but I hear that they found his body near Upton Park railway station. And the reason that I think his death is significant is that he died from strangulation."

"Excellent," said Higgins. "I hoped you would say that."

"What do you mean?"

"When we first met, I told you I would only give you a certain amount of information. I have a theory, but that is all it is. The Metropolitan Police do not share my views. I needed to know that you would come to the same conclusion entirely through your own investigations. And you have, which strengthens my opinion that these crimes were all carried out by the same person."

"So, you knew about Florrie Rolph and the boy?"

"Of course. But I was less sure about those two murders than the others. There are patterns, but also discrepancies, not least the small matter of gender, in Barratt's case."

"The dates clinched it for me," said Lawrence. "Factoring in Florrie and William's deaths means a killing occurred at least every two years, or more since 1890."

"Exactly," said Higgins. "Follow me,"

He led Lawrence into his research room, ignited the wall lamp and pulled a box from the top of the desk. "Here it is," he said, lifting a folded page closer to his eyes. "They found six-year-old William Barratt in September 1897, lying on an open piece of ground given over to a builder. He was alive when found but died soon after. The boy lived in St Leonard's Road, Bromley by Bow, some four miles from Upton Park. William was well-nourished and loved by his family. So, the coroner came to the inescapable conclusion that his murderer decoyed him from the vicinity of his home."

"But why?"

"Therein lies the question," sighed Higgins. "As you know, young Barratt met his death by strangulation, but that is not all. The killer removed the boy's shoes and socks, then beat him on the chest with his bare fists. Whether he died from strangulation or the bruise on his heart was impossible to tell."

"So, he killed him for the thrill of it," said Lawrence. "I take it he was not..."

"The killer only removed his footwear," said Higgins, sparing Lawrence an awkward question. "But whether the murderer gained sexual gratification from the act, is another matter."

"There are enough similarities, don't you think?"

"Yes."

"But what we can do about it?"

"We need to look for commonalities between the dead children," said Higgins. "I am down to my last dozen newspapers," he added, nodding towards the much-reduced pile. "I'll finish them tonight. Then we'll know we have accounted for all potential victims."

"Wouldn't you know that by now?"

"You'd be surprised how many children were harmed during this decade," said Higgins. "I take nothing for granted."

"Where to start?" mused Lawrence, staring at the map on the wall.

"West Road," said Higgins with certainty.

"I've already been there, and I don't much like the look of one of the estate agents."

"We should consider anyone connected to the building trade."

"Or someone dwelling in West Road," said Lawrence. "But how can I find out who was living there when the girls died?"

"It will be on the census records," said Higgins.

"Yes. But I won't be able to look at them. You'd need to be in government."

"Or the local council."

A glance passed between them, and Lawrence smiled in satisfaction. "Isabel Smith," they both said in unison.

# CHAPTER 21

## *A Murder of Crows*

***Thursday, March 2, 1899***

*Dear Michael*

*I am struggling to write this letter, for the trembling in my hands –
a movement so uncontrollable that I can barely hold the pen. My
home, my refuge is now my prison. I am fearful of venturing outside,
at least not while it is dark. I hope I can face it in the morning. Thank
goodness that Daisy is with Norma or I would have no choice. And
the thought of setting foot outside these four walls is more than I can
bear. My head is swimming, and I feel as if I am watching myself
from afar. The room is blurry, unclear. It must be the shock of
tonight.*

You will remember reading of my encounter with Reverend Winter in the graveyard, and I told you I had found a key in the disturbed earth by Ella's grave. Well, tonight I learned its purpose.

Today should have been a good day. I arrived home from Norma's in good spirits, eager to attend a rare evening of bridge at The George Hotel. I was getting ready when I heard an almighty clatter of metal as if someone was banging pans together. I looked out of the window, but there was nothing out of the ordinary. So, I went downstairs to check if something had fallen over in the kitchen. Everything was as expected, and I carried on getting ready. No sooner did I set foot on the stairs than the noise began again. This time, there was no doubt about where it was coming from – it was right outside my back door. I hastened towards the kitchen, and from there went outside into the yard. By now, it was a little after seven o'clock, and though dark, I could see the outline of an unfamiliar shape a few feet from the house. An eerie silence replaced the banging sound, and I gazed at the shape with trepidation wondering what it was and why it was in my garden. As I took a tentative step closer, a yowling shriek pierced the chilly night, and a cat sprang from the fence and darted towards the gate. I clutched my heart, terror coursing through me, and in a rush of nerves, I fled for the rear door to find a source of light. I lit the largest lantern with a shaking hand, and steeling myself, raised it aloft and retraced my steps.

As I approached the object, my fear vanished, replaced by idle curiosity. For the item lying upon the hard earth, was a small tin trunk about a foot and a half long, inlaid with circles and swirls and with a large clasp lock on the side. I set the lantern on the floor and tried to pick it up. The trunk lifted easily, and I tucked it under my arm and carried it inside, holding the lantern in my other hand. Intrigued by the strange discovery, I placed it on my kitchen table and examined it. On closer inspection, the swirls and circles turned out to be scrolls and skulls. I lifted the hasp to reveal a lock beneath, and I tugged it, but it would not open. I soon realised that, in the *absence of a hand axe, I would only find out what was inside with the aid of a key.*

*I sat there for five minutes, Michael, staring at the box. Then I lifted it again and shook it slightly. Something soft bumped against the side. Though no longer frightened, the unsolicited gift troubled me. It had not been there that morning, of that I was sure, but when was it delivered? It must have been late as I had used the front door that evening. But why leave a locked box without a note, and how was I supposed to get into it?*

*I stopped to make myself a cup of tea and collect my thoughts. Ten minutes later, and with a groggy head, I stared at the box again. By now, I had a headache, and the skulls started blurring together. Then, one came sharply into focus, bringing a sudden horrible sense of foreboding. I had seen a similar skull very recently. It had formed part of the key which I had found on Ella Morse's grave.*

*I slowly reached into my bag and located the key which had lain there since its discovery and I held it next to the lock, comparing the shape. It looked like a good fit. Ignoring the goosebumps crawling across my skin, and the panicky thud of my heart, I slid the key into the lock where it nestled, daring me onwards. I licked my lips, closed my eyes and turned the key. The lock opened with a satisfying click. All I had to do was open it. Pandora's box – a box from which no good could possibly come. For a moment, I contemplated putting it out with the rubbish. It would only take moments, and I would never know what was inside. But I am nothing if not curious, and I knew that I would always wonder if I didn't look. So, taking a deep breath, I flung the lid open and peered inside.*

*The smell hit me first, Michael. Death, of course. Death and decay. And the sight I saw you would know only too well. For you have been there, and you have seen it – two dead crows, with maggots crawling through their putrefying bodies. I screamed, ran, and locked myself in the bedroom where I am penning this letter now.*

*I have stopped pretending to be brave. I am terrified, Michael. I have never been more scared in my entire life. And if I am sufficiently recovered to stamp and post this letter tomorrow, then you will know I have survived the night.*

*If not, I remain your friend always.*

*Violet*

# CHAPTER 22

## *Telegram*

*Tuesday, March 7, 1899*

From: Rev Farrow, c/o The White Hart Inn, Swaffham
To: Lawrence Harpham, c/o 55 Buxton Road, West Ham

Lawrence. No time to explain, but Violet has been living in
Swaffham until recently. We have corresponded, but now she has
disappeared, and I think she is in danger. Come quickly – wire
confirmation by return.

Yours

Michael

# CHAPTER 23

## *Break-In*

*Wednesday, March 8, 1899*

"So, you see, short of tripping over the killer in the act, it's the only chance we've got."

Lawrence Harpham was sipping coffee in Isabel Smith's office at the Municipal Buildings while trying to explain his lack of progress.

"But you believe there is a murderer?"

"Undoubtedly. A very cunning, ruthless degenerate man who won't stop until we catch him."

"And you think this man was responsible for all the deaths?"

"I believe so," said Lawrence.

"And the disappearances?"

"Logic would suggest so, but I am less certain. Geographically, it fits the bill."

"How are you getting on with Samuel?" asked Isabel.

"Very well. He's a little odd though. I wish you had warned me about his head."

Isabel smiled and put her empty coffee cup on the desk. "I didn't want you jumping to any conclusions about his character before hearing what he had to say."

"I'm not judgemental."

"Yes, you are. I remember your reaction when I told you that the new inspector was a little portly. Too much food makes a man lazy, you said, if I remember rightly."

"That's different."

Isabel raised an eyebrow.

"Anyway, how did it happen?"

"What?"

"Higgins ear and whatever is or isn't behind that blacked-out lens."

"Someone attacked him with a brick," said Isabel. "Long before I knew him. Back in the early nineties, I think. A case of mistaken identity, as I understand it."

"Poor chap."

"Yes, he was, and unlucky enough to become the focus of a witch hunt. It had something to do with a crime – a serious matter. I don't know the details, but a group of men chased Higgins, beat him and left him for dead. He was in the hospital for over a month. The surgeons did their best but could not save his sight, and he lost an ear. All very unfortunate and avoidable."

"Did they catch them?"

"The attackers? Yes, they did. And unbelievably, Higgins forgave them. He pleaded in court for leniency, saying that if he'd done what they thought he had done, then their actions were justifiable. It must have carried some weight as the judge reduced their prison sentences."

"I said he was strange. I'd have turned the key and left them to rot."

"It's not his way," said Isabel. "So, you and Samuel agree about these deaths?"

"Yes. Completely," said Lawrence. "But the investigation, such as it is, has all but stalled. Higgins has plotted the murders on a map. We know that West Road plays an important part in the mystery. It would help to know who was living there when the murders and disappearances took place. I've met one or two of the current inhabitants, both estate agents, as it happens, but they won't remember everyone who lived there. We need records."

"What records?"

"The eighty-one and ninety-one censuses would be helpful."

"You know they're not open to the public, don't you?"

"I guessed as much. But it would be beneficial to have them."

Isabel sighed. "The records are in the repository in Chancery Lane, but I can't get you in there."

"Under any circumstances?"

"No. It's not possible. You're not entitled to that information. But..." Isabel said, chewing her lip as she considered the dilemma, "there may be another way."

Isabel stood, turned to her right, and reached for a hanging cord which she pulled. Lawrence heard a shrill jangle in the distance. Moments later, a young girl appeared in the doorway clutching a clipboard and pen.

"Yes, Miss Smith," she said.

"Can you fetch Miss Ponsonby and Miss Cream?"

"Right away, miss."

"She's an improvement on the last one," said Lawrence. "You never told me what happened."

"And I never will," said Isabel, shuddering. "I think it's enough to say that your judgement of Miss Worthington's character was correct. She could have drowned in her officiousness, as you so admirably put it."

Lawrence tried and failed to conceal a grin, remembering the sanctimonious receptionist with whom he had locked horns during the Silvertown investigation.

Isabel was about to reprimand him when a knock at the door interrupted her. Lawrence watched open-mouthed as a tall slim woman dressed in trousers and a waistcoat marched through the door. Her sultry, perfectly groomed companion wearing a slick of scarlet lipstick followed.

"Ladies, this is Mr Harpham."

Lawrence stood and immediately offered his chair to the dark-haired woman.

"No need. They won't be here long," said Isabel before the girl could answer. "Now, ladies. Are you familiar with the public records office in Chancery Lane?"

"Yes, ma'am," said Miss Ponsonby.

"Miss Smith," said Isabel, with the air of a woman who has given the same reply on many previous occasions. "Now," she continued, scribbling furiously on a piece of paper which she signed with a flourish then folded and placed in an envelope. "Take this," she continued, tucking the flap inside, "and give it to Mr Grace. He may rail against the contents of this letter, but he will abide by them, and you will need his help. Ask for the census records for West Road, West Ham. You have until six o'clock tonight to take down as much information as you can. Then pay a runner to deliver it to Mr Harpham at – where are you staying, Lawrence?"

"Fifty-five Buxton Road, West Ham."

"Very good. Deliver it there, and each of you, please take half a day off next week for your trouble."

"Consider it done," said Miss Ponsonby tweaking the knot in her tie.

"Shall I write it down?" asked Lawrence.

"No need," said Isabel. "Miss Ponsonby has an excellent memory. She forgets nothing."

"Perhaps I'll deliver it myself," said Miss Cream, with a slow, deliberate wink at Lawrence who spluttered as he battled for an appropriate response.

"That will do," said Isabel patiently. "Off you go and good luck."

Lawrence waited for the door to close. "She was wearing trousers," he said to Isabel.

"I noticed."

"And did you see what the other one did to me?"

"It isn't the first time, and it won't be the last," said Isabel. "Don't worry about trivial matters. Misses Ponsonby and Cream are excellent women. Quite the best. Their talents go to waste in the typing pool, which is where they work on a quiet day like this. But if I have any covert clerical work, I call on them first. Miss Ponsonby apprehended a thief last year, alone and in dangerous circumstances. As for Miss Cream, don't let her glamourous appearance fool you. She speaks four languages and wields an épée as skillfully as any man."

"They sound overqualified for the task at hand," Lawrence admitted.

"And they are, but if I need speed and ruthless efficiency, I can do no better. If it's possible to get this information in the time allotted, they will do it."

"I can't thank you enough," said Lawrence. "It's too kind."

"On the contrary, you are helping me," said Isabel. "I have slept more peacefully, knowing that someone is finally taking an interest in those poor girls."

"I'm surprised you didn't put Miss Ponsonby and Miss Cream on the case," said Lawrence.

"You know, it never occurred to me, but they have certain qualities," she mused, her words trailing away as she considered the implications.

"I'll leave you to it," said Lawrence, scraping his chair back. He walked to the window and looked outside. "Drat. It's raining," he said.

"Would you like to take my carriage?" asked Isabel.

Lawrence raised an eyebrow.

"It's a new driver," Isabel continued. "Obviously."

"Have you got an umbrella?" asked Lawrence.

Isabel nodded.

"I'd rather take that."

#

The rain teemed down for ten minutes while Lawrence made his way towards Holborn intending to catch the first available train to West Ham. But the rain abruptly stopped as Lawrence neared the station and he reconsidered. As the weather brightened, his mood did too. Having nothing else to do with his day, he made the most of his time in London and re-familiarised himself with the sights. Lawrence dined at midday in a little restaurant off the Cornfields and continued promenading around London. When he ran out of things to do, he caught a late afternoon train back to Maryland station, whistling as he walked the short distance to Buxton Road. Lawrence was musing on his day when he turned into number fifty-five to find the door wide open and several police officers standing in the hallway.

"Who are you," asked a red-haired constable when he saw Lawrence.

"I'm lodging here," said Lawrence. "Where are Mr and Mrs Ward?"

"Is that you, Mr Harpham?" Agnes Ward's voice drifted from upstairs accompanied by the wail of her youngest child.

"Yes. What's going on and can I help?"

"Wait a moment."

Lawrence stared at the two officers while he waited for Agnes until she ran breathlessly downstairs without her infant. The crying continued from above.

"I've put Mabel in the crib," said Agnes. "Otherwise, we will get no peace. She'll settle in a minute."

"What's going on?" repeated Lawrence.

"We don't know yet," said the rounder of the two police officers. "Something to do with this, I presume?" He nodded towards a series of deep gouges in the front door near the lock which Lawrence had somehow overlooked.

"Yes," said Agnes. "I went out earlier to post a letter which reminds me; there's a telegram for you upstairs, Mr Harpham. Then I ran a few errands and noticed these marks when I returned."

"It doesn't look like anyone got in," said the red-haired policeman, running his hand over the damaged door. "The lock is still intact."

"This one is," said Agnes, "but come through to the kitchen and look at the back door."

The two officers traipsed through the hallway and into the back of the house with Lawrence trailing behind.

"Dear, oh dear. What do you think happened here, PC Ainsworth?"

The constable knelt and examined the tiled floor, before opening the back door and peering outside.

"The culprit broke the glass with a heavy object and gained entry through the back door. He committed the crime alone, and cut his hand while in the act, Sarge."

"Good work," said the sergeant, approvingly.

"How do you know?" asked Agnes.

"Simple. There is only one set of footprints on the path and glass inside the door. Add to that the drops of blood on the floor and a dirty great hole in your window, and it's easy to deduce what happened. He tried to jemmy the front door open, which indicates the man was a stranger and didn't know to try the back entrance first."

"Then how did he know that Mrs Ward was out?" Lawrence stepped forward and made a quick visual examination of the scene.

"I don't suppose he did," said the sergeant. "I expect he took a chance and robbed the house. I doubt it's the first one he's tried. Anything missing?"

"Well, that's the strange thing," said Agnes. "We own nothing of value, except for the silver tea service on the dining table and it's still there."

"What have they taken?"

"Nothing that I can see."

"You're wrong about the footprints," said Lawrence.

The sergeant drew himself to his full height and put his hands on his hips. "And what makes you think that?"

"Because I made them last night. Look closely, and you'll see that they lead from the shed where I left my bicycle. And the specks of blood on the floor belong to Mr James Ward who cut his hand on a tin a few nights ago while feeding the cat. You shouldn't jump to conclusions."

The sergeant glowered at Lawrence. "Mind your own business," he snapped. "Haven't you got somewhere to go while we speak to Mrs Ward? This matter doesn't concern you."

Lawrence ignored him and returned to the hallway, where he inspected the damaged lock. He must have missed it earlier because the door had been open. But having examined it from the outside, the scratches on the paintwork were worse than the structural damage. Theatrically so. And why had there been such a visible break-in when nothing was missing? Or was it?

Lawrence raced upstairs to his room and opened the door. The curtains were still closed, the bed untouched, but the neat stack of papers was slightly askew. Not enough for most people to notice but Lawrence was fastidious. Someone had disturbed them. Lawrence rifled through the newspapers, but there were so many that he couldn't tell if any were missing. He couldn't imagine a burglar sitting down and quietly reading so something else must have attracted his attention. The rest of the room appeared undisturbed. It was tidy, everything was in place, and nothing seemed untoward. And then he realised. The dressing table was empty, and it shouldn't have been. He had left nine pieces of paper representing the missing and murdered children in date order on the desk last night. On top, was a tenth page on which he had written all the commonalities between the crimes. It was a comprehensive list, and he had hoped to compare it with the results of the census records when they arrived.

Lawrence sat down on the bed, contemplating why someone would take the papers. Then, with a sudden sinking feeling, he patted his jacket pockets, frantically trying to locate his notebook. To his relief, Lawrence felt the firm edges through his inside breast pocket. So long as he had the information from his notebook, he could replicate the missing pages.

If Agnes was right and nothing else had gone from the house, there was only one inescapable conclusion. Someone had entered the property with the sole purpose of finding out what Lawrence knew. And given that he was purporting to be an undercover reporter working on a series of historical crimes, he must be getting close to the truth. Though God only knew how considering the lack of suspects. He ought to go downstairs and tell the police officers about the missing papers. But they would only impede his investigation. He decided instead, to re-read his notes and wait for the census transcription to arrive.

# CHAPTER 24

## *Making Sense of the Census*

"I hope it wasn't serious," said Agnes Ward as Lawrence joined the family at the dinner table. It was six thirty, and James Ward had been back from the foundry for half an hour. Having washed and changed, he was looking forward to his evening meal, almost forgetting the lodger in their midst. He visibly started when Lawrence came through the door.

"What do you mean?" asked Lawrence, answering Agnes while watching James.

"The telegram. I trust it didn't bring bad news?"

"Can't have been worse than a man arriving home to find he needs to buy two new doors," muttered James Ward. "It's a poor state of affairs."

"What telegram?" asked Lawrence frowning.

"I told you earlier. A telegram came for you this morning. I put it on your dressing table."

"I didn't see it."

"Has it fallen on the floor?"

The intruder took it, more likely, thought Lawrence gloomily, spearing a forkful of beans. It was tempting to leave the meal table and check his room in case the telegram had against all the odds, fluttered under the bed, but he knew it wouldn't be there. It was in the same location as the pieces of paper by now and likely destroyed. Lawrence had no way of knowing who'd sent it or what it contained. He put thoughts of the communication from his mind and carried on eating the delicious cottage pie that Agnes had prepared.

The meal continued with Lawrence and Agnes making polite conversation. The two eldest children quietly ate while James grumbled about the break-in. Lawrence hadn't mentioned the missing paperwork and had no intention of doing so. James Ward was not as keen on taking lodgers as his wife and Lawrence had already upset him earlier in the week. Ward still hadn't forgiven him for the press runner arriving early and waking the children. Not that Lawrence had had any control over it, but he couldn't afford any more trouble at the house. If Ward thought that Lawrence was responsible for the damage to his doors, Lawrence would be out on his ear and looking for alternative accommodation. Feeling guilty, but not enough to do anything about it, he kept his counsel.

James Ward's mood improved as his stomach filled. By the time Agnes cleared the plates away and returned with a large bread and butter pudding and a jug of custard, he was starting to relax. He was regaling Lawrence with a tale about the foundry cat when a rapping at the door followed by a voice bellowing, 'delivery', startled him.

James Ward was out of his chair and bounding up the hallway before Lawrence had the chance to say that it was probably for him. Ward returned to the dining room with a scowl on his face and tossed a brown envelope at Lawrence.

"Whoever it was, left this on the doorstep," he muttered, digging into the remains of his dessert.

Lawrence tucked the package under his chair and finished his pudding, waiting for Ward to resume his story. But in apparent disapproval of the interruption to his meal, Ward ate silently and Agnes, sensing his mood, did the same. As eager to examine the census as he was to escape the uncomfortable atmosphere, Lawrence excused himself as soon as he finished pudding.

Back upstairs, he placed the package on the dressing table and took a futile look under the bed. There was no sign of the telegram there or anywhere else in the bedroom. Replacing his jacket with a robe, Lawrence plumped up the pillows and settled on the bed. He opened the envelope to find a brief note from Miss Ponsonby. 'Mission accomplished – all information successfully transcribed. Destroy after use.' Inside were pages of writing, in at least six different hands. God only knows how they had managed it. But the women must have harnessed several of the staff in the public records office to finish the transcription. Lawrence wondered how Isabel had gained the cooperation of the man in charge. Something untoward, he supposed, but speculation was pointless, and it might be better not to know. Still, it was very much to his gain.

Lawrence split the records into two piles, one for the 1881 census and one for 1891, took out his pencil and ruled his notebook into several columns. He'd already given considerable thought on how to manage the volume of information and had a fully developed plan. West Road was central to the earlier murders and disappearances so Lawrence would focus on any occupants who were on both sets of census records. The nature of the outrages meant that he could rule out women and children, which narrowed things further. Finally, he would note down all occupations. Though it would be too risky to eliminate anyone at this stage, householders who had connections to property or building work would be at the top of his list. Lawrence hoped that by the time he had finished, the list would be manageable, and he could confidently investigate.

The hours ticked by as he scribbled furiously, and the list grew line by line. He was still writing at midnight and turned to the last page of the 1891 census hoping the number of houses in West Road had reduced. They had not. There were still one hundred and five, and no amount of wishful thinking would change it. Gritting his teeth, Lawrence continued through the night. Finally, just before three o'clock, he finished and through bleary eyes, examined his list. It contained twelve names. Only twelve. He sighed and reclined in his bed, holding the page above him and angling it towards the bedside lamp. Lawrence had asterisked two of the names, William Donaldson and John Manisier, men with whom he was already acquainted. Both had lived in West Road for over a decade. Both had access to empty properties. Lawrence had instinctively liked Donaldson and had formed a lesser opinion of Manisier. Even so, they were at the top of his suspect list. Beneath were George Gill, a carpenter, Philip Harris and Frederick Tuff, bricklayers, and two labourers named Thomas Smith and Benjamin Snow. Below Snow and underlined, was Walter Veitch, decorator and paper hanger. The remaining men had non-building related occupations. They included Harry Edwards, a railway guard from Bury St Edmunds, who Lawrence vaguely knew but didn't realise had moved to West Ham. He gazed at his notes, wondering which of them to pursue first. But when the lines started blurring, tiredness overcame him, and he fell asleep still clutching his pencil.

# CHAPTER 25

## *The List of Suspects Grows*

### *Thursday, March 9, 1899*

Lawrence woke at an embarrassingly late hour to a dilemma. Should he ask for breakfast or quietly slip from the house and start questioning the men on his list? Fortunately, Agnes decided for him, having heard his soft footfall on the stairs. She approached him by the front door with a cup of tea in her hand.

"Have this," she said, thrusting it towards him. "And don't worry about the time. You can rise whenever you wish."

Lawrence regarded her kind face. She was not yet forty, he surmised, yet deep frown lines and the beginnings of crow's feet were prematurely ageing her. Mabel squirmed in her arms, and she changed position and rocked the baby as she spoke.

"Do you want something to eat?" she asked.

"I don't want to trouble you, and I'm going out," said Lawrence.

"I can make you a ham sandwich," said Agnes. "You can eat it while you walk."

Lawrence salivated at the thought. Starting the day tired and hungry was not an ideal combination for successful detecting. "I'll hold the baby if you like," he said.

Agnes nodded and passed the child over, and Lawrence continued to rock her, patting her back gently as he walked up and down the hallway. Her eyes fluttered and closed, and within seconds she was asleep. He smiled and watched the gentle rise of her chest as she breathed, remembering his daughter Lily at that age. But unusually the thought did not fill him with despair. Holding this child filled him with a feeling of contentment he had not experienced in years. Perhaps it was not too late to have a family of his own.

Moments later, Agnes disturbed his reverie as she scooped her baby from his arms and handed him a brown paper bag.

"Off you go," she smiled. Lawrence left the house intending to proceed straight to West Road, but a smart Gil Cooper dressed in a suit emerged from his front door and waylaid him. Lawrence sighed as he realised he would have to stop for a chat.

"You're looking very smart," said Lawrence, as Gil approached him. "Not at work today?"

"No," said Gil. "I wish I was."

Lawrence regarded him thoughtfully. The man was unusually taciturn, and Lawrence struggled for something to say.

"I'm on my way to a funeral," said Gilbert.

"Oh. I'm sorry to hear that."

"Woodgrange Park cemetery," said Gil, as if Lawrence ought to be familiar with the location.

"I see."

"A work colleague died," Gil continued. "Sad affair. He was only young."

"Well, don't let me hold you up," said Lawrence, "and please accept my condolences."

Gil nodded and walked in the same direction as Lawrence who slowed to avoid any further awkwardness. He was just re-tying a perfectly well-tied shoelace when he heard a call in the distance.

"Oi, mister." A familiar voice hailed him from further down the road. He turned to see the press office runner Stanley coming towards him at a rate of knots.

"Are you looking for me?"

"Of course, I am. Why would I be hollering at the top of my lungs? The governor wants to see you."

"Governor?"

"Mr Higgins."

"He's not the governor."

"He's my boss. Same difference. What does it matter? He wants to see you, and he says it's urgent."

"I was going in the opposite direction."

"Do as you please then. Mr Higgins paid me to deliver the message, and I've done my bit."

Stanley turned to go.

"Do you know what it's about?"

"Yes. Mr Higgins tells me all his plans," he said sarcastically.

Lawrence sighed. "Tell me exactly what Mr Higgins said."

Stanley put his hands on his hips and shook his head. "He said, Stanley, find Mr Harpham and tell him I have some important news. Don't delay. He will want to hear this immediately."

"Hmmm. I suppose I'd better come."

"Then I'll tell him you're on your way."

"I'll fetch the bicycle. I expect I'll get there before you."

Lawrence was as good as his word and was already sitting at Higgins' desk nursing a cup of tea when Stanley ran breathlessly into the building.

"A good boy, that one," said Higgins.

"A touch impertinent though."

"He does as he's told, and that's rare these days," said Higgins, scratching the side of his head beneath his spectacles and revealing the edges of a nasty scar. "We took on two boys before him, both bone idle and incapable of following instructions. Neither lasted long, and one had the brass neck to send his mother to ask for his job back. I told her a few home truths about her lazy little lad. Stanley could do with a lesson in manners, but I can't complain about his work, and he's very industrious."

"It's not for me to comment," said Lawrence, restraining himself. He didn't like Stanley and unlike Higgins, could find no redeeming qualities in the boy. "Anyway, are you going to tell me what you want? I was on my way to West Road with a list of people I need to talk to."

"Who?"

"These twelve," said Lawrence removing his notebook and pushing it towards Higgins.

"Where have they come from?"

"The census transcription," said Lawrence. "These men have lived in West Road for over a decade. They were there during the Carter/Seward disappearances and Millie Jeff's murder."

"Interesting," said Higgins, stroking his chin. "Remind me to check my cards before you go, and we'll see if there's a match."

"Your cards?"

"Yes," said Higgins gesturing dismissively in the direction of the research cupboard. "You're a long way ahead of me, now that you know the occupants of West Road, but I've kept a box of cards containing details of names relevant to the murders. Friends, relatives and anyone with geographical connections to where the girls lived or where they found their bodies. It's quite extensive."

"Show me."

"Not now," said Higgins. "I have more pressing news. I've finally completed my trawl of the newspapers and found something noteworthy. There are a couple of minor articles on two barely reported crimes which happened before I became interested in the case. I'd like to know your thoughts." Higgins opened a brown folder on his desk and pushed two newspaper clippings towards Lawrence.

Lawrence picked up the first and read.

*Daily Mail, 15th May 1882*

*Another disappearance of a singular kind is also reported from West Ham. It concerns a little girl named Susan Luxton aged six, the daughter of a railway mechanic living in Victoria Terrace, West Ham Lane. On Monday afternoon last, the girl accompanied a playmate home to Station Street, Stratford. She was told to go straight home and said she would but never reached Victoria Terrace. She was afterwards located in a workhouse in the city. About half past six on a Monday evening, the child was found near Ludgate Circus by a policeman. She was alone and did not know her road home, and he took her to the police station and thence to the workhouse. The child remembers nothing of what took place from the time she left her playmate's house until the police officer gave her a cake at the station. It is believed that she was drugged in Stratford and while insensible removed to London. The child could not have possibly walked from Stratford to the city in two hours.*

"Well?" Higgins eyed Lawrence eagerly.

"I'm not sure," said Lawrence. "Stratford station is a little out of the way."

"It's about a mile, as the crow flies," said Higgins.

"Oh. I didn't realise. In that case..." Lawrence re-read the article, this time more slowly. "This incident must have happened around the time of the disappearances?"

"Less than a month after Mary Seward vanished," said Higgins.

"But Susan was a lot younger than Mary."

"Yes. That aspect bothers me too. But Susan's age fits in with the Walthamstow murders. Do you think her kidnapping is part of the sequence?"

"I don't know," said Lawrence, shaking his head. "If anything, it makes me think that the murders and the vanishings were entirely separate."

"But it suggests a method, doesn't it?"

"Most definitely. Someone could have drugged Eliza Carter and Mary Seward and removed them to the city. But who and why? And how did a small defenceless child escape the clutches of a kidnapper?"

"Precisely," mused Higgins. "I don't know. It's not clear, but I feel it matters. Read the next one."

Lawrence picked up the second cutting. "February 1890," he said, "The month after Amelia Jeffs died."

"Read on."

Lawrence obliged and read aloud.

*The attempted outrage at Walthamstow where a girl named Kerridge was enticed into a house on February 1st was referred to Detective Inspector Wildey. He, together with Sergeant Forth, made inquiries. They do not in any way conceive this outrage to relate to that perpetrated on the girl Jeffs the previous night...*

Lawrence broke off. "The previous night?"

"Quite," said Higgins. "It wasn't a month apart – only a day."

"Then, there can't be a connection. Not with the distance involved. The man would have sated his urge when he violated Amelia."

"Finish the account."

*...the Walthamstow incident, as it is called, clearly indicates how easily a girl might be lured into an empty house by a plausible tale. In this case, a well-dressed middle-aged man inquired at a shop as to where he might get a servant girl. He told a story that he had recently taken a house in the neighbourhood and wanted to engage a servant before his furniture was brought into the house. He was referred to one girl's house, and as she was away from home, the man was introduced to Kerridge's house. He saw Kerridge, repeated the story, and she went with him to the empty house. He then got her upstairs by a pretext that he wanted some rooms cleaned. His attempts at outrage were happily frustrated for Kerridge fought him*

*and succeeded in getting away from the house. The matter was reported to the police, and a search was made. To date, her attacker has not been located.*

"No," said Lawrence, returning the article to Higgins. "There's a slight chance that Susan Luxton is part of this, but nothing in the article suggests the Kerridge girl's involvement. And consider the timescale. It's impossible. You are making the crime fit the theory."

"Nothing?" asked Higgins.

"Well, obviously the crime happened in Walthamstow, but that's the only connection."

"Is it?"

"Apart from the attempted outrage."

"And?"

Lawrence sighed. "And it happened upstairs in an empty house."

"So, three points of interest."

"The Kerridge girl lived."

"So did Elizabeth Skinner."

"How old was Kerridge?"

"I don't know. It doesn't say. Old enough to be a servant and strong enough to fight off her attacker."

"The police stressed there wasn't a connection with Amelia Jeff's slaying."

Higgins snorted. "After nine attacks, eleven if you count Luxton and Kerridge, the Metropolitan Police released the only men arrested within days. I hold little stock by what they think."

"But was there enough time? Could one man commit such a crime and be in another location ready to commit the same foul act in less than twenty-four hours?"

"How did you get to Walthamstow?"

"By bicycle."

"How long did it take?"

"About twenty minutes."

"There's your answer. Of course, one man could do it. Whether he did, is an entirely different matter. But I mean to find out."

"Why?" asked Lawrence.

"I don't follow?"

"I don't either. Your interest in these girls seems excessive. The cuttings on the walls of that room, for instance." Lawrence nodded towards the research cupboard. "That must have taken hours of your time, not to mention wading through hundreds of newspapers. It's more like an obsession."

Higgins coloured. "I want to see justice done," he growled.

"Obviously, but you haven't said why."

"Because I'm an excellent reporter and a decent human being," said Higgins. "There's an unresolved story here, and somewhere in the immediate locality, a wicked man is free to kill without restraint. The police are worse than useless, and somebody has to bring him to account."

"Accepted and understood," said Lawrence. "Can I take the cuttings?" he asked, nodding to the folder.

"No. I haven't made copies, but I've written the salient points here. Higgins passed a sheet of plain paper containing a brief list of names and dates to Lawrence.

"I'll take it away and think about it," said Lawrence. "It's all I can do."

"But first, come with me, and we'll check through my cards," said Higgins. "You might as well have all the facts to hand."

\#

"Show me your list again," said Higgins sitting at the desk in the research room. He reached for a small six-drawer oak cabinet by his side and opened the first drawer which he'd filled with filing cards.

Lawrence handed over the notebook and Higgins worked his way down the list, checking each name against the alphabetic records.

"Not much there," he said when he had finished. "But you can rule out Benjamin Snow. He died in 1896, and this one," he continued pointing to Thomas Smith," died a few years after."

"It helps a little," said Lawrence.

"But does it?" Higgins reclined on the wooden chair and gazed at the wall with his head cocked to one side.

"I think so," said Lawrence uncertainly. "We're down to ten men."

"Well, I don't agree," said Higgins. "Excuse my bluntness, but I think you're barking up the wrong tree."

"You were the one that suggested the importance of West Road," said Lawrence. "Please don't tell me that all the work on the census has gone to waste. God only knows what strings Isabel pulled to make it happen."

"No. It was a necessary and valuable acquisition of data," said Higgins. "It's your interpretation of it, that I'm not so sure about."

Lawrence shook his head, angrily. "Why?"

"Think about it," said Higgins. "Look at the wall chart and pay careful attention to where the girls lived."

Sighing, Lawrence advanced towards the first of the three covered walls. "Where should I look?" he asked sullenly.

Higgins nodded towards the longest wall where he'd indicated the residence of each girl using a pin and a piece of coloured string. Lawrence noticed that there were four new strings. Two showed the location of their houses and another two pointed to the area of Susan Luxton's abduction and the Kerridge girl's attack.

Lawrence stared at the wall, wondering what Higgins wanted him to deduce from the mess of strings. Except for the Luxton and Kerridge locations, the information wasn't new. Beginning with the first disappearance in 1881, Lawrence followed the orange lines. He muttered under his breath as he thought out loud, counting off the girls on his fingers. By the time he reached Annie West's death in Walthamstow in 1892, Lawrence had understood. With or without the Luxton and Kerridge cases, the result was the same. The killings had started in West Ham but had moved towards Walthamstow. Yet the later murders happened between the two locations.

"Of course," said Lawrence. "I can see why the Kerridge attack is so important. If it forms part of the series, it shows the date our murderer found a new hunting ground."

Higgins nodded.

"And it sets a pattern for the future killings which are, as we know, nearly half an hour from West Road using a bicycle, bus or tram. Not far, but not convenient either which suggests that the killer might have moved home."

"That's what I was thinking," said Higgins. "If you take every location into account, someone can easily reach them from a point between West Road and Walthamstow. Though where that point lies, is anybody's guess."

"Which makes my list redundant," said Lawrence.

"Not necessarily," said Higgins. "Hang onto it, by all means."

"But you're saying we need a second list with those men of the right age who were present in the 1881 census but not in 1891."

"That would be a good use of your time," said Higgins.

"I don't think I can face another night of research." Lawrence rubbed his eyes. He was bone tired and though ready to conduct a day of investigation, was less enthused about poring over census records.

"I don't mind doing it," said Higgins.

"The records are back at my lodgings."

"Then it's over to you. Keep me informed of your progress."

Lawrence nodded and left the building before wearily mounting his bicycle. Had he been more alert, he might have noticed the actions of two people watching as he cycled up the road. One figure gestured, and the other acknowledged instructions to follow.

# CHAPTER 26

## *What Happened in West Road?*

"You're back. Thank goodness," said Agnes Ward as Lawrence stepped into the hallway of fifty-five Buxton Road.

"Why? What's wrong? Has there been another break-in? I hope not. I don't think your husband will suffer any more disruption to his house."

"No. Nothing like that. A man called for you."

"A man? For me? Nobody knows I'm here. What did he look like?"

"About your height, sandy hair and wearing a dog collar."

"That must be Michael, an old friend of mine. But I can't think why he has come all this way. How was he?"

"Agitated," said Agnes. "And keen to find you. He kept asking when you would be back. I said I didn't know."

"Did Michael say what he wanted?"

"No. Only that he needed to speak to you urgently."

"I wonder if something has happened to Francis," mused Lawrence. "When will he be back? Where did he go?"

"I don't know," said Agnes, "and I told him you were heading to West Road, so I daresay he's gone to find you."

"Blast it. When did Michael leave?"

"About half an hour ago."

"Then, there's no point in trying to catch up with him. He'll have arrived at West Road by now and realised I'm not there. He'll either come straight back or go to wherever he's staying. It's probably best if I remain here and get on with things."

"I'll let you know if he turns up," said Agnes.

Lawrence climbed the stairs, went to his room and removed his coat, hearing a rustle from his pocket as he sat on the bed. He reached inside and pulled out the brown paper bag containing the ham sandwich that Agnes had made earlier. He had forgotten all about it. Lawrence unwrapped the sandwich and though a little squashed, he ate it with gusto as he began compiling the new list of names.

The census records transcribed in varying hands were in no particular order. It had made last night's task time-consuming and would be no less tricky now. Lawrence squinted over the words, blinking back tiredness, but the longer he worked, the heavier his eyes grew. He was only ten minutes into the job when his attempts at fighting tiredness failed, and he woke with a start half an hour later when his notebook fell off the bed. Shaking his head, Lawrence advanced to the window and, despite the chill in the air, flung it open, determined to stay awake. As he looked outside, a shape darted away from the lamppost on the other side of the road. The fleeting movement happened so quickly that Lawrence wasn't sure whether he'd imagined it. But it was discomfiting, and he couldn't shake off the feeling that someone was spying on him. Lawrence retreated out of sight and waited silently by the open window, but the watcher did not reappear. Assuming that it was his imagination playing tricks, he returned to the task at hand.

Lawrence had not appreciated how many men were working in the building trade in 1881. He soon realised that the second list would be longer than the first and began the cumbersome task of transcribing names – John Reeves, painter, William Pallant, bricklayer, Thomas Lanaway, carpenter. Name by name, the list increased, and moment by moment, Lawrence grew ever more tired. After falling asleep for a second time, Lawrence went for a walk to wake himself up. He popped into the kitchen where Agnes was preparing a meal and asked her to make sure Michael stayed at the house if he reappeared while Lawrence was out. Then, he made his way towards the cemetery to get some fresh air and gather his thoughts.

It was after five o'clock by the time Lawrence returned to the house, and the welcome smell of roasting meat greeted him by the door. James was not yet home, and the evening meal was about an hour away, time enough to go back upstairs and resume his task. But almost as soon as he returned, he heard a rap at the front door and opened it eagerly expecting to see Michael. Instead, a glum-looking Gilbert Cooper was standing on the doorstep. "Here," said Cooper, passing him a bag of pastries. "The wife made them," he continued as he walked into the hallway. "Where's Agnes?"

"I'm through here," Agnes called.

Gilbert Cooper walked towards her and Lawrence opened the paper bag, raising an eyebrow at the misshapen objects inside. Had they belonged to him, Lawrence would have disposed of them at the earliest opportunity. He placed the bag on the dining table, intending to disappear upstairs while he had the chance, but Cooper reappeared before he left the hallway.

"Have you got a moment?" Cooper asked.

"Not really," said Lawrence making for the stairs. "Why?"

"Ah, that's a shame. I could do with some company. Agnes is busy, and Hannah, my wife, is messing around in her shop. It's been a hard day."

"I can imagine," said Lawrence, saying a mental goodbye to the idea of resuming his work before dinner. Gilbert looked miserable. He had changed out of his smart suit and was back in his paint-strewn overalls, which smelled as if they needed a good wash. Lawrence had only known Gil Cooper for a few days, but if Gilbert was desperate for his company after such a brief acquaintance, he must be in a bad way. The least Lawrence could do, he supposed, was take a break and listen to the man.

"Inside or out?" asked Lawrence, gesturing to the door.

"In," said Gil. "James will be back shortly, and he'll want his dinner."

"Of course. Join me in the dining room, and we'll talk."

Lawrence sat in his usual place at the foot of the table, while Gilbert Cooper took the chair to his right. He opened the bag of pastries and poked one moodily. "Here. Try them," he said.

"No, thank you," said Lawrence, suppressing a shudder. "I'd rather not spoil my appetite."

"We don't eat until eight," said Gil, taking a bite. He chewed for a moment then spat a small, hard object onto the table which pinged onto the floor. Gilbert did not explain, and Lawrence refrained from asking. Instead, he made a mental note to dispose of the pastries as soon as Gil had left before one of the Ward children found them.

"Tough day?"

Gil nodded and stared at the floor. Lawrence tried again.

"Did you know him well?"

"Who?"

"Your workmate."

"Not really. But it's always sad when people die – puts you in mind of your own mortality, doesn't it?"

"Naturally," said Lawrence.

"Did he leave a wife?"

"I don't want to talk about it," said Gil.

"Right." Lawrence sat for a moment, wondering about the pointlessness of the encounter. He understood why Gil might want companionship but sitting in silence was awkward and uncomfortable.

"Tell me what you've been up to," said Gil. "Take my mind off things."

"Not a great deal," said Lawrence, unwilling to give too much away.

"Talk to Donaldson again?"

"No. I haven't seen either land agent."

"I've been thinking about it myself," said Gilbert. "And racking my brains. Donaldson's a decent chap, but Manisier – well that's a different matter. I'm sure he had something to do with the Portway house sales."

"I know he did. He showed me the property. Or to be more accurate, he gave me the keys."

"I don't mean now. Back in 1890 when the Jeffs girl died."

"Are you sure?"

"No. I can't be certain, which is why I haven't mentioned it before. But something is nagging in the back of mind. There were always people in West Road – policemen and reporters, some we knew and some we'd never seen before. My memory is fuzzy after all this time. But there was something about Manisier."

"Who might remember?"

Cooper pursed his lips. "Phil Harris might. Perhaps Wally Veitch."

"They're on my list," said Lawrence indiscreetly.

"List?"

"Not an actual list. Just the people I'd like to talk to."

"I thought you'd nearly finished?"

"Almost."

"Can I read it?"

"The story? Not yet," said Lawrence. "It's mostly research notes. I'll write it up properly when I get back to Suffolk."

"When will that be?"

"Sunday at the latest."

"Right. Well, if I were you..."

Gilbert did not deliver the piece of advice on the tip of his tongue. The front door opened, and James Ward strode inside.

"Good day, Gil," he said, placing his hat on the stand in the hallway. "Time for dinner," he continued, looking pointedly at the mahogany wall clock.

"Right you are," said Gil, rising to his feet. "I expect I'll see you again before you go, Mr Harpham."

"I'm sure you will," said Lawrence, about to leave the table.

Agnes rushed through and greeted her husband. "Don't get up," she said to Lawrence, before addressing James. "Dinner will be ready in five minutes. Just time for you to wash and change, my dear."

#

Agnes Ward's roast pork was one of the best meals Lawrence had eaten. He managed a second helping before starting on the pudding of treacle tart and custard. By the time he had finished, he was full to bursting and even less keen on the idea of spending the evening in his bedroom making lists. Besides, Gil Cooper's information was weighing heavily on his mind. Lawrence was unconvinced that the Kerridge attack was the work of the killer. Nor was he wedded to Higgins' theory that the murderer had moved houses. The idea had merit – a great deal of merit, but it was by no means certain. Yet if John Manisier had been selling new properties in Portway when Amelia died, it warranted further investigation. And what better way of finding out more than using a visit to Harris and Veitch as a pretext. Lawrence briefly returned to his room and noted the addresses of the two men. Harris lived at number seventy-six and Veitch at number thirty-five. So, Harris had lived opposite Amelia Jeffs in 1881, and Veitch lived opposite the family in 1890. It was inconceivable that they did not know each other, and the two men might have vital information.

This small nugget of information excited Lawrence out of proportion to its relevance. His detective instincts were in full flow, and he was confident that West Road played a leading role in the mystery. He weighed up the prospects of staying indoors to research against going out to investigate and decided on the latter. It was nearly seven o'clock and the perfect time of day to catch families at home. He only needed to work out a plausible story to explain his interest. Harris was a bricklayer and Veitch a paper hanger. Perhaps he could start by offering them work. He decided to walk to West Road and flesh out the details on the way.

Dusk was falling when Lawrence left Buxton Road and had settled into nightfall by the time he arrived. He walked past William Donaldson's house at the junction of West Road and Portway fighting the urge to call in. Donaldson had made him welcome during his previous visit, and Lawrence wasn't sure what reception he would get from Harris and Veitch. But he didn't want to intrude into their evenings by calling late and decided to bypass Donaldson and get on with it.

Number thirty-five was on the right-hand side about a third of the way up. Lawrence hesitated briefly outside the small front yard while he double-checked his notes. Then he approached the front door and knocked loudly. Lawrence waited at the doorstep listening for the sound of footsteps in the hall but heard nothing above the raucous laughter coming from inside. He knocked again, this time with real effort and, within moments, a young lady opened the door.

"Yes?" she asked.

Lawrence stumbled over his words, not sure whether to ask for her father or husband. "Is the man of the house about?" he asked lamely.

She turned away from him. "Dad," she yelled, "there's someone at the door for you."

Walter Veitch was a small, rat-faced man with a greying moustache and a thin neck. His face, half-shaven but in all the wrong places, looked as if it would benefit from a new razor or an urgent visit to the barber. "What do you want?" he asked, eying Lawrence suspiciously.

"A decorator," said Lawrence.

"At this time of night?"

"Well, no – but soon. I'll pay well."

"Who told you about me?"

"Gilbert Cooper," said Lawrence, hoping it wouldn't inconvenience Cooper at a later date.

"Oh. Fair enough. Good of him to think of me. Come inside and tell me all about it."

Lawrence entered the cramped terraced house, making his way towards the back room. He peered around the door to see a woman of Walter's age and five adult children, seated around the fireplace.

- "Not there," said Walter Veitch. "You'll get no peace. Back this way." He gestured towards the parlour and opened the door. "Sit."

Lawrence perched on the edge of a green floral sofa noting its threadbare arms and prepared to embellish his story.

"Right," said Veitch. "How big is your house and how much of it do you want to decorate."

"I'd like to paper the hallway," said Lawrence.

"Just the hallway?"

"And the stairs and landing."

"A big job," said Veitch, leaning back and flashing a toothy smile. "I'll do it at the weekend. Not Sunday, obviously."

"I'm sure a Saturday will be suitable if the price is right," said Lawrence. "I take it you are in employment during the week?"

"Yes. I work for a builder."

"I noticed a lot of new houses in this area," said Lawrence. "In fact, I considered renting one before deciding to improve my property. I saw one of the three-storey houses near the park.

"Which one?"

"Number one hundred and twenty-six."

"Bad luck," said Veitch. "Did Manisier show it to you, or was it his stuck-up wife?"

"Manisier," said Lawrence. "Though I spoke briefly with his wife. She seemed nice enough."

"She'll be putting on a face – all charm and good grace to her customers, but there's a proper harridan beneath the surface."

"What do you mean?"

"Oh, let me count the ways," said Veitch, raising his index finger. "One, she's a busybody, two, she complains about everything, three she's a troublemaker, four she thinks she's a cut above everybody else. Is that enough? Or have I said too much? You're not friends with them, are you?"

Lawrence resisted the temptation to pretend a close acquaintance with Mrs Manisier. It was on the tip of his tongue to claim kinship, but he wouldn't get what he wanted out of Veitch if he antagonised him. "No. I've never met either of them before this week, and now that I'm no longer in the market to rent, I don't suppose I'll see them again."

"Lucky old you. Unfortunately, I can't avoid the Manisiers, living as close as I do."

"Mr Donaldson didn't seem that keen, either. Are they universally disliked?"

"Ah, you've met Jock Donaldson, have you? No. Any problems between him and Manisier comes from professional rivalry. With me, it's personal."

Lawrence badly wanted to ask what the problem was but felt it would be a question too far. He couldn't quite judge Veitch's personality though the man was cocksure and full of himself. Lawrence couldn't imagine anyone else having the audacity to call William Donaldson, Jock. And Veitch was obviously doing it for effect. The little man sat with his arms firmly crossed, and an eyebrow raised, almost in challenge. Veitch was either a shocking gossip or cleverly testing the validity of Lawrence's story. Only careful interrogation would reveal which.

"I suppose you'll want to choose the paper," said Veitch.

"Naturally."

"And I'll want to see your place before we talk about price."

"Is that necessary? I can give you a rough idea of the size."

Veitch snorted. "Not a chance. People have caught me that way before, and they'll only fool me once. You could invent the measurements to keep the price down. I want to see the building myself, or you can find someone else."

"There's no need for that. You can come to the house," said Lawrence calmly, surprised at his sudden hostility.

"Wait here then."

Walter Veitch sprang from the chair and strode from the room, leaving Lawrence alone and somewhat perturbed. He was contemplating the lack of creature comforts in the parlour when Veitch returned, clutching a battered journal.

"What did you say your name was?" asked Veitch, smoothing a page.

"I didn't. But it's Lawrence Harpham."

"Address?"

"Fifty-five Buxton Road."

"I know the house."

"Does that mean you won't have to see it?" asked Lawrence hopefully.

"There are no exceptions. Tuesday week, alright?"

"Yes," said Lawrence, relieved. He would be long gone by then though he must remember to cancel the appointment before returning to Suffolk. It wouldn't be fair to add this to the list of domestic matters to be dealt with by the long-suffering Agnes.

"I'll come after work. About six-ish. It will only take five minutes."

"Good. Thank you. I need to see a man about a garden wall."

"You won't have to look far if you want a brickie," said Veitch. "The road's full of them."

"I know. My next call is to Mr Harris."

"Phil Harris?"

"Yes. Do you know him?"

"We all know each other," said Veitch impatiently, as if explaining the blindingly obvious. "Those of us that have lived here longer than five minutes, that is. You won't get him, though. He's at the Friendly Club tonight."

"Friendly Club?"

"Society," said Veitch. "Meets every third Tuesday. At least it used to." He glowered at Lawrence, who seized the initiative.

"But not now?"

"I wouldn't know." Veitch spoke slowly and with feeling, mauling the pencil as if he was trying his best not to snap it.

"You're not a member?"

"Not anymore. Manisier put paid to that years ago, insufferable little man."

"Ah. Were you blackballed?" It was an audacious question, but Lawrence wouldn't see Veitch again with any luck, and it was worth the risk.

"You could say that," growled Veitch. "His interfering wife said I'd been thieving from the club and by the time they worked out that it wasn't me, the damage had been done."

"To your reputation? That's unfair. Surely they should have reinstated you."

"They would have if I hadn't knocked out the chairman," said Veitch.

Lawrence almost laughed. Walter Veitch was stick thin and looked in need of a good meal. The thought of him being on the business end of good punch was as unlikely as it was absurd. "Did you really," he asked, inserting a note of admiration.

"Too right," said Veitch. "And Manisier nearly got the same. I would have done it if they hadn't dragged me off."

"Quite understandable. And a very public argument, by the sound of it."

Veitch rose and walked towards the door. "It's no secret that I dislike Manisier," he said. "But I'm done talking shop. The night is running away."

"Thank you," said Lawrence. "I'll see you Tuesday week."

#

Having learned that Philip Harris was at the Friendly Club, Lawrence had no further business in West Road and strolled back. He took a circuitous route, subconsciously delaying his return to Buxton Road having no excuse to avoid finishing the second list once he arrived. James Ward had offered him use of the back door if he chose, but Lawrence generally refrained. It seemed only polite to acknowledge his hosts and let them know when he was in the house. Tonight was different. He needed to devote the rest of the evening to administrative tasks and must avoid human interaction at all costs. Any excuse, any reason for prevarication, and he would

160

need to eat his frog tomorrow. He must complete the job now, and he had better get on with it. But as Lawrence approached his room, a piece of paper pinned to the front of his bedroom door drew his eye. He opened it to find a scribbled note from Agnes.

*Dear Mr Harpham*

*Your friend came back again and was most unhappy to find you out. He will return at nine o'clock tomorrow morning. Please make sure you stay here as he says he will wait until he sees you, no matter how long it takes. He has asked me to tell you that it's urgent. If you cannot help him, he will contact the police.*

*Mrs A Ward*

Lawrence scratched his head, baffled at the tone of the note. For Michael to turn up out of the blue implied something important, and he only now began to appreciate the urgency. After all, Michael had surprised him when on church business in London on previous occasions, and those had been social matters. But this latest development was worrying. Lawrence couldn't think of any situation where contacting the police was the only alternative to his help. If the problem was desperate, the authorities should have been Michael's first port of call.

Lawrence thrust the note into his pocket and flung his coat on the bed. Time was not his friend, and it was now or never. He grabbed the census records and spread them over the dressing table, having learned from bitter experience, not to write sprawled across the bed, or that is where he would wake up with the task unfinished. His room was chilly, but he opened the window anyway, his only nod to comfort removing his shoes and releasing the collar of his shirt.

An hour later, he'd finished the list. In the end, it was surprisingly easy as he'd already extracted many relevant records. And as Lawrence examined the piece of paper in his hand, he realised that he hadn't needed a list after all. The answer was staring him in the face as it had done since he'd arrived. Lawrence didn't know how or why, but he was damn sure he knew who. But with Michael coming tomorrow and an urgent situation brewing, he had to act quickly. He must share his findings tonight.

# CHAPTER 27

## *Quandary*

Lawrence stood in the garden staring at the remains of his bicycle in disbelief. "What in God's name...?" he exclaimed, dragging the broken cycle to the rear door and closer to the light. He leaned over and ran a hand over the bowed wheel before spotting the saddle dangling uselessly from the frame. To add insult to injury, one pedal hung at an unnatural angle while the other was missing altogether. Not only was the cycle damaged beyond repair, but the destruction was quite deliberate. "Damn it," said Lawrence, hurling the bike over in a fit of temper. It clattered against the yard and knocked into a metal urn which spun into the rear door. Lawrence grimaced at the ungodly sound, hoping that James Ward was somewhere else. But a moment later, the door opened to reveal the tall and angry form of his host.

"What is going on?" yelled Ward.

"Someone has broken my cycle," said Lawrence.

"So, you thought you'd retaliate by destroying my already damaged back door, did you?"

"It was an accident. I dropped the cycle in shock." Lawrence cringed as he told the outright lie, but now was no time for honesty.

"Right. Well, you'd better tidy it up then. Where are you going at this time of night? It's nearly ten o'clock. I can't have you wandering around the house in the small hours waking the children up."

"I won't," said Lawrence. "I must go out. Something has happened, and it won't wait until morning."

"I don't like the idea of you coming in late. It's getting too noisy around here."

Lawrence bit his lip to stop himself saying that most of the shouting was coming from James. If he hadn't already woken his children with all the bellowing, they'd sleep through anything. But he didn't say it. James Ward was angry enough, and Lawrence needed a bed for at least one more night.

"I won't be long, and I promise you won't hear me. If there were any other way, I'd wait until morning. But from the tone of your wife's note, I fear I'll be leaving sooner than I thought."

"Yes. I got that impression too. Your friend was very keen to see you. Alright. I'll leave the key under the mat. But please do not let me down."

"Right you are." Lawrence straightened the urn and propped the cycle carcass against the shed. Then, closing the back gate as quietly as possible, he set off into the night.

#

Lawrence was in two minds which direction to take. One way led to inevitable confrontation and the other to a place he could leave a message. But at this late hour, nobody would be there to read it, and they wouldn't arrive for work until he had departed. The delay would be risky and could cost lives. Lawrence mulled it over as he walked along but had decided by the time he reached the end of Buxton Road. Alone and with hardly any proof, he plumped for the latter choice. It wasn't ideal, but it was the lesser of two poor options.

He had only ventured half a mile when the unexpected sound of lightly running feet disturbed his concentration. He whipped his head around, but the streets were dark and empty, the footsteps disappearing into the distance. Then silence. A few more yards, and he crossed paths with a couple of men, weaving their way home after a night of revelry, their voices booming, brash and welcome. A cat mewed, then silence. A gust of wind, a rustle of leaves and the soft patter of rain petered into another spell of quiet. Lawrence raised his collar and wrapped his scarf over his mouth. The drizzle was light, but already liberally covering his raincoat as the temperature plummeted. He shivered and kicked a stone down the path – anything to create the illusion of noise, of crowds. Lawrence imagined the daily swarm of people. Why was it so quiet? Ten o'clock wasn't late. He usually enjoyed walking alone, but not tonight. Maybe it was the urgency of his mission or the responsibility of conveying what he instinctively knew with little in the way of facts. Perhaps it was something else, a certainty that his mission would not go according to plan. And why should it? He hardly had a plan, let alone time to construct a comprehensive course of action.

And then he heard it – a shuffle, an echo. It could be close or not. In the dark, he couldn't tell. He spun around, walking backwards as he peered through the gloom into the dimly lit road beyond – nothing. Another rustle, a sudden shriek and he stopped still, hardly daring to move. He loitered, breathlessly watching, waiting. Then a shape darted across the road; rusty fur captured momentarily in a chink of light from a bay window as a fox slunk down an alleyway and out of sight.

Lawrence steadied himself on a nearby railing, clutching the cold iron as he caught his breath, grateful for the metallic chill on his palm. It represented something real and not lurking in an irrational part of his subconscious. He faltered, tempted to return to Buxton Road, face James Ward's wrath and tell him what he knew. But would Ward pass it on? And would he pass it to the right person? If

Lawrence made a poor choice, the suffering could be endless. No. He needed to get a grip of himself and get on with it.

Hands in pockets, Lawrence strode against the increasing wind, choosing not the most direct route, but any road with a light source. Soon he found his way to the main thoroughfare, one thankfully with working gas lamps and he remained on it for another half a mile. But as Lawrence approached the end of the street, the lamps became less frequent, until he reached a spot where his only choice was to turn into another dark and unlit road. He considered lighting the small candle stub he habitually carried but disregarded the idea. It was a waste, and he might need it later. Besides, some windows were bare, but in other houses, the owners were less careful. An open curtain here and there provided a little light – not much but enough for comfort.

Eventually, even that vanished. And as Lawrence turned into a road near to his final destination, he realised he hadn't been there before. He'd got himself lost, and although he knew the direction he was going, he didn't know which route to take to get there. And the rows of terraced houses had petered out into scrubland. As his eyes adjusted to the darker surroundings, he realised that if he continued, he would have to walk alone across an empty field. A left turn would take him back the way he'd come, but if he turned right, he would come close to where he needed to be. But even with the meagre light from the pale moon, Lawrence soon realised that if he took that route, he would pass a row of newly built houses ahead. Swallowing his fear, he turned right anyway and marched towards the houses, whistling confidently. At least he hoped he sounded confident. An outward show of bravado would see his demons off and stop him from being afraid. Yes, he was alone, and it was unnerving, and that was all. But as Lawrence reached the far side of the row of houses, sighing with relief, he heard footsteps coming from behind. Then a plank of wood in the small of his back knocked him off his feet, and he fell, face first, into a puddle.

Seconds later, with a mouthful of dirty water, a chipped tooth and a spinning head, Lawrence reached out and tried to look up. A wave of nausea engulfed him, and he put his head down for a few moments ready for another try. This time he took his body weight on the palm of both hands and stared anxiously ahead. A faint light sparkled in the puddle below. Just as the reflection caught his eye, a shadow loomed behind him and whipped a rope around his neck. Lawrence clutched at his throat, clawing the harsh fibres as he fought for breath. His lungs screamed with pain as the rope tightened, and moments later, the light faded.

# CHAPTER 28

## *Suffer the Innocent*

Lawrence hunched over his office desk, contemplating a solution to Loveday's proposal. She wanted them to live in London, and he would rather sweep the streets than agree. His hand rested near a bottle of cheap whisky standing near to a scratched glass with a chip on the rim. Lawrence needed a drink, and soon. He was hungry and tired, but a splash of the amber liquid would see him right. He reached out a hand, but it didn't connect with the bottle. Damn it. He was thirsty, and he couldn't even pour himself a drink. Then the door opened, and the bell chimed. He looked up, and Violet was standing there, smiling at him, telling him not to worry. Everything would work out. 'Violet,' he mouthed, but he couldn't form the words. Her face fell, and he tried again. 'Violet, I'm sorry. Forgive me,' but the sound never came.

'Time to wake up, Mr Harpham,' she said. But her tone was oddly formal, and her voice sounded gruff and masculine. Then Lawrence understood. He had been dreaming, and the encounter with Violet was only a distant memory. He groaned and opened his eyes to find himself in the parlour of an unglazed empty property. The dimly lit room was as cold as the grave. His eyes focused on a lantern on top of an old packing crate. Beside it were two forms, one standing and the other recumbent on the floor, head bound, and hands tied. Lawrence stared transfixed at the standing man. 'What in God's name are you doing here?"

"Sit down," said Samuel Higgins as he watched Lawrence vainly attempt to struggle to his feet.

"What's happened to me? Why are my legs bound? And my throat is so tight I can hardly breathe."

"That's because you were choked into unconsciousness," said Higgins, in a matter-of-fact tone of voice." By rights, you ought to be dead."

Lawrence rubbed his fingers over the uneven welts on his throat as he assessed his position.

"How did you find me?"

"Young Stanley and I had an arrangement. He's been following your every move since you left the print works. He's earned himself a tidy sum of money for his trouble."

"But why?"

"Because you're an intelligent chap and it was only a matter of time until you did what the police could not."

"We were working together. There was no need."

"Oh, but there was every need."

"I don't understand."

"And there's no reason why you should. Let me enlighten you. I'll tell you a story."

Lawrence glanced at the bound man who was now squirming on the floor. His voice sounded muffled, and Lawrence guessed he'd been gagged. Not that he could easily tell what was beneath the sack that covered the man's head. Anything could have happened while he was unconscious. The man's groans turned to whimpers as Higgins stood and kicked him in the stomach.

"Stop it," commanded Lawrence, but Samuel Higgins responded by stamping on the man's hand. A muffled scream, from inside the hood, masked the sound of knuckles crunching beneath Higgins' boots.

"You'll kill him."

"Correct. But not yet. Now, are you comfortable?"

"Hardly. It can't have escaped your notice that someone has tied my legs together."

"Sorry about that. I can't have you interfering. It's freezing on the floor. Get up, there's a good chap and hop onto that other crate. You'll catch your death of cold lying on the floor."

Lawrence eyed Higgins with suspicion as he pushed himself to a standing position and shuffled across the room."

"I know it's undignified, but you'll thank me later. We'll be here for a while."

"Not if I have anything to do with it," snapped Lawrence. "I trusted you. Just get on with this story if you must."

"Very well." Higgins removed the lantern and perched on the crate opposite Lawrence.

#

"Once upon a time..." Higgins began to speak.

Lawrence groaned. "Don't do that. It's facetious. You've knocked me out, tied me up and the least you owe me is a serious explanation."

"My dear chap," said Higgins. "You are under a gross misapprehension. Yes, I bound your legs, but I did not harm you. Nor would I, as you will appreciate if you hear me out."

"Go on then," croaked Lawrence, flexing his bound feet. "It's cold, and I'm in pain." He winced as he ran his hands across his throat."

Lawrence blinked as Higgins raised the lantern and held it towards him.

"I'm not surprised," he said. "You've got a nasty rope burn. You'll need some salve at the very least, if not medical attention. Here, take this." Higgins reached into his coat pocket and thrust a flask towards Lawrence.

"What is it?" asked Lawrence, eying the battered metal.

"Brandy," said Higgins. "Not the finest, but it will help."

"How do I know it's not poison?"

Higgins shook his head sadly. "I truly have lost your trust. I mean you no harm, Lawrence."

"Then untie me."

"No. But I promise I won't harm you."

Higgins unscrewed the container and left it on the ground near Lawrence.

"Go on," he said, nodding towards the brandy.

Lawrence bit his lip, grabbed the flask and gulped greedily, sighing as the liquid trickled down his damaged throat.

"Better?"

"A little."

"Then I'll begin again. I live alone," said Higgins, "but that was not always the case. I had a wife once and was a happily married man with a daughter of my own. We lived in Stratford Road. Do you know it?"

"Yes," said Lawrence. "It's at the top of West Road. Odd that you didn't mention it before. That puts you right in the heart of the vanishings."

"Yes, it does, and I was as concerned about the disappearances of Eliza Carter and Mary Ann Seward as anyone else. Everyone was talking about it – everybody feared for their children. It was different for me. My daughter, Rachel, was a little older and had left school. She's dead now; God rest her soul – died in childbirth many years ago. It would have been her first had the child lived, but there were complications. Anyway, all you need to know is that Rachel was my only child."

"I'm sorry," said Lawrence sincerely. "I know what it's like to lose a daughter. You have my deepest sympathies."

"It was a long time ago," said Higgins. "God took her for his own. It was a natural death and I have learned to live with her loss. But only her loss, you understand. Not the rest of it."

Higgins returned to the second packing crate and sat heavily with his head in his hands. He was silent for a moment, and Lawrence watched him brooding until a groan from the man on the floor broke his reverie.

"He's waking up," said Lawrence.

"Good. I want him to hear this." Samuel Higgins approached the man and heaved his body to a sitting position. The man flopped against the wall with his head tilted uncomfortably to one side.

"Not quite awake," Higgins continued, manipulating the figure into the corner where he sat him in a more natural position.

"Better," said Lawrence.

Higgins grunted. "As I was saying, my life then was quite different – a wife, a child, normality. I was content with my lot and nothing could have prepared me for what happened in 1890."

"That was the year Amelia Jeffs died," said Lawrence.

"Exactly," said Higgins. "When Amelia died, a part of me died with her. My life changed irrevocably. Pass me the flask, will you?"

Lawrence slid the metal container across the floor. Higgins knocked it back and wiped his lips. "I haven't talked about this for years," he said.

"Is Isabel aware?" asked Lawrence.

"She knows very little," said Higgins, "and this revelation will prove deeply shocking. It's unfortunate."

"What are you talking about?"

"Never mind. I was telling you about Amelia. I knew her fairly well. She was a kind girl, very sweet. I remember her rescuing a baby starling after a mauling from a cat. The bird was in a bad way. It should have died, but Amelia nursed it back to health. She was like that."

"Were you acquainted with her family?"

"I knew them, but not well. Rachel minded little Edie once or twice and occasionally Amelia. Well, having a daughter of my own,

I love little girls and often stopped to speak to them when they were playing on the road. So, I knew the children very well, but not so much the parents. Back then, I worked for a different newspaper, and my route to work took me through West Road. I usually carried sweets in my pocket and would treat the girls whenever I saw them. And not only the Jeffs girls, but many other local children. They're such innocents, Lawrence. Easy to chat to, full of interesting ideas and observations. And in case you were wondering, I didn't confine my attentions only to little girls. I made friends with the boys too. God blessed Olga and I with only one child, and I would have welcomed a brood of them, but it was not to be. And with so many friendly children nearby, it was not a tragedy."

"Your interest in the children was fatherly?"

"Of course." Higgins frowned. "It's a fair comment. I enjoyed their company for the most innocent reasons. But everything changed when Amelia died."

"I think I can guess what happened."

Higgins nodded. "I'm sure you can. I passed Amelia outside her house in West Road on the night she died. I was not the last to see her – Lizzie Harmer ran into her a few moments later outside number thirty, and by then I would have been almost home. I thought nothing of it until the following day when the rumour mill started grinding, and word went around that Amelia was missing. Her father began searching and he couldn't find her. You've read the reports – you know what happened. Days went by with no news. Everyone was looking for Amelia – in their outhouses, in the park, in the scrubland by the building site. They spared no effort to find the girl. Speculation was rife, as you can imagine, and after a few days, people who had always trusted each other, started thinking the unthinkable. Could someone have abducted Amelia and was it one of their own? Finally, they found her body on Saint Valentine's day, strangled and violated. There was an uproar, Mr Harpham. Speculation turned to accusation and suspicion to certainty. Amelia's killer was a man, and they considered any man under the age of eighty a viable suspect.

Two days after Amelia died, I walked my usual route to work and encountered young Cyril Hicks as I had done many times before. I handed him a toffee, and his mother ran from the house and snatched it from his hand, shrieking at me to leave her child alone. Her actions horrified me and her words cut to the quick, revealing unbridled concern about my motives. Shaken, I decided not to hand out any sweets until more time had passed. But children don't think like adults. They still ran up to me, clustering around excitedly and looking for kind words and treats. And like a fool, I gave in to my better judgement. Within days, the finger-pointing began, suspicion settling on me like maggots on a corpse. The curtains twitched when I walked past, parents called their children inside when they saw me approach. The road emptied, and I changed my route to work, but it didn't help."

Higgins took another gulp of brandy. "Has anyone ever ostracised you?" he asked.

Lawrence shook his head. "No."

"You can't imagine the loneliness. It was already quiet at home. Rachel started in service only weeks before Amelia died and lived with the family in Cricklewood. Olga was still with me then. But gossip is insidious. Words shouldn't hurt, but they do. The whispering started, each wicked suggestion infiltrating every part of our lives. We had no extended family. Both my parents were dead, my only brother living in Leicester and Olga's kin in Europe. As the devilish accusations gained traction, our friends peeled away. People stopped speaking and I narrowly avoided losing my occupation. Had my editor not been a principled and rational man, I would have, for my colleagues turned their backs on me.

Then one day two women cornered Olga in the corner shop at the end of West Road. They said they'd seen me talking to Amelia Jeffs, and not only Amelia but Mary Seward too. Olga spoke up for me, ridiculing the idea that anyone could remember what happened on the day of Mary's disappearance all those years ago. But, Harpham, people remember what you tell them. They repeated the stories so often that they quickly became fact. And before long, Olga couldn't walk down the street without catcalls and stone-throwing. We held our nerve, carried on, tried to live life as best we could, but it never stopped. By the spring of 1890, I was a social pariah and Olga, my accomplice. And just when I thought it couldn't get any worse, this happened."

Higgins pointed to the blacked-out lens with a shaking finger. "Do you want to see it?"

Lawrence shuddered. "I'd rather not."

Higgins grasped the fraying elastic holding the glasses on his head and stared at Lawrence as if in two minds. Then he lowered his hands. "It's not a pretty sight," he said. "I won't subject you to it."

"What happened?" asked Lawrence, confronting the unavoidable.

"It was a day like any other," said Higgins. "Except it must have been busier than usual as the light was failing when I returned, so I must have worked long hours. It was late spring and, by then, I'd taken to alternating my route between several streets leading home. It was the only sensible way to avoid a frightening and potentially embarrassing confrontation."

"I can imagine." Lawrence was starting to feel sympathetic towards Higgins despite his better judgement. He had seen enough in his time to know that rumour and innuendo could finish a man. "I'm only surprised that you didn't move."

"I would have but Olga didn't want to. She liked the house and thought that moving would only make me look more guilty."

"I expect she was right."

"She usually was," said Higgins. "And had she known of the colossal lapse of judgement that her husband was about to make she would have moved heaven and earth to prevent it."

"What did you do?" asked Lawrence.

Higgins put his head in his hands. He sat quietly for a moment, sighing as if he would give all he possessed to go back in time and reverse the consequences of his ill-considered choice.

After a moment, he raised his head, and a tear trickled down his cheek. Lawrence stared, not knowing what to say. He opted for continued silence.

Higgins spoke in a faltering voice. "The route I chose took me down the Portway, crossing the top of West Road near the park. On the corner of the junction near Donaldson's house, I passed little Alice Houghton playing by the road with a friend and almost stopped to speak to her. It was getting late, and before Amelia's death, I wouldn't have hesitated to tell her to run along home before nightfall. But I thought twice and carried on walking without acknowledging her presence. Well, to my surprise, I felt a soft squeeze. Alice had caught up with me and slipped her hand into mine. She said hello and asked how I was, and then, in a sad voice, she asked why I didn't like her anymore and what she had done to upset me. It broke my heart, Harpham. But how could I explain it to her? Children should stay innocent for as long as possible. I could not tell her the truth for fear of distressing her or making her fearful. What I should have done is to walk away. What I did was give her a few sweets. And that decision changed my life forever."

Higgins stood and paced towards the open window, placing his hands on the ledge. "I went home, had my supper and was settling down for the evening when I heard a hammering at my door. Olga looked up in surprise and told me not to answer it, but stupidly I assumed someone was in trouble and thought they might need my help. I didn't stop to consider an alternative and flung the door open. But when I looked outside, nobody was there. I shut the door behind me and walked up the path to take a better look to see if the local children were playing knock down ginger. Then, just as I was about to go back indoors, someone seized me from behind, and a group of men bundled me away. They covered my head with a hood and marched me off. I had no idea where they were taking me – West Ham Park as it turned out. I could not see them, but I could hear them whispering about the dreadful methods they would use to make me talk. And as they approached the park, their voices grew louder and more confident. Darkness had fallen, but even through a hood, I could feel the difference between the lamplit street and the terrible emptiness of the park. I was friendless and alone, and all I could do was wait and hope that I could talk my way out of it. I stood unbalanced as they removed their hands and lingered nearby. I could feel their presence and knew they were watching me, and their silence only increased the terror. For a fleeting moment, I hoped they had seen the folly of their behaviour, but then I heard heavy breathing, and someone coughed.

" 'Who are you? What do you want?' I asked determined to break the silence, then suddenly a kick to my solar plexus knocked the breath from my body. I dropped to the floor, winded and writhing in terror."

"Filthy pigs," said Lawrence, now unable to hide his empathy. "That's no kind of justice. What did you do?"

"Nothing. How could I? One of them leaned over and removed the hood. He held a lantern over me, waiting until I could catch my breath long enough to speak. Then he told me he would kill me if I didn't confess to Amelia Jeff's murder. Well, of course, I said I hadn't done it, and he said he'd heard that I'd seen her that night. I knew it would be worse if I lied so I agreed that I had seen her, but that I hadn't harmed her."

"Did you know him?" asked Lawrence

"I'd never seen him before in my life," said Higgins. "Not him or any of his friends. They were young men, a bit rough around the edges, but not the sort who run in gangs. Anyway, I assured him I wasn't responsible for Amelia's death, and he accused me of trying to lure Alice Houghton away from her family by giving her sweets. I told him exactly what had happened and suggested he ask Alice who would confirm my story. At that point, he spat in my face and kicked me between the legs. I screamed in pain, Harpham. God help me, but at that moment, I was on the verge of confessing if only to make it stop. But my screams enraged them further. One man stepped forward and put his hand over my mouth while pressing my nostrils. I was gasping for air, fighting to breathe. The man with the lantern told him to stop and sat down beside me while the others stood above. He said he was the cousin of Alice's friend, the girl I had seen playing with her in Portway. The story his relative relayed gave an entirely different interpretation of my actions. Her family had told her never to accept things from strangers, repeating the rule often since Amelia's murder. They had instructed her to tell a grown-up if anyone she didn't know offered her anything. So, he couldn't care less what Alice said, his cousin's story was all he needed. There must be a motive for going around giving young girls sweets with no good cause. He called me a filthy pervert and asked how I wanted to die. My teeth were chattering with the cold, and I'd urinated in fear. I was alone in the dark, at the mercy of strangers, and I didn't know whether I'd survive the night. But in the end, I could not bring myself to lie. If I'd lied, they might have taken me to face proper justice, but I would not confess to something I hadn't done, nor would I choose the means of my demise. So, I said nothing, and they took it in turns to kick me and beat me until I was half dead. Then, one of them found a brick near the pathway and slammed it on my temple, shattering my skull and eye socket. The pain was unendurable and within moments, thankfully, I lost consciousness."

"God, that's awful," said Lawrence. "I don't know what to say."

"Then say nothing, old chap. That's not the worst of it. One man must have had a rudimentary conscience and anonymously called a doctor. They told him where to find me, and it didn't take long before the doctor transported me to the hospital. I spent weeks there while they repaired what remained of my face. After a few days Olga came to visit me, but weeks went by, and she didn't return. I pressed the nurse for an early discharge, and when that wasn't forthcoming, I walked out anyway and went home. There, on the mantlepiece was a letter from Olga. Never a strong woman and always on the wrong side of squeamish, she couldn't bear the thought of my broken face. Nor could she stand any more accusations. She had left to start a new life. I never saw her again. And that, Harpham, is my story."

Lawrence gestured for the flask. Higgins slid it towards him, and he took a slug. "I'm sorry," Lawrence said, almost lost for words. "But answer me one thing, if you can. When Isabel mentioned your injury, she said that you had forgiven your attackers and even spoke up for them at the trial. Why?"

"Because fear motivated their actions. Someone had taken two girls and murdered another. Though in all innocence, I had behaved unwisely. Had I committed the act of which they accused me, there would be justification for revenge. So, whose fault was it?"

"Theirs," said Lawrence. "That's not how justice works."

"But it doesn't work, does it?" said Higgins. "Here we are eighteen years on from the first disappearance, and we're still none the wiser. The police have failed. Ten crimes against children remain unpunished. Those men may have got it wrong, but at least they tried."

"They ruined your life," said Lawrence. "I don't understand."

"No, they didn't. He did," said Higgins glaring towards the sitting, hooded form of the bound man breathing heavily in the corner. "All that remains is to find out why."

# CHAPTER 29

## *How & Why*

"Go on then," said Higgins. "You've heard my story. Now I want to hear yours."

The man shifted uncomfortably on the floor but said nothing.

"Your story. Now," said Higgins, menacingly, as he approached the bound man and smiled. "Now," he said again.

"Water," gasped the man. "I'm parched."

"Story," said Higgins. "Or I'll cut you."

"You wouldn't," croaked the prisoner.

Higgins slid his hand into his jacket pocket, removed a long, sharp blade, and held it in the lamplight. "This knife should do the trick," he said.

"Steady on," said Lawrence. "There's no need for that."

"He's bluffing," snarled the bound man.

Higgins knelt and put his face close to the hood. "I'm not, you know," he whispered.

The man squirmed, and for seconds nothing happened. Then with lightning speed, Higgins grabbed the man's hand, slammed it on the floor and pushed the knife-edge onto his little finger using his body weight to slice through the bone. A scream pierced the air and Lawrence leapt from the crate. "For God's sake, no!" he yelled, trying to keep his balance.

"Sorry, Harpham," said Samuel Higgins, wiping the blade on his trouser leg. "I'll get to the truth one way or another."

"Then untie me. This is ridiculous."

"I can't. You'll try to stop me, and it's too late."

"I can't watch this."

"Then don't," said Higgins. "I'll take you into the back room, but I thought you'd want to know what happened."

"I do," said Lawrence. "I'll hear the truth, but I don't want to see a man tortured, no matter what the provocation."

"Sorry, I can't help you," said Higgins. "He'll lose another finger every time he doesn't answer me – and worse if he prevaricates for much longer. You can either listen or sit elsewhere. Your choice but I'm losing patience, so decide."

"I'll stay," muttered Lawrence, trying to ignore the whimpers of the bound man on the floor. He clutched his damaged hand in the other and rocked pitifully.

"Good. Then we'll begin." Higgins paced towards the second packing crate and kicked it towards the man, then sat with his legs splayed and his hand on his chin. "Let's start with Eliza Carter."

"I didn't do it. I didn't hurt Eliza," said the man.

"Come now," said Higgins, stroking his finger down the knife blade. "That won't help you."

"Really. I didn't. It was nothing to do with me, and neither was the other girl."

"Mary Seward?"

"Yes, Mary. I swear I didn't touch them."

"So, Amelia was the first."

Silence.

"I'm waiting."

"Yes," whispered the man.

"Speak up. I can't hear you."

"Yes, damn it. She was the first. I killed Amelia Jeffs."

"How?"

"I choked her with a scarf."

"And?"

"What do you mean, and?"

"What else did you do?"

Silence, then the man in the hood started sobbing.

"What else?"

"I... I. God help me."

"You'll need his help if you don't answer me now."

"No," said Lawrence.

"Yes," said Higgins, reaching for the man's hand. He grasped it firmly and stroked the blade across his palm."

"I had my way with her," shrieked the man. "I took Amelia there on the floor and used her as a woman."

"Yes, you did, didn't you," said Higgins. "You filthy dog. And then you left her, and cowardly crept away to let others, that is me, suffer for your unspeakable actions. Actions, which I will punish in due course. But for now, let's talk about why."

The man sighed and put his hands to his hooded head. Blood trickled down his wrist, pooling into his cuffs. "If I tell you, do you promise not to hurt me?"

"Don't be ridiculous. You're tied up and at my mercy. Why would I make promises I can't keep?"

"Then don't torture me. Make it quick."

"Coward."

"Whatever you say. I don't care anymore. What I've done is monstrous. He made me."

"He? What do you mean? Please don't blame it on disembodied voices."

"That's not what I mean," gasped the hooded man, before lapsing into a coughing fit.

"Start at the beginning," said Higgins. "I want every last detail, and if I get it, then you get to keep the rest of your fingers."

"Take the hood off."

"Not yet. Perhaps if you start convincing me – now, your murder spree started with Amelia?"

"No. It started with Eliza Carter, but I didn't do it."

#

"Someone abducted Eliza Carter and Mary Seward," said the man.

"Hold the front page," said Higgins, sarcastically. "We know."

"I mean people traffickers took them."

"That's only a rumour," said Lawrence, adjusting his position on the crate.

"No. It's the truth, and I know because I saw it happen."

"You saw someone kidnapping the girls?"

"Not the two elder ones. The abduction I witnessed was Susan Luxton's."

"The little girl found at Ludgate?" asked Lawrence

The man's hooded head bobbed up and down. "Yes, her. I didn't know what I'd seen until I read about it in the papers, but then it all added up, and I realised what had happened to the older girls."

"Do you know who took her?" asked Higgins.

"Oh, yes. I knew them very well," said the man with a touch of satisfaction.

"And like a good law-abiding citizen, you informed the police".

"Not exactly."

"Not at all," snapped Higgins. "You let it happen, and you didn't say a word."

"I said a lot of words," said the man. "And it kept the wolves from my door for many years."

"You blackmailed him," said Lawrence.

"Such a nasty word," said the man. "And no. I blackmailed her."

183

Higgins and Lawrence exchanged glances. "Her?" they said in unison. "Who?"

"Ha. Not so clever now, are you?"

Higgins unseated himself, picked up the dismembered finger and plopped it onto the man's lap.

"What's that?" the man asked in alarm, patting his stomach.

"A reminder to keep you on track," said Higgins calmly.

The man recoiled. "Alright. Sorry. The laundress in West Road," he said. "She was the contact."

"Contact?"

"The go-between. She got the girls and drugged them, and then her accomplices took them by cart to Ludgate."

"But Susan escaped?"

"No. She was too young for that. The old woman saw a bobby at the station and took fright. She abandoned the girl there and legged it and never risked another after that day. But I told her what I'd seen and that I'd squeal if she didn't pay me to keep quiet."

"She can't have had much to give you," said Higgins. "A laundress is hardly a gold mine."

"They'd paid her well for the girls," said the man. "And I suppose I had most of it, in the end."

"So," said Higgins, conversationally. "Explain why you decided to violate and murder Amelia Jeffs eight years after a spot of blackmail. It's quite a change of tactic."

The man grasped his finger stump and sighed. "Give me a handkerchief or something. It's still bleeding, and I feel faint."

Lawrence rummaged in his pocket. "Pass him this," he said, handing a silk square to Higgins.

"It's more than he deserves," muttered Samuel, but took it anyway and dropped it on the man's hand. He seized it eagerly and wrapped his bleeding appendage.

"You were saying..." Higgins continued.

"I was short of money," said the man. "Times were tough, and I didn't have a job. They'd laid me off."

"Your occupation?" asked Higgins.

"House painter," muttered the man, "as if you don't know."

"We were only nodding acquaintances if you remember. I wasn't sure where you worked. But I know as well as you do that houses have been going up thick and fast for the last few decades and house painters are in demand. Why weren't you?"

"None of your business. I needed money and that's all you need to know."

"You can have that one," said Higgins. "But that's your last chance. You needed money having bled the laundress dry. What did you do next?"

"I went to Ludgate," said the man, "and hung around for a few days. I'd heard there were still traffickers even after all that time, but I didn't come across any at first. Next day was a different matter, and I met a man who was looking for them too. He wanted a girl, you see, for domestic purposes. He was there the following day when I returned, and we got talking. I said he should advertise in the newspaper and he laughed at me. He said he had certain urges for girls that he couldn't legally satisfy. Well, I seized my chance and asked him how much he would pay if I got him a girl myself. And the sum he offered was extraordinary. I said I would do whatever it took and arranged a time and place to meet him a week later. The trouble is that kidnapping is harder than you think. You've got to find the right person, be in the right place at the right time and get your mind prepared. I'm not a violent man – at least I wasn't then. It took a lot of courage."

Higgins snorted. "Courage. You worm. There is nothing courageous about what you did."

"Alright. But it wasn't easy. And I couldn't do it that week. I found someone, but I couldn't bring myself to touch her. And Mr Carnaby was very particular about the type of girl he wanted. Not too young, but not grown up and most definitely an innocent. I'd got nowhere with it by the time we arranged to meet up, and I asked him for another fortnight to find her. But when I still hadn't come up with the goods, he got angry and gave me one more week. If I didn't bring a girl by then, I could forget all about it. Well, I was desperate for the money, and it was now or never."

"Never would have been a better option," Lawrence interjected, but the man ignored him.

"Charles Jeffs had lived in West Road for over a decade. He'd moved houses once or twice but never far away, and I came to know his routines. I knew he would send Millie for a fish and chip supper that night because he always did. And I knew she would go along the Portway. Sure, it was dark, but it was darker still going the back way across the scrubland. Luckily, my house was right next to the entrance to the unused land, which led directly to the rear doors of the new houses. I didn't work there at the time, but my mate Tubby Warner had employment as a paperhanger, and he told me everything I needed to know to get in. You see it's a perk of the job to use the builds for shelter when married workmen go out tot hunting. They want more than a thrupenny upright and need somewhere comfortable to take the girls. Well, one of the finished houses is ideal, especially one that's watertight and not due for immediate occupation. Tubby had a sweetheart and was taking her to the Portway house to get her to give up the goods, and he said that the keys were under the stone, as usual."

The hooded man stopped, took a deep breath and scratched his chin through the sacking.

"Are you still listening?" he asked.

"Oh, yes," said Samuel Higgins, his lips set in a thin line. "I'm taking in every word. Do carry on."

"I didn't plan it," said the man. "But I was getting desperate for the money, and I thought I would go out and see if the Jeffs girl left home as usual. Their new house was almost opposite mine but too far to see from my window. So, I slipped out and loitered a few doors down. It was just before half past six. I was only waiting a matter of minutes when the door of number thirty-eight opened, and there she was. It was a sign – a sign for me to act. And without planning it, I ran down the alleyway and onto the scrubland at the rear of Portway. There was only one stone big enough for a key, and sure enough, it was underneath. Quick as a fox, I unlocked the rear door, and ran to the front of the property, opening the door just in time to see Millie walk by. I looked up and down the road. It was empty, so I called her name. She turned and smiled. She knew me, you see. Had done since she was a girl, and she asked me what I was doing there. I told her that our cat had crept in and had her kittens upstairs in the bedroom, but they were in a bad way, and I needed to take them home. I asked her if she would help me. She didn't hesitate and followed me into the house and upstairs like a lamb to the slaughter. And when we arrived at the top floor bedroom, I pointed to the cupboard and said the kittens were in there. She opened the door, and I stood there for a moment, paralysed with the sudden realisation that I hadn't planned what to do next. I had the girl, but how was I going to subdue her and get her to Carnaby? I slammed the door shut, and she screamed in fright, then after a few moments, she asked me to stop playing pranks and let her out. All the time, my mind was racing. If I could subdue her, I could keep her in the house overnight, and possibly for a few days longer. Then Carnaby could collect her from here. How he did so was his problem and not mine. But how was I to keep her quiet? The only thing I could think of on the spur of the moment was to knock her unconscious. I looked around for something suitable, but the room was empty, and I couldn't go looking for an object as there was no lock on the door and no way to fasten it. Then Amelia started screaming. She yelled at the top of her lungs and hammered on the door. Anyone walking by would hear her and I realised I would have to act quickly. I yanked the door open, put my arm around her neck and clasped my hand over her mouth. But the little vixen bit me, drawing blood and almost causing me to let go. She fought like a tiger, biting, scratching and narrowly missing my eye. She wouldn't stop. If only she'd stayed quiet, I would have let her live. It was her fault – hers, do you hear?"

"So, you killed her," said Lawrence.

"I had no choice in the matter."

"Tell me what you did," said Higgins. "Every detail, don't forget."

"As I said, she wouldn't shut up. She was wearing a coat and scarf, and I grabbed the scarf and tightened it a little. The screaming stopped, and she relaxed in my arms, so I released it, and she started fighting me again. I threw her on the floor and straddled her body, pulling the scarf until she stared bug-eyed back at me. Her nose started bleeding, and she frothed at the mouth, so I let it go again, hoping that she would fall into unconsciousness. But it didn't happen. When I released the scarf, she struggled, and when I tightened it, she looked half dead. I couldn't make it work. And there was an unexpected side effect. As I controlled her breathing, holding her life in my hands, I lost my original purpose in waves of pleasure from this new power. Amelia Jeffs hung between life and death for my amusement for the best part of half an hour. From that day to this, I have never recaptured the thrill of that first time."

The man's voice had changed in tone and timbre as he dreamily stroked the palm of his hand with his thumb while reliving the memories of his first kill.

Higgins jumped to his feet and without hesitation, kicked the man between his legs.

The man howled in pain and curled into a foetal position, smearing blood from his finger stump over the floor. "Why did you do that? You asked me for details," he cried.

"I didn't ask you to enjoy it," snapped Higgins. "And you've missed an important point. Did you violate her before or after she died?"

"After," muttered the man. "I did it when I realised that I had taken things too far. I had killed her for pleasure instead of using her for money. She was a good-looking girl," he continued as if seeking justification. "And if I hadn't, Carnaby would have."

"Carnaby wouldn't have known she existed without you," said Higgins, "assuming there was any such man."

"Of course, there was," said the man. "He tried it himself the very next day."

# CHAPTER 30

## *Who?*

"Carnaby? Who did he kill?" asked Higgins in surprise. "There were no other murders committed the month that Amelia died."

"That's because he didn't succeed," said the man. "Turns out he wasn't as clever as me."

"What do you mean?"

The hooded figure coughed again, a raspy, tickling sound that went on and on. "For God's sake, take this sack off," he complained. "I can't breathe. My throat is so dry that I can hardly talk and there's a lot to tell."

"Very well." Higgins walked towards him, pointing the knife. Lawrence flinched and looked away, but Higgins sliced through the cord and removed the sack. "You haven't changed much," he said, staring into the pallid face of Gilbert Cooper.

"That's more than I can say for you," said Cooper, grimacing.

Higgins moved his face to within a few inches of Cooper's. "This should have happened to you," he said. "Mind your manners."

Cooper recoiled. "I didn't do it."

"You caused it, but let's not dwell on that for now. Tell me about Carnaby. What did he do?"

"He tried to capture another girl," said Cooper. "I suppose he couldn't wait. Kerridge, her name was. He pretended to hire a servant and got her into a house. But he couldn't hold onto her, and she escaped."

"We know about the Kerridge girl," said Lawrence. "How do you know it was Carnaby?"

"It stands to reason," said Cooper. "He wanted me to get him a girl, and the day after I got one, he did too."

"Did you talk to him?"

"No. We never met again. But every time I got a girl, he got another. One for one, tit for tat. Him then me. It was a game you see."

"Then why did you start killing in Walthamstow?" asked Higgins.

"I know why," said Lawrence. "And that's the message I was on my way to deliver, Samuel. That's why I was hot-footing it to the print works so I could leave it for you."

"I wasn't sure," said Higgins. "Stanley fetched me as soon as you were on the move, just in case. Well, if you know, then tell me why?"

"Because he moved to a new house," said Lawrence. "Isn't that right, Gilbert?" The sneer lingering on Lawrence's face did not bypass Cooper.

"Don't look so disappointed in me, Mr Harpham," said Gilbert Cooper. "You have lied too. You're no more a reporter than I am."

"You believed me at the beginning."

"Yes, stupidly. But it didn't last long. I wised up to you quickly, and it was pure bad luck that that brick didn't dash your brains out."

"Never mind that," Higgins interjected. "You moved where?"

"Buxton Road," said Cooper.

"Where you're lodging?" Higgins turned to Lawrence.

"Yes. A few doors down. I've been swapping ideas with this fellow ever since we started," said Lawrence. "It didn't occur to me until tonight that it might be him, though all the clues were there."

"Clues?"

"Paint-spattered overalls, living close enough to follow me and the damage to the bicycle. Who else could it have been? Hardly anyone knew it was there."

Cooper sneered. "I could hear you coming a mile off on that thing. And yes. I moved to Buxton Road because I ran out of money. The rooms were smaller and cheaper than those in West Road, but then my wife started running a shop, and she did alright. I worked when I needed to, and we managed, but I never forgot Amelia Jeffs or the way it made me feel. A year later, I took a contract on a building site in Walthamstow and worked there for the best part of three years, cycling to work every day. One Monday evening, I was riding home and I'd just gone down Markhouse Road when I heard two people screaming at each other. I looked up to see a young girl fleeing the house barefoot with no coat or hat. Her mother shrieked like a banshee, cursing at her daughter and telling her not to come back. The woman was in her cups and didn't care enough to go looking for the child. Without further thought or a plan in my head, I left my cycle in an alleyway and followed the girl, watching as she walked barefoot to Collingwood Road. I loitered nearby as she knocked on the door of her friend's house and waited for half an hour until she left and walked to the house of another. I nearly gave up. It was bitterly cold and were it not for the memories of killing Amelia I would have gone home. But the girl moved on again, walking towards Low Hall Lane and I knew I was onto a winner. The area was familiar. I had walked there a few times, and I knew it was dark and lonely – just the right place to have my way."

"With a ten-year-old girl? Aren't you the big man?" Higgins slammed the knife into the packing crate, where it stuck, blade quivering in time with his rage.

"I told you. It was a game. A dare."

"You said you never saw Carnaby again?" Lawrence struck quickly, determined not to let the reprehensible creature before him get away with any detail.

"And I told you it didn't matter. It was part of the game. Words weren't necessary."

"Who killed Elizabeth Skinner?" asked Higgins

"Carnaby."

"Florrie Rolph?"

"I did."

"William Barratt?"

"Carnaby, obviously. I wouldn't touch a boy."

"On that basis, you killed Mary Jane Voller," said Higgins. Cooper nodded.

"And by process of deduction, Carnaby killed Bertha Russ."

"Exactly." Gilbert Cooper crossed his arms and regarded Higgins with an air of satisfaction, like a man who had finally mastered a stubborn animal.

"Except it couldn't have happened, now could it?" said Lawrence.

"Well, it did."

"Then why did you follow me to Lawrence Avenue and attack me with a brick?"

"It was Carnaby," said Cooper sullenly.

"You admitted doing it only five minutes ago."

"I misspoke. Carnaby did it."

"What does Carnaby look like?" asked Higgins, flexing the knife blade with his fingers.

"Watch that," said Lawrence. "It's wobbling, and I don't want a blade in my face."

Higgins tugged the knife from the packing crate and rested it on his lap. "Carnaby. What does he look like?"

"I can't remember," muttered Cooper.

"Try. Or you might lose another little piggy," said Higgins, testing the knife blade. "Still nice and sharp," he continued as a welt of blood oozed from his index finger. He sucked the blood off slowly and purposefully. "Answer me."

"About my age, greying hair, thinnish. Seemed quite well-to-do."
"Why?"
"He wore a smart suit and polished boots."
"Interesting," said Lawrence. "I met a man who looked exactly like that a few days ago."
"Well, bully for you," said Cooper.
"I told you to mind your manners," said Higgins.
"You said nothing about minding them with him," said Cooper, teeth exposed as he spat the words out.
"I seem to have upset you," said Lawrence calmly. "Could it be that you recognise my description?"
"No, I don't."
"I was referring to the day you turned up at my lodgings suited and booted for your friend's funeral."
"Bertha Russ' funeral," said Cooper, "except I got the wrong day."
"Oh my. You are an extremely sick man," said Higgins. "And what excuse can you possibly have for seeing young Bertha interred?"
"I wanted to catch up with Carnaby."
"Why?"
"To stop him from killing. If he ends the game, I can too. Do you think I still enjoy killing those children? It was never the same after Amelia. But while Carnaby plays, I must. There is no choice."
Higgins fished into his pocket and pulled out a silver cigar case, then buffed it on the bottom of his jacket. "Look," he said, holding it to Cooper's face. "What do you see?"
"My reflection," said Cooper uncertainly as if awaiting a trick.
"Quite. Your reflection and Carnaby's too," said Higgins.
"No. It's not true – I couldn't. I wouldn't. I only did it because he did."
"You attacked Amelia Jeffs before Carnaby attacked the Kerridge girl, assuming he did. And I'm starting to doubt that."
"How did you feel in the days after Amelia died?" asked Lawrence.

Cooper put his head in his hands. "Powerful," he said finally. "But wrong. It felt wrong. Her friends and family were all around me, talking about the murder every day. Everywhere I went, everyone I saw. There was no getting away from it. The guilt, I mean. If only they had let it lie. If only I could remember the good bits."

"Are you thinking what I'm thinking?" asked Higgins.

Lawrence nodded.

"You read an article about the Kerridge girl a few days after Millie's murder, didn't you?" asked Higgins.

Cooper nodded.

"Did it make you feel better?"

"Less like a monster," said Cooper. "Which I wasn't. Amelia Jeffs was an accident."

"She was an accident and the others were part of the game," said Higgins.

"Well, yes," said Cooper. "Exactly that. It wasn't cold-blooded murder. None of this would have happened but for Carnaby."

"But take away the elusive Mr Carnaby and what remains? Seven cold and calculated killings by one man."

"No," said Gilbert Cooper.

Higgins sprang from the crate and advanced towards Cooper, looming in front of him with a face contorted in rage. "There was no Mr Carnaby," he snarled.

Lawrence stared at Higgins, watching his face redden as his white fingers clasped the knife handle.

"You are Carnaby. Carnaby is you. You read about the attempted outrage of Kerridge, and your sick mind created Carnaby, so you didn't have to confront the evil that lives inside you. The existence of Carnaby meant that you could carry on killing at will without blame or responsibility. You killed Bertha Russ, didn't you?"

"No," said Cooper, recoiling from his accuser.

"Yes, you did. Admit it, you pathetic individual. You lured her away and strangled her, just like Millie Jeffs. And you stuffed her poor little body into a cupboard."

"No. It was Carnaby."

"And you committed a carnal act on her body."

"No. Not her. She was too young. I didn't do it to her."

"Then what did you do?"

"I wanted it to be like it was with Amelia. I saw the child leaving the house all alone, and I followed her. She stopped for a moment, and I seized the opportunity and took her under my arm, but she bit me and got away. I chased her, threw her to the ground, and covered her head with my jacket. I only wanted to stop her from screaming, but she carried on relentlessly, first squealing and then moaning, so I held it harder until she stopped moving. And when I took the jacket away, I realised that I had held it there too long. She'd stopped breathing, and that was that. She died close to where I'd been working. Disposal of her body required a bit more thought than usual, so I hid her for a day or two. Then I took her to another empty house and left her in the cupboard. But I did nothing to her body, I swear."

"Finally," said Higgins, licking his lips and attempting to keep his temper. "Now nod your head, where appropriate. Did you kill Elizabeth Skinner?"

Cooper stared mutely.

"Once again, did you kill Elizabeth Skinner?"

"Yes." The word was barely audible.

"Louder."

"Yes," hissed Cooper

"William Barratt?"

"It was an accident."

"Did you kill him?"

"Yes."

"And Bertha Russ."

"I already told you."

"Say it again."

"Yes."

"So, you killed seven children and withheld vital information from the police about the three abducted girls?"

Cooper opened his mouth.

"And before you answer, I will not be responsible for my actions if you dare repeat that it wasn't your fault."

"I killed them. Yes, I killed them. There is something wrong in my head."

"Evidently," said Higgins. "You are incurably mad. Now, what would we do with you if you were a rabid dog?"

"I'm not," said Cooper. "Take me to the police if you must. I will confess."

"You might," said Higgins. "But despite our hard work, there isn't much in the way of proof; not irrefutable proof that will stick. And they'll probably put you in an asylum which, though far from comfortable, is more than you deserve. No, if you were a mad dog, they'd destroy you. And I consider it my civic duty to oblige."

"You can't," said Lawrence.

"I can and must," said Higgins. "I have devoted my life to finding the cause of my misery and tonight two lives will end."

"Don't, Higgins. He's not worth it. For God's sake untie me, man."

"No, Harpham. It's for your own good. Have you any further questions to ask of this animal before I dispatch him?"

"I can't think, damn you, Higgins. You can't make this sacrifice."

"It's the only way," said Higgins. "And I'm glad of it."

"You're barking mad," snarled Cooper. "Let me out of here." His voice rose, and he began screaming, pleading for his life.

Higgins walked behind him and held a knife to his throat. Cooper shut up.

"Stay here," Higgins said to Lawrence, as he dragged Cooper backwards into the hallway.

"No." Lawrence stood and tried to hop from the packing crate, but the bindings around his legs were so tight that he fell to his knees. He scrabbled at the rope trying to release the knots, but Higgins had taken no chances, and Lawrence could not dislodge his bonds.

"Stop," shouted Lawrence, dragging himself to the doorway. But the hallway was empty, and the house silent. Lawrence waited for a moment, wondering whether Higgins had the nerve to go through with it. Moments later, he heard the soft tread of boots coming towards him.

"Oh God," said Lawrence, as Higgins strode into view, blood dripping from the knife. "Is he...?"

Higgins nodded. "It was swift," he said. "He didn't suffer. Pity. But I'm not out for revenge. I only wanted to put right a wrong. Seven wrongs, actually."

"It didn't have to be this way," said Lawrence.

"Come now. You know better than that. Can you give your full assurance that justice will prevail?"

Lawrence didn't speak.

"Exactly. Too much risk. I'm leaving for my lodgings, now where I have stored a large quantity of laudanum. If you would be so kind as to give me an hour or two to get home and compose a note to my aunt, I will dispatch myself to my maker by the end of the day. This," he continued, passing an envelope to Lawrence, "is for young Stanley who may well find himself unemployed because of my actions. It will tide him over until he finds a new position. I trust that you will make sure it reaches him. It only remains for me to leave this." Higgins took the knife and placed it by the front door. "You can cut yourself free while I make my way home. It's been a pleasure," said Higgins, offering his hand.

"Don't do this," said Lawrence.

"Envelope to Stanley. Don't forget," said Higgins, touching his forelock as he left the room.

# CHAPTER 31

## *Lost and Found*

It took a full ten minutes before Lawrence managed to cut through the thick rope binding his legs together and a further ten to marshal his thoughts. The house was freezing, and he was chilled to the marrow, legs cramped and aching from where Higgins had tied him. But his physical pain was the least of his problems. The bloody knife was evidence that harm had come to Gilbert Cooper, but to what extent? Should he check on the man to see if he was still alive, or would that make matters worse? If Cooper lived, then morally, he should try to save him. The best option would be to walk away and pretend the events of the last two hours had never happened. A more sensible and less curious man than Lawrence might have done just that. But he couldn't leave without knowing, without being sure. God forbid that Cooper had only suffered a minor injury. He might leave the house, seek medical help and start killing all over again.

Lawrence heaved himself to a standing position and flexed his legs, pacing backwards and forwards to test his strength. And when he was sure that his legs would carry him to the back of the house, he cautiously proceeded in that direction.

The rear door was ajar, and Lawrence carefully pushed it open before lighting a gas lamp which, to his relief, was in working order. The gloomy glow illuminated a prone figure lying face down on the floor. Lawrence flipped the body over with the toe of his boot, exposing a deep gash in Cooper's neck, almost severing his head from his body. Blood pooled around Cooper's head, and his clothes were crimson. Lawrence turned away, trying to ignore the metallic smell of fresh blood as his stomach churned. He returned to the kitchen and glanced at his shoes, noticing the tread of bloody footprints behind him. Sighing, Lawrence felt for his handkerchief before remembering that he had already given it away. Lawrence needed to leave and soon, but not smeared with evidence of a crime. God forbid someone saw him and assumed he was the culprit. Lawrence patted his coat pockets but found nothing of use. All he had was the clothes he stood up in, his wallet and his emergency tin. He opened it in desperation, gazing at a box of matches and his folded beard and moustache set. There was only one option. Higgins wasn't the only one who would be making sacrifices tonight. Seizing the beard and feeling sadder than was reasonable at the destruction of an inanimate object, Lawrence began. He wiped his footprints from the kitchen floor and cleaned both shoes removing all evidence of blood. Then he slunk from the property, picking his way through the alleys and passageways, avoiding all major roads and lit areas.

Lawrence was in turmoil as he staggered towards West Ham. He desperately wanted to track Higgins down and stop him before it was too late. But he didn't know where Higgins lived and was sure he wouldn't thank him for any intervention. Samuel Higgins had known suffering that no man should ever bear. He had lost his child, his wife, his reputation and half his face to a man without conscience or feeling. Higgins' actions, though criminal, were wholly understandable. But as an investigator and a man paid to bring wrongdoers to justice, Lawrence ought to make sure he held Cooper's killer to account. At the very least, he should report Cooper's death and unmask him as a murderer. But it only took a few moments for Lawrence to decided not to do either and let justice take its natural course. And given the poor showing of the West Ham police force to date, Lawrence doubted they would get any further than finding and identifying the body. He felt a flicker of guilt when he realised that the West Ham vanishings would forever remain officially unsolved. But that situation was no different now than it had been since Eliza Carter first disappeared.

Though it was late and there were few people around, Lawrence took the long route to Buxton Road taking extreme care to remain out of view. He arrived home well past the time agreed with James Ward. Fortunately, the key was still under the mat, and Lawrence removed it, turning it gently and padding up the stairs silently to avoid waking the household. Breathing a sigh of relief, he collapsed on the bed and fell asleep fully clothed.

#

### Friday, March 10, 1899

Lawrence slumbered through the night, not hearing James Ward's light tread on the stairs as he left for work. He did not rouse when daylight flooded through his open curtains or hear the cries of baby Mabel as she battled teething pain. Lawrence didn't wake until a quarter to nine and only then when his shoe fell off and thudded onto the floorboards. He pushed himself onto an elbow, rubbed his eyes and gazed around the room, momentarily wondering where he was. Then his eyes wandered to his uncharacteristically dirty nails. He picked at the substance beneath and grimaced at the sight of congealed blood as the memories of the previous night flooded back. Groaning, Lawrence undressed and poured a jug of water into the bowl. He soaped his hands and arms, paying particular attention to his nails then reached for his tin and removed the bloodied beard. Lawrence's spirits rallied as he examined the hairy, matted mess, noting that the spring and wire attachment remained intact. He decided to try and save it, scrubbing gently at the beard and teasing hairs from the coagulated blood. Then he tossed the scarlet water from the bedroom window. Lawrence left the false beard to dry on the edge of the bowl hoping that Agnes would not enter the room and re-fill the jug, only to mistake it for some half-dead creature. Satisfied with the fruits of his labours, Lawrence was contemplating a shave when he heard a furious hammering at the door. Someone opened it immediately, presumably Agnes. There was a brisk exchange of words and a firm and determined tread on the staircase. Then the door to Lawrence's bedroom swung open followed immediately by Michael.

"There you are," he said. "Why didn't you reply to my telegram?"

"Good to see you too," said Lawrence, offering his hand while feeling slightly uncomfortable at his shirtless torso.

Michael returned the shake for the briefest moment.

"Anyway, what, telegram?" asked Lawrence.

"I wrote to you days ago."

"That's right. Agnes said she had seen a telegram, but someone ransacked the house and it vanished. I didn't get to read it."

"Then you don't know?"

"Don't know what?"

"It's Violet. She's missing."

Lawrence stared incredulously. "She's been missing for the last three years," he said. "We've spoken about it often and at length. Have you come all this way to remind me?"

Michael sat on the bed as Lawrence opened the wardrobe and took out a clean shirt.

"Is that blood on your trousers?" he asked.

Lawrence inspected his thigh. "God. I thought I'd got it all. Turn away there's a good chap." He disrobed and bundled the trousers into his case, before donning a fresh pair.

"Are you decent?" asked Michael, staring into the corner of the room. "There's an urgent matter we need to discuss."

"Yes. You can turn around. Shall I ask Agnes for some tea?"

"No, you will not," said Michael brusquely. Violet is missing, and we must find her."

"I've spent years looking for her," snapped Lawrence. "Her continued absence is not for want of trying."

"I wish you had read the telegram," said Michael. "It would have made this so much easier. I found Violet. We've been corresponding."

Lawrence stared open-mouthed. He shook his head and tried to speak, but the words wouldn't come. "You can't – you would have told me."

"I'm sorry," said Michael. "I did, but she made me promise not to tell anyone and especially not you."

"Where is she?"

"That's the problem. I don't know. Violet was in Swaffham."

"But that's hardly any distance away. Why couldn't I find her?"

"Because she didn't want you to. Look, I'll tell you another time. The point is that she's gone missing again."

"How do you know?"

"She had some trouble – bad things happened to her, and then she stopped writing after regularly corresponding at least several times a week. I left it for a while, but then I thought about the dead crows and her terror in the last letter. I knew it wasn't safe to leave things any longer, so I jumped on the train and went to her house. But she wasn't there and didn't seem to have been for a while. That's why I wrote to you from the hotel. The next day I located her place of work. I spoke to a waitress, but she was new and had never met Violet. She said that her employer hadn't seen Violet for several days and was worried about her. Naturally, I asked to speak to the woman, but she was buying supplies in Norwich. So, I boarded the first train to West Ham and came to look for you."

"Crows? Dead crows like the ones we found in Fressingfield?"

Michael nodded.

"You should have contacted me as soon as you read about them."

"I know. I know. But I didn't want to break Violet's trust. I'm a man of God. If I give my word, I must keep it."

"I'm not blaming you," said Lawrence, advancing to the wardrobe and removing his remaining clothes. "Give me a hand packing," he said. "We must leave at once."

# CHAPTER 32

## *A Puzzle*

The journey to Swaffham seemed endless. The two men spoke in fits and starts, their conversation punctuated by flurries of explanations, then periods of brooding silence. Exhaustion overwhelmed Lawrence. Though tired to the bone, his physical pain fell short of the anguish caused by Michael finding Violet and not telling him. Lawrence felt betrayed and abandoned. He had known Michael all his life, whereas Violet had only met Michael nine years ago in Fressingfield. Michael was a family friend, known to Lawrence's father and uncles. He doubted Michael had ever met any of Violet's relatives. Yet when the time had come for Michael to choose, he had kept faith with Violet, protecting her secret from the very person who had spent hours pondering over her whereabouts and days trying to track her down. It was all very well hiding behind the 'man of the cloth' persona, but why should that trump the loyalty of friendship?

"I don't understand," Lawrence had said plaintively, staring from the carriage window, but not seeing the passing landscape.

"I cannot betray a confidence," Michael had countered, trying unsuccessfully to defend himself for the third time. It cut no ice with Lawrence.

"How long would you have left me to wonder?" he asked as they pulled into the station.

"I've only known her location for a few months," said Michael, "and I haven't seen you at all during that time. It's not as if I have lied or misled you. It hasn't come up for discussion."

"No. And I don't suppose it would have, but for Violet's second disappearance," Lawrence had muttered.

"Which you should concentrate your efforts upon," snapped Michael. "You're too self-indulgent. Violet is in trouble and needs our help."

Lawrence sighed. Michael was right, and he knew it. But other than a vague explanation bordering on the ludicrous about a dead dog and the bloodstain on his trousers, Michael was oblivious to Lawrence's recent ordeal and the effects it was having on his mood. And that was the way it must stay. Lawrence was well equipped to file the affair away in the deepest darkest recesses of his mind. But Michael was the owner of a busy and insistent conscience. One word and he would feel the need to report the killing, which would risk revealing Lawrence's part in it. Lawrence was confident that the Wards hadn't heard him come in. He hoped that by the time they found Cooper's body, there would be enough uncertainty over the time of the killing, not to suspect their former lodger. So, he didn't challenge Michael when he tersely reprieved him for a self-serving attitude and tried to rise above it. After all, it was satisfying to keep a secret from Michael, given the current circumstances.

The train chugged into Swaffham station at four twenty-eight, two minutes later than scheduled. Lawrence raised a rare smile at the sight of the knapped flint station building with its brick quoins and stone window surrounds. The good old Norfolk architecture cheered his soul, and he felt relieved to be away from the rows of red brick terraced houses in West Ham. Suitcase in one hand, and clutching his coat, Lawrence negotiated his way down the platform and out of the building.

"Hold on," said Michael, trying to keep up with Lawrence's rangy pace. Lawrence ignored him and strode towards a waiting carriage, agreeing on a price with the driver before anyone else could.

"Where are we going?" he asked as Michael caught up with him.

"Violet's house is on the Norwich Road," said Michael. "Though it's hardly worth bothering with transport. It's only a short walk."

Lawrence boarded the carriage in no mood for further discussion on the matter. He had no intention of walking any further with his suitcase in tow. A bare five minutes later they arrived outside a tidy flint cottage set diagonally opposite the extensive churchyard. Underneath the two ground-floor windows were two wooden boxes in which green shoots were starting to flourish.

"Very Violet," murmured Lawrence, eyeing the property as he paid the driver. "You'd better be right, Michael, or she's about to get the shock of her life when I turn up."

"Don't you think I know that?" asked Michael. "And if she opens the door and roundly castigates me, I'll accept it, as long as she's safe. But I don't think she will answer.

"Let's do it the right way first," said Lawrence, hammering on the door with the flat of his hand. They waited and listened, but silence reigned. Lawrence knocked again, this time rapping on the window too.

"Hmmm," he said, resting his suitcase on the floor, and peering through the letterbox. The hallway was empty, but several envelopes littered the mat. "She's not been here for several days," he said.

"I know," Michael replied. "I'm worried."

Lawrence stroked his chin. "We'd better use the rear entrance," he said, taking his case and making his way towards the side gate. He clicked the latch, and the gate swung open, revealing a small, but pretty cottage garden beyond a gravelled yard.

He peered into the only accessible window, but there was no sign of life. "Right," he muttered. "Now I need to find the means to get in."

"Don't destroy anything," Michael pleaded. "I know in my heart that Violet is in trouble, but in the unlikely event that she has gone to stay with relatives, please treat her house with respect."

"Oh ye of little faith," said Lawrence, as he started searching the yard.

"What are you looking for?"

"A gnome – it's an ugly little thing with an accordion," said Lawrence.

"Why?" asked Michael.

"Just look for it," said Lawrence. "Ah. Don't bother. There it is." He pointed to the end of the yard, by a flower border. Michael walked over and attempted to pick it up. "It's heavy," he said, lifting the ornament and dropping it down again. Do you want it?"

"No," said Lawrence, impatiently. "Look underneath. Violet's had it for years. It's where she used to keep her spare house key, and I'm hoping she hasn't changed her habits."

Michael tipped the cast iron gnome backwards and grinned as he retrieved a weighty door key.

"Excellent," said Lawrence reaching his hand out. He took the key, unlocked the door, and heaved his suitcase into Violet's kitchen. "I'll leave it here," he said to Michael. "You might want to do likewise. If we can't track her down, we may end up staying here tonight."

"I don't know if we should," said Michael. But Lawrence had glanced across the kitchen and moved on to examine two wooden doors in the hallway. He unlatched the first, revealing a steep staircase and proceeded upstairs, lowering his head in the cramped space which led to a tiny landing. The largest room was evidently Violet's. He smiled at the tidy white bedspread with its array of embroidered yellow flowers, wondering how it looked so neat when Violet was not. The bedside table was more in character, piled high with a tower of books, dog-eared and loved, a reading lamp, and a half-filled beaker of water. Lawrence tipped it towards him, wrinkling his nose at the tiny dust particles.

"I can't decide whether that should worry me," he said, holding it towards Michael.

"What do you mean?"

"She can't have used it for the best part of a week," said Lawrence. "Violet is usually messier than this room suggests. I would automatically empty my glass if I were going away, but I can't be sure if Violet would. There's nothing else in this bedroom suggesting foul play. Let's see if there's anything in the second bedroom.

Michael left first and opened the door to the smaller room where Lawrence joined him. What they saw left them temporarily lost for words. The room contained a single bed covered by a pink candlewick bedspread with a doll in the centre. A brightly painted toy box in the corner groaned under the weight of an assortment of wooden toys. Curtains covered in daisies framed the little window overlooking the garden and children's picture books covered the windowsill.

"She must have a relative staying with her," said Lawrence after a moment's silence.

"Yes," said Michael. "She has a cousin, doesn't she?"

"Several, I believe," said Lawrence. "I am surprised, though. She has never spent much time with the younger members of her family. Too busy investigating, I suppose."

"And she couldn't do it when she lived in," said Michael. "It's one of the downsides of being a companion."

Lawrence grunted. "Let's see what there is downstairs," he said, lowering his head again. They entered the comfortably furnished living room. It was a homely place with cushions and antimacassars spread haphazardly over the furniture. Both pictures hung slightly askew from the rail and Lawrence felt an urgent need to straighten them. He made his adjustments, then stepped back and surveyed his work. They were now both perfectly aligned, and he breathed a sigh of relief until he caught sight of a vase of flowers on the side table. The vase was devoid of water and full of crispy flowers.

"Not good," he muttered. "Violet might be untidy, but she loves her garden, whether indoors or out. She would have given those away before letting them die. Wherever Violet has gone, it's safe to say she didn't plan it. I wonder where she keeps her paperwork?"

"There's a bureau in the hallway," said Michael.

"Ah, yes. So there is." Lawrence took a last glance around the room before closing the door. He proceeded to the small writing desk opposite the stairs where a brass key hung from the lid. Lawrence inserted it and opened the desk before pulling out the struts that held the writing area firm.

"Oh dear," he said, surveying a mess of items pushed back into the rear of the desk. A cream lined page and an envelope lay beneath a fountain pen, which had rolled from its stand. Black ink had leaked from the nib of the pen onto the blotter, and the inkstand had fallen over.

"It looks as if she was writing a list," Lawrence grunted, thrusting the page at Michael.

"Hmmm. She's only written a few lines and didn't get any further."

"It's not dated either," said Lawrence. "No use at all." He rummaged again, then turned to Michael.

"What's that smell?" he asked, wrinkling his nose.

"What smell?" Michael sniffed the air. "Oh, yes. I see what you mean. Perhaps it's the flowers?"

"They were as dry as a bone," said Lawrence. "This smells like rotting food."

He walked into the kitchen and opened the door of the larder. "Urghh," he said, covering his mouth before retrieving a block of mouldy cheese and a loaf of stale bread which he tossed outside.

"You can't leave them there," said Michael, in disgust.

"I'm not going to. I don't know where Violet keeps her rubbish, but it can wait until we leave the house. Now, back to business."

Lawrence returned to the desk and opened the inner drawer, but after a moment he began sniffing the air again. "It's a different smell," he said. "Far worse than cheese." He spun around and examined the second door by the entrance to the stairs. Then grasping the handle firmly, he wrenched it open. The odour hit them like a freight train, causing both men to reach for their handkerchiefs and hold them over their mouths. Squashed inside the cupboard was a small tin trunk covered in skulls and scrolls.

"Don't open it," said Michael. "It's full of dead crows."

Lawrence tried to pick it up, but his left hand failed him as it had so often before, and the trunk slammed down again.

"I'll do it," said Michael.

"No, damn it," Lawrence said through gritted teeth, as he tried again and this time successfully carried it into the yard.

"I don't understand why it was in the cupboard," said Michael. "What was she thinking?"

"I doubt she was," said Lawrence. "She'd have been terrified. Who wouldn't? And with the history behind those crows..." He shuddered, trying to block visions of Violet in mortal dread.

"I suppose we have to open it?"

Lawrence nodded. "We must in case there's anything else inside. I suppose it's pointless asking if you have a flask about your person?"

Michael raised an eyebrow.

"Just a thought. Right. Stand by." He raised the lid and looked down on a putrefying black mass peppered with plump maggots.

"Stick?" he asked, looking away.

Michael stepped towards the vegetable bed and removed a pea stick. "Will that do?"

Lawrence nodded and used it to push the feathery mess into the corner of the trunk. "No, nothing," he said. "No clues at all. Who on earth could have done this?"

"That's why I searched you out," said Michael. "I don't know where to start. Dozens of people knew about the Fressingfield crows. Think about it. There were those involved in the case, our acquaintances, most of the village and anyone else we've subsequently told."

Lawrence closed the lid and moved the tin trunk towards a wooden outhouse with the toe of his boot. "You're right. It could be a number of people, but one thing's for sure. Whoever did this meant to frighten the life out of Violet. They knew her well enough to be sure it would scare her. And from what you've told me, Violet was already fearful."

"I have never known her so terrified," said Michael. "When I first read her letters, I thought she might be having a nervous breakdown. But as time went on, it became clear that someone was targeting her. And what he did to her is unnecessarily melodramatic when you think about it."

"What do you mean?"

"Well, first, there was the moving stone. It's moved before, and from what I hear, they have reinstated it several times. But someone had gone to great lengths to make it seem to have turned. He physically wrenched it or dug out the foundations, which is no mean feat. The thing is heavy and cumbersome. And if that wasn't enough, they piled earth around it so that anyone who regularly passed by would inevitably notice. And if that person approached the stone and examined the grave, they would find a key – a key that opens a tin trunk covered in skulls."

"I see what you mean," said Lawrence. "The whole thing is stage-managed and none of it coincidental. He timed it so that Violet and only Violet would see the gravestone. But why?"

"Why indeed? To frighten her, I suppose."

"But nobody knows she is here," said Lawrence.

"Perhaps she's been investigating in the village and has upset someone."

"No. That can't be it. How would anyone else know about the crows?"

"Or it could be a horrible coincidence."

Lawrence shook his head. "Not a chance. As you say, the whole thing has been stage-managed. Every detail counts. The watcher is someone that Violet has upset in the past."

"But why are they seeking revenge now?"

"Because, like you, they've only just found her."

"Of course," murmured Michael. "But who and why?"

"Did you say you've spoken to her friends in the tea room?"

Michael nodded. "Not the manageress, unfortunately. She'd have been a bit more use, but the waitress said she was on a business trip and she may not be back yet."

"Not much point in going back there then. We need to look for Violet, and I've no idea where to start."

"She must still be in Swaffham," said Michael.

"I hope so," said Lawrence, thinking about Eliza Carter and Mary Seward. "Not all missing people are found."

"Don't think like that," said Michael. "Of course we will track her down. It's one thing taking someone from their home, but quite another transporting them across the county."

"You'd be surprised," said Lawrence, darkly. "But as you say, let's be optimistic and assume she is still in town. Where would she be?"

"I don't know."

"You wouldn't have her letters with you?" asked Lawrence.

"Of course," said Michael. "I knew you'd ask at some point, so I brought them to West Ham." He opened his bag and produced a sheaf of papers.

"Perfect. Make me a cup of tea, will you while I read them?"

Lawrence didn't wait for a reply, but proceeded to the living room, kicked off his shoes and reclined on the settee with his feet on the antimacassar. Ten minutes later, Michael appeared bearing a mug. "No milk," he said. "I hope you don't mind it without."

"I'd prefer it with a splash of brandy, but if I can't have that I'll take it how it comes," said Lawrence, moving to a seated position. "Now, this is very helpful, Michael. These letters are quite revealing."

212

"Good. Do you think we will find her?"

"We will," said Lawrence. "Violet is in grave danger, and I will not let her down again. I owe her everything and my behaviour towards her was unforgivable."

His voice quivered, and Michael sensed that he was close to tears. Lawrence had been belligerent earlier, his behaviour flippant. For a while, Michael had worried that his attitude towards Violet had hardened over the passing years. But it was clearly a business-as-usual act designed to hide his true feelings. Beneath it all, Lawrence was hopelessly worried and trying to put a brave face on it.

"Have I missed anything?"

"No. You have faithfully recounted everything Violet told you, but the letters reveal a pattern. It's funny, you know. When we started investigating together, I was impulsive, and Violet was analytic. I used my instinct to solve puzzles, and she relied on logic. But the years brought us closer together somehow. We watched and learned from each other, and during our latter cases, I tended towards fact and Violet towards feelings. And so, I know that if she thought someone was following her, then there would have been a good reason for it. And given what turned up in the trunk, it's fair to conclude that Violet has been under scrutiny for weeks. Whoever watched her was doing it from a nearby vantage point. She never saw him, but she felt him. So, he was either skilled in tracking or more likely, he lived nearby."

"Of course," said Michael, brightening. "You must be right. There is no other explanation, and it is so mundane. Nothing supernatural about it at all."

"Quite," said Lawrence. "Now, we've got two choices. We can either leave it until morning, locate the local land agent and ask what properties he has rented out lately, or we can visit the churchyard tonight. Personally, I would prefer the latter."

"It will be dark soon," said Michael, peering from the window.

"I know," said Lawrence, "but we don't know who's got her and why. I'm reluctant to leave it any longer."

213

"It won't be easy. There are many houses in which he could have hidden Violet."

Lawrence shook his head. "I don't think so. The house must be in sight of the churchyard. There can't be that many. We need lanterns and this," he continued, removing a gnarled stick propped against a coat stand. "Quite why Violet has a shillelagh in her hallway, I don't know, but it could be jolly useful."

# CHAPTER 33

## *In Hot Pursuit*

"Have a care," snapped Lawrence as Michael tripped in a divot on the church path, falling into Lawrence and knocking him flying.

"It's the lamp," protested Michael. "It's not producing much light."

"I'm not surprised. It's filthy," said Lawrence, examining the glass. "And this one isn't much better. They'll have to do, though. We haven't got time to stop and clean them."

"But all the time in the world to go prowling around the churchyard after dark."

"With good reason," said Lawrence. "We need to find Ella Morse's resting place."

"Can't it wait until morning?"

"I think we decided it would be too late by then."

"Too late to look for Violet, not the grave."

"It's the same thing," said Lawrence. "Finding the grave will give us the best chance of locating Violet."

"Will it?"

"Of course. Whoever was following Violet knew she walked past the cross every day, and they used it to attract her attention. Well, he must have been watching, and I wouldn't mind betting he can see it from his house, especially with the aid of a pair of binoculars. Now, do you know where the gravestone is?"

"Sorry. I've no idea. I didn't know it existed until Violet first mentioned it."

"Then this could be a long night. It's best if we split up. It shouldn't be difficult to identify the cross when we track it down if it's still askew."

"Right you are," sighed Michael, resigned to the task despite his better judgement. The two men peeled off in different directions.

Lawrence trudged wearily towards the front stone standing tall and proud before him. All the other grave markers lay obediently in line and had not moved since the day they were first erected. He passed another row and another. Then Lawrence stifled a yawn, hardly able to believe that this time the previous night he was with two men, both of whom were now deceased. Lawrence had seen Gilbert Cooper. He was stone dead when Lawrence turned him over to check, not that anyone could have survived his injuries. Whether Higgins had followed through with his plans, was unknown. But Higgins was an honourable man with little left to live for, and in all probability, Lawrence was the only survivor of the night's encounter. He shuddered at the thought as he passed yet another row of crumbling lichen-covered tombstones. Fifteen minutes later and scowling with frustration, Lawrence saw a light coming towards him. He ducked behind a tree until he was sure it belonged to Michael. "Any luck?" he asked, raising his lamp in acknowledgement.

"No. Not a thing," said Michael. "But the stone must be here."

"Unless they've put it back in line," said Lawrence.

"The disturbance would be obvious; at least it would be if we were looking during daylight hours." Short of saying 'I told you so', Michael's tone could not have been more dismissive.

"Ah, but wait," said Lawrence, raising his lantern again and directing the beam to the nearby row of gravestones. "And there it is," he added smugly, as the light glanced off a stone cross standing at right angles to the other graves, nestling by the corner of the church. "We were near it all along."

"So it is, and exactly as Violet described."

"It's odd though," said Lawrence. "There seems to have been a great deal of digging, yet this stone looks as if it was on the move long before the most recent disturbance."

"Exactly as the legend suggests," said Michael. "Even in this poor light, you can see that the stone has changed position many times."

"Best not think about it while we're standing in the lee of an unlit church," said Lawrence, turning up his coat collar. "Things are unsettling enough as it is."

"Where do we go from here?"

Lawrence turned away from the cross. "The church is blocking the view from the rear which makes the problem easier," he said. "If my theory is correct, we are looking for a property that's visible from here."

"Or would be visible, if it wasn't so dark," said Michael, peering into the blackness in frustration.

"It doesn't matter," said Lawrence. The house must be parallel with this side of the church. We need to find it. Follow me."

He strode into the darkness, leaving Michael behind. "Wait for me," he called.

"Shhh," said Lawrence. "No more noise. We'll creep past these houses and see if anything looks awry."

They walked down one side of the road and back up the other, then Lawrence stopped and leaned against a red brick house, wearing a puzzled frown on his face.

"What?" asked Michael.

"That's not right," said Lawrence, pointing to a flint covered terraced cottage.

"It looks perfectly normal to me."

"No. Not right at all."

Michael looked again. "I don't see it."

"Someone's boarded the front window up."

"So?"

"Look at the chimney."

A wisp of smoke drifted into the night sky.

"Perhaps they can't afford to get it repaired," said Michael. "It's only a little cottage and may need maintenance."

"It doesn't feel right. I'm going to take a look."

"Don't rouse them," said Michael.

"I don't intend to. Are you coming?"

Michael sighed. His conscience was already troubling him, and he had done nothing wrong – yet. But he was with Lawrence – impulsive, foolhardy Lawrence. Trouble was only ever one ill-considered action away. But Violet was in danger, and that was more important. "Please be careful," he said. "I have more to risk than you."

"I know," said Lawrence. "And I understand if you would rather stay here. I can manage things alone."

"No," said Michael. "I asked for your help, and the least I can do is stick with you."

Lawrence nodded. "Lights out for a moment," he said. Both men turned the screws on their oil lamps which spluttered and died. Then the men tiptoed through the ungated side entrance and into a small rear garden.

A dim glow illuminated the back room of the house as Lawrence advanced to the window. He peered through the glass, struggling to identify the contents of the room beyond. But as his eyes grew accustomed to the gloom, they settled on a domestic tableau inside. A man, just out of view, reclined with his legs crossed under the table. He was tucking into a plate of food in front of him with gusto. Lawrence craned his neck, trying to glimpse the man's face, but no matter how hard he tried, that part of the room remained frustratingly out of view. Directly in front of the man and at the other end of the table, a pale-faced woman sat silently. She nibbled tiny amounts of food from a fork as if repelled at the repast before her. Her face, drawn and haggard, was as familiar to him as his own. She hadn't changed in all these years, and Lawrence felt a rush of short-lived joy as he regarded her. It was Violet, not the happiest looking Violet he'd seen, but she was well and unharmed and eating an evening meal by the look of things. He turned to Michael. "Look. She's perfectly safe," he murmured.

Michael frowned as he took his turn at the window. "She looks uncomfortable," he whispered. "And who is with her? I can't see him from here."

"A gentleman friend," said Lawrence, smile falling away. "That's why she hasn't been home and with no consideration for the consequences. She's throwing her reputation away."

"No," said Michael. "That's not Violet's way. She's not enjoying herself. Look at her face."

"Move then." Lawrence nudged him impatiently as he fought for the window space.

"I see what you mean. She's picking at that food in a very un-Violet-like way. She usually eats like a horse."

"Don't be flippant," Michael hissed. "She looks terrified."

Lawrence sighed and stared inside again, eyes darting across the room. A lace cloth covered the table, and an elaborate candelabra stood centrepiece. It illuminated two platters of food, one a joint of meat and the other laden with vegetables. Violet, resplendent in an elegant navy dress, wore a pearl rope necklace and a matching brooch. Yet for all the finery around the table, the house was in poor repair. Stains coated the broken mirror above the fireplace, and plaster crumbled from the walls. The olive wallpaper curled below the picture rail, and the room looked dirty. Michael's instinct was correct, and something inside was badly wrong. "She's wearing a lot of jewellery," said Lawrence, thinking aloud.

"She doesn't usually care for it," said Michael.

"I know. I bought Violet a bracelet once, and she never wore it. I thought she was superstitious. She's wearing pearls and I'm sure she doesn't like them."

"Do you think we should make ourselves known?" asked Michael.

"No. Violet is safe, and we know where she is. Besides, she won't be happy with you for telling me where to find her. Perhaps we should leave both of them alone and keep an eye on things for the next few days, just in case."

"Yes. Violet is there of her own free will and can easily leave if she wants to. I'm sorry, Lawrence. I've dragged you away from London for nothing."

"Oh no," Lawrence gasped and clapped his hand over his mouth.

"What's wrong."

"I've changed my mind. We're going in. But we need to wait for a moment."

"Why? What's happened."

"It's better if you see for yourself. Look at the chair Violet is sitting on."

They swapped places, and Michael exhaled, shaking his head. "Oh, Lawrence. Are those ropes?"

"Yes. That scoundrel has tied her legs to the chair."

"It's worse than that."

"Why? What have you seen?"

Michael pointed, and Lawrence craned over his shoulder. Propped against the far corner of the fireplace was the unmistakable form of a shotgun.

#

"There are two of us and only one of him," whispered Lawrence. "We can overpower him."

"No. The gun is only a step away. If he lunges towards the fireplace, he will reach it long before we can get there. If only Violet were free to move. Do you think we should fetch help?"

"What if he takes a potshot at her before we get back?"

"That's not very likely. They've been together for days, but I suppose we should err on the side of caution. Yes. A rush of people might cause him to act irrationally and who knows where that might end?"

"Act irrationally?" hissed Lawrence. "There's more food on that table than six people could eat in a week. He's made Violet dress to the nines, and she is wearing jewellery for dinner in a workman's cottage. Not only that, but she's tied to a chair and dining with a man sitting two feet away from a shotgun. Whoever he is, the man's a lunatic. He's not going to behave rationally, and we will need to take some risks."

"Considered risks," said Michael.

"Of course," snapped Lawrence. "Now, let me think. He's going to leave the room at some stage..." His words trailed away as the man leaned forward and reached for a wine decanter. Lawrence craned his head, waiting with bated breath for the man's face to appear. But just as Lawrence glimpsed his jacket collar, the man reclined again. Then he slid the decanter back down the table, its contents vastly reduced.

"Damn it. Why can't we see him? He's a cool fellow, and that's a fact," said Lawrence, gritting his teeth in frustration. "Well, he'll need a visit to the gentleman's room very shortly if he continues quaffing wine at that rate."

"Yes, he will," agreed Michael. "But will he let Violet stay where she is?"

"I expect so," said Lawrence. "What's the point of moving her? She can't go anywhere. He doesn't know we're watching him and has every reason to feel safe. We need to find a way inside. I'll see if there's any give in the window frame."

Lawrence quietly tugged the frame, but it didn't budge. "That's not going to work," he said. "Try the other side, Michael."

"No. Same here. It's latched from inside."

"Right," said Lawrence. "I'll just..." But whatever he was going to say next was lost in a crash of noise as the lantern slipped from his hand and bounced off a stone trough. "Hide," he hissed, grabbing the light.

Seconds later, the rear door of the cottage slammed open, and the silhouette of a man brandishing a shotgun loomed ahead. Lawrence crouched by the side of the ramshackle shed, hoping that Michael had found somewhere to conceal himself. The man walked forward, shrouded in darkness and Lawrence breathlessly watched as footsteps crunched through gravel. The man negotiated the short distance to the end of the yard, turned and surveyed the property.

Clouds hung moodily in the night sky, obscuring all but the brightest stars and a sliver of moon. Lawrence used what little light was available as he scanned the area, searching for signs of Michael. Then, out of the corner of his eye, he caught the unmistakable glint of metal only feet from Violet's captor. The man would see Michael, if not tread on him at any moment. Lawrence reached blindly for an object and grasped a handful of gravel which he threw over his head and into the next-door neighbour's garden. The stones ricocheted off the low metal roof of an outhouse, exploding in a torrent of unexpected noise. The man wheeled round, raising the shotgun to his shoulder, its outline just visible in the low light. Lawrence resisted the urge to peer at the man's face as he paced towards the door. Then he shrank back into the side of the shed with his head down and his collar up to keep his pale extremities hidden. The sound of falling gravel had roused the neighbours, and a door opened in the next-door cottage.

"I can't see anything, Joan," said a voice.

"Well, I heard something, Harold. Call Smokey."

"Smokey. Come here, puss-puss. Where are you?"

A faint mewling preceded the scratch of claws as the sounds of a cat clambering over walls and roofs reached their ears.

"There he is. Nothing to worry about," said Harold, ushering the cat inside. The door shut with a faint click followed by the clunk of a solid bolt.

Lawrence waited silently to see what Violet's captor did next, but he seemed satisfied at the sight of the cat, lowered his gun, and opened the door. As soon as he went inside, Lawrence darted over to the window and lightly drummed his fingers against the pane before the man had time to reach the table. Violet turned her head at the sound, and her eyes narrowed as she peered outside, trying to see what was going on. As Violet stared confusedly towards the window, Lawrence regretted his impetuous decision. Violet could no more see him than he could see her captor, but now she knew that somebody was outside and was trying to stay invisible. Friend or foe – she would have no way of knowing. Lawrence hoped that she would employ her sharp intellect to piece together Michael's involvement, if not his own.

"Is she alright?" Michael had reappeared and was crouching by Lawrence again.

"Yes," said Lawrence. "I think so. That was a close shave."

"I'm a bag of nerves," said Michael. "He was almost on top of me. I couldn't see a thing, yet there was a familiarity about the man I can't account for."

"What was it? A smell? A sound?"

"I don't know. A feeling, I suppose."

"Well, that's no help," said Lawrence bluntly. "Oh, what now?" He looked up and held his hand out as a fat raindrop fell on the bridge of his nose. "It's raining. That's all we need."

"What are we going to do?"

"Wait," said Lawrence. "It's all we can do."

Half an hour later, they were still loitering by the window, watching the static scene inside. Violet had long since pushed her plate away and was sitting in silence. There was no sign of movement at all from the other end of the table. Lawrence placed his ear as close to the window as possible and listened. Moments later, he touched Michael's arm. "He's asleep," he whispered.

"Shall we go in?"

"It's still too risky. But Violet's awake. We need to attract her attention."

"Don't make any noise."

"I won't." Lawrence retreated to the side of the shed where he had left the lamp, removed his tin, and lit the wick. Then he tiptoed back to the window and lifted the lantern towards Violet. She saw it immediately and turned to face them. Then, hoping she would not cry out in shock, he moved towards the light so she could see his face. Her eyes widened, but she kept tight control over her features, giving nothing away. Her eyes darted towards the window and back with a sense of urgency that Lawrence instinctively understood. The lantern was too bright. He lowered it a little, and her eyes stilled.

"Is he asleep?" he mouthed.

Violet didn't move.

"Take this." Lawrence thrust the light towards Michael, and once unencumbered, he put his hands together by the side of his head and mimed sleep.

Violet gave an imperceptible nod.

"Where is the gun?" he mimed.

Her eyes darted towards the end of the table.

"Who is he?"

Nothing. She didn't move.

Lawrence pointed towards the man and held both hands palms up.

Violet's facial features didn't change, but she moved her hands slowly, pointing first to the brooch and then to the pearls. Finally, she adjusted an earring.

"What does she mean?" whispered Lawrence.

"That the jewellery is important," said Michael.

Lawrence looked again. He'd already known that the jewellery didn't belong to Violet, but there was something disconcertingly familiar about it.

He turned to Violet and shrugged his shoulders. She stared at him with soft, sad eyes – eyes brimming with empathy, tearful and intense.

"She's upset, not angry," he said. "I doubt she's pleased to see me, yet there's no sign of resentment."

"I expect she's relieved," said Michael. "She must have been terrified."

When Lawrence looked back into the room, Violet was staring straight down the table, but her hand was still clutching the brooch. She turned it towards the window as she sat impassively, revealing for the first time a dark stone in the centre of the pearls. And suddenly, with heart lurching realisation, Lawrence understood.

He gasped and spun towards Michael ashen-faced. "Oh my God," he said.

"What? What's happened?"

"They're Catherine's. How did I miss it? The necklace, the earrings. They all belong to my dead wife. I haven't seen them since she died. I didn't even know they were missing. What are they doing in there and why the devil is Violet wearing them?"

Michael stared incredulously. "Violet didn't know Catherine. How is this possible?"

"It's not her doing," said Lawrence. "It wasn't fear in her eyes, but compassion."

"Look, he's moving."

The crossed legs under the table vanished as Violet stared ahead with a fixed expression. Moments later, they heard a door closing inside.

"It's now or never," said Lawrence.

# CHAPTER 34

## *As Bad As It Gets*

The two men stood either side of the back door relieved that their access inside was now unimpeded by a lock since the man's earlier foray into the garden. Lawrence, still carrying the shillelagh, stowed the lantern by a flowerpot and brandished his weapon as Michael opened the door. They crept nervously through the passageway, hoping to secure a non-violent rescue. Michael gently pushed the dining room door, which was still ajar, stepping back to allow Lawrence first access. Lawrence peered inside to see Violet still tied to a chair at the bottom of the table, but alone in the room. The seat where her captor had been was empty and the shotgun had gone. Lawrence rushed to her side, kneeling as he began the tricky task of untying her bonds. "Are you injured?" he whispered.

"No. But you should go. There isn't time. He's quite mad, Lawrence. He will kill you."

"Stay still. Michael, come and help."

Michael was at Violet's side by the time Lawrence finished the sentence, trying unsuccessfully to free Violet without touching her flesh.

"Now is not the time for modesty," snapped Lawrence. He watched in frustration as Michael blindly fumbled with the knots, his eyes averted from Violet's legs.

"Don't worry about it," said Violet. "I'm so pleased to see you both."

"That's one leg free," said Lawrence. "Come on, Michael."

"Done." Michael stood and held out a hand to Violet. "Let me help you up."

Violet stood, swaying uncertainly. She reached down and rubbed her calves. Deep grooves streaked her legs where the ropes had cut in.

"Can you walk?" asked Lawrence.

Violet nodded.

"Then hurry. We don't have much time."

Violet took a few steps forward, then stumbled as Lawrence and Michael instinctively reached to support her. They each took an arm and propelled her towards the door, towards safety. Then, as freedom seemed within their grasp, the unmistakable form of a rifle appeared through the door, followed by its owner.

"What a touching scene," said a familiar voice. "Walk backwards towards the fireplace and sit on the floor. Go on."

Lawrence gasped in shock, and Michael stood, ashen-faced, lip trembling and almost on the verge of tears.

"You!" exclaimed Lawrence. "But why?"

"Floor now," said their captor, pointing the rifle directly at Violet. "I don't want to spoil her face, but she doesn't want me. God knows I've tried. And if I can't have her, then she might as well be dead." He paused for a moment. "Or disfigured," he continued, menacingly.

Lawrence took Violet's hand and retreated towards the fireplace before sitting on the cold, hard floor as instructed. Michael remained standing.

"And you," said the man. "Don't think that blood ties will help."

"But we're brothers," said Michael. "You've been like a father to me."

"It didn't stop your betrayal."

"I don't understand."

"You didn't tell me you'd found her." Francis nodded towards Violet.

"I didn't tell anyone. Violet asked me not to."

"Then it's a good thing I found your letters, or I'd never have known."

"How? You've been abroad for months."

Francis Farrow laughed as he raised the shotgun again. "Sit down with your friends," he snarled, stroking the trigger.

Michael stood motionless then took an uncertain pace forward. Francis pointed the shotgun at Violet again.

"I'm a crack shot, don't forget," he said.

"I can't believe this is happening," said Michael, as he joined Lawrence and Violet. "He's gone mad."

"Don't be so offensive," snapped Francis. "I'm perfectly rational. Now, let me pull up a chair, and I'll tell you all about it. And then I'll decide what to do with you. The first thing you should know is that I haven't been abroad at all. I've been the length and breadth of England looking for Violet, stopping only to visit your respective residences. And you, the detective, were worse than useless," said Francis, glaring at Lawrence. "I've read your notes. You didn't get anywhere, did you? Then I thought I'd visit Michael's rooms just in case and wasn't that a good decision? He had recently encountered Violet, and she'd conveniently written a letter with her address on it."

"But why did you want to find her so badly?" asked Lawrence.

"Because I love her. I wanted her, and she abandoned me just as she abandoned you," said Francis.

"You don't love me," said Violet. "It was an obsession. It started when we were in Felsham, and you must have realised how uncomfortable I felt. I tried to stay away from you and reduce our contact. But you kept finding ways to see me, and I soon realised that it would come to a head. I tried to let you down gently, Francis, but you wouldn't have it, and I worried about how you would react if I publicly rejected you. Lawrence was getting married, and he didn't need me anymore. I had responsibilities that I needed to live up to, and my safety was paramount. So, I sold my house and left. And if I hadn't bumped into Michael, you'd never have seen me again."

"Enough." Francis spat the words as he glared at Violet. "You don't know what love is. I have pursued you, searching every day since you left. Lawrence gave up, but I did not. You haven't given me a chance, Violet. I could make you happy. You'd want for nothing."

"But she doesn't love you," said Lawrence.

Francis stood, face contorted with rage and fired a single shot towards the window. The glass exploded, sending shards tinkling into the outside yard. "Shut up, or the next shot will be in her head," he snarled, snapping open the gun and loading another cartridge.

"For God's sake, Francis," Michael appealed. "What has happened to you? The person standing before me isn't the loving brother I've known all my life."

"You know nothing about me," retorted Francis.

"But you've always been so happy-go-lucky."

"On the contrary, I've known nothing but disappointment. My life is an empty shell."

"Hence all the toys," said Lawrence.

"Toys?" Michael looked bemused.

"New cars, expensive carriages – objects filling a gap in his life. Why didn't you take a wife like any normal man?"

"I did," said Francis, lip curling.

"I don't understand. You never married."

"Were you behind the moving stone?" asked Michael, changing the subject at an inopportune moment.

Francis grinned wolfishly. "Yes. Clever, wasn't it? I took a cottage here the day after I read your letter. At first, I thought I would announce myself to Violet, and gradually re-introduce myself back into her life. But I wasn't sure how she would react, so I decided to frighten her a little. Then she would be receptive to a friend, especially one who could offer protection. I watched her instead, noting her preoccupation with the Morse stone. After asking around, I soon heard the story of how the damn thing had travelled over the years."

"And you moved it again," asked Michael.

"To a point. There was something in the legend. The stone travelled unaided – tree roots or subsidence, I suppose. Quite unsettling to see it misaligned. And equally uncomfortable digging it up at night, which I did, of course."

"I suppose you left the key and the crows?" asked Lawrence.

"Naturally. And by then, I'd thoroughly scared Violet as I intended. Yet when I arrived at her cottage, she didn't want to come with me. She didn't seem pleased to see me at all, and it took a lot of persuading to get her to agree to join me the following day. Eventually, she capitulated, and I employed a local woman to cook us a meal. She left, immediately before Violet arrived and we ate and talked without an audience. Then I told Violet how much I had missed her and asked her to stay. She refused, just like that. Wanted to collect the child, I suppose. I would have let Violet go if she'd agreed to return later, but she said it was best if she didn't come back. And I knew that if I allowed her to leave, I would never see her again. I had no choice, Harpham. Don't you see?"

"You took her prisoner?"

"Yes, he did," said Violet. "I have been here for days living this half-life tied up and with no control over my destiny. But I need to go. If you ever loved me, Francis, then release me."

"No. I haven't gone to all this trouble to be alone again."

"Find another woman, Farrow," said Lawrence. "She doesn't want you, and she never will."

"No. Violet is irreplaceable."

"And what did you mean about having a wife? You've never had a wife."

A slow, satisfied smile slid across Francis' face. "Oh, but I did. I had yours."

#

"What the devil do you mean, man?" asked Lawrence, eyes flashing with anger. "Don't talk about Catherine. You're not worthy."

"It's you that didn't deserve her," said Francis. "Always away – leaving her alone while you swanned off on your investigations."

"I was a police officer," said Lawrence. "We both were. You of all people know the demands of the job. God knows you went away often enough yourself."

"That was different. I had no wife or obligations."

"Catherine understood the burden of my employment when she met me."

"It didn't stop her being lonely."

"How do you know how my wife felt? And why is Violet wearing her jewellery?"

"Because I took the jewels when Catherine died. My colleagues recovered them from the house, and as a serving officer, I had full access to the evidence. I kept them and a few other trinkets besides."

"Why didn't you tell me? They were mine. I should have had them."

"You didn't deserve them."

"Francis. The fire wasn't my fault. I have done nothing wrong. Why are you behaving like this?"

"Harpham. You are entirely to blame. You are the reason Catherine died. You and you alone."

"Don't listen to him," said Violet, her eyes filling with tears. "Don't. He's poison."

Francis Farrow reclined in the wooden chair his legs splayed as he held the rifle on the floor with the barrel pointing to the ceiling. He scratched his head as he fought for composure. "Catherine wasn't yours. She was mine," he said. "She loved me, and I loved her, passionately, body and soul. We wanted to be together."

"Don't you dare suggest that Catherine was unfaithful. She was a loyal and constant wife."

"We were lovers," said Francis. "For years. She despised you and thought you were weak. But her family name was everything. She couldn't divorce you without a scandal, and we kept our love a secret."

"No. Impossible. Catherine wouldn't have betrayed me." Lawrence clutched his hair grimacing in anguish.

"She wrote letters to me while I was in Ipswich with messages under the envelope flap. How do you think I replicated them?"

"You sent those crests to me? I thought I was going out of my mind."

"That was my intention. You were getting too close to Violet, and I wanted her. Nothing could have made me happier than when Loveday came back on the scene. Well, nothing except having Catherine back, that is."

"I don't believe any of this. I would have known." Michael was sitting bolt upright, arms around his knees and staring at Francis as if he was a stranger.

"You were away at university, little brother," said Francis, scornfully. "What would you know of my affairs?"

"Why am I the reason Catherine died?" Lawrence spoke quietly, fearful of the response.

"Because we were desperate to be together, and while you were still husband and wife, it would never happen. Catherine couldn't divorce you without ruining her good name, so I planned to dispose of you, naturally keeping the details from Catherine. I didn't want her involved."

"My disposal. Were you going to kill me?"

Francis nodded. "Yes. It was the only way – nothing personal, old man. Well, actually, that's a lie. Of course it was personal. I hated you, Harpham. Not while we were at university. But I had my sights on Catherine from the moment I met her, and if I'd known the two of you would fall in love, I would never have introduced you. I don't know how I got through your wedding day, let alone acted as best man, watching you marry the woman I loved. Watching you steal my life from under my nose. As time went on, my hatred grew until I could barely control my loathing. I contemplated all the ways I could kill you and finally settled on fire."

"It was you?" Michael stared at his brother in horror.

"Yes. I set the fire. Catherine was going away to visit her family, leaving him in the house alone." Francis scowled at Lawrence as he stroked the barrel of the shotgun. "Only she didn't go, and I didn't know. And worse still, he wasn't even there when I lit the match. There was I thinking all my problems would soon be over and the next day I realised I had lost everything. Lost it all, yet still he lived."

"You killed my family. You killed Catherine, and you killed Lily. You murdered my daughter."

"My daughter," shouted Francis. "Lily was mine, not yours. For four long years, I let you claim paternity, but she was my child. You never had a daughter."

Michael gasped, and the room fell silent, the full horror of the words settling over them like a poisonous fog. Then Lawrence sprang from the floor and sprinted towards Francis. "I'm going to kill you, you murderous bastard."

Francis pointed the shotgun, but Lawrence's speed had surprised him. Lawrence reached for the gun, knocking it from Francis' grasp. It rattled to the floor. Lawrence tried to grab it, but Francis was quicker and rammed the butt in Lawrence's face. Lawrence crashed to the floor, blood streaming from his wound, but he didn't seem to notice and scrambled to his feet. "I'll kill you," he said again, advancing towards Francis.

"Stop, or I'll shoot her. I mean it." Francis pointed the gun towards Violet again.

"You'll only get one shot, and then I'll have you," snarled Lawrence.

"But she'll be dead."

"Go on. Shoot me." Violet slowly got to her feet.

"Sit down," barked Francis.

"No. Shoot me." Violet took a step forward.

"Violet, stop." Lawrence managed to control his rage for a moment, but Violet took another tentative step.

"I'll shoot." Francis waved the gun wildly, finger turning white against the trigger.

She took a deep breath and advanced again.

"You've done it now," snarled Francis pressing the trigger as Lawrence rushed forwards. He launched himself at the gun, tipping it off course as the shell exploded from the barrel and ricocheted off the fireplace. Cursing, Francis ran towards the door and took another shot at Lawrence. The bullet met its mark and Lawrence fell backwards with the impact of the shot. The last thing he remembered was Violet leaning over him, tears running down her face.

# EPILOGUE

## *Epilogue*

***Thursday, March 23, 1899***

"Good morning, Mr Harpham." The nurse pulled open the curtains with a forced smile on her face. "What a lovely day," she said.

He stared at her, unblinking. "I'm glad you think so." His voice was monotone, the inflexion neither rising nor falling – a grey voice in a grey and pointless world.

"The sun is shining, and the daffodils are out."

"I don't care, and I'd appreciate it if you shut the damned curtains. I don't care for daylight."

"It's good for you," said the nurse. "Now, what can I bring you for breakfast."

"Nothing," said Lawrence.

"I'll choose for you then.," said the nurse, seemingly unaffected by his mood.

"I won't eat it."

"As you wish. But I'll bring something just in case you change your mind. I'll be back in a moment."

Lawrence sighed and wished they would leave him alone. He hated being in the hospital, the forced cheerfulness of everyone around him and the fact that he was still alive. One inch to the right and Lawrence would be in the ground by now. And he might as well be dead. His life had ended the moment Francis had claimed Catherine and Lily for his own.

The doctors had heavily sedated Lawrence during his first few days in the hospital. But as he'd regained consciousness, the pain of Francis Farrow's revelation settled on him like a malevolent wraith. It seeped into his thoughts, ruining former happy memories, and destroying all trust. Had he really known Catherine and had she ever loved him? Wracked with self-pity, Lawrence had sobbed for days, driven to distraction at the thought of it. Physician after physician had attended his bedside, trying to lift his mood, but nothing helped. Eventually, a mind doctor arrived and prescribed something that took the edge of his depression. But only the edge. His thoughts turned inwards, burning like acid through his brain. Rest came only with the aid of sleeping draughts, but the time asleep and temporarily unaware, made his life immeasurably harder. Each day, a torrent of terrible memories would accompany his morning rouse to consciousness. Every time he opened his eyes, he remembered his loss more acutely than the day before. Tonight, he intended to refuse the sleeping draft altogether and sleep fitfully instead. Then he would know what was coming the next day, and it wouldn't be such a dreadful shock.

Michael had visited the previous week, sitting with Lawrence for a bare ten minutes. The matron, with her starched collar and equally stiff demeanour, had shown no sympathy when Michael had asked for more time with his friend. She'd pursed her thin lips and marched him out, brooking no further discussion. And it happened at the exact moment that Michael was trying to explain to Lawrence that just because Francis had said those things, did not make them true. But in his heart, Lawrence didn't need telling. It was obvious as soon as the words were out. Lily wasn't his child and never had been. And once the thought had embedded itself, he marvelled that he had ever missed her resemblance to Francis.

On one particularly rational day, Lawrence wondered whether Francis had forced himself on Catherine, and she had conceived Lily in consequence. But how would he ever know? The words Francis had uttered became the truth from the moment they left his lips as there was nobody left to contradict them. Only Francis himself had the power and he would never use it. A man capable of tying a woman to a table, hoping she would settle into domestic bliss against her free will, lacked the capacity for introspection. Whether or not it happened, Francis believed his interpretation of the affair with Catherine. Lawrence would never know for sure and the little family he'd thought he had was only an illusion. Lawrence had never had a daughter and only a partial claim to the affections of his wife. Lawrence might as well be dead and not for the first time he contemplated purchasing a fast-acting poison.

A crash interrupted Lawrence's musing, and he turned a careless eye towards the bed beside him where a young man had dropped an empty metal jug on the floor. He grinned ruefully at Lawrence, who turned his head away and stared blankly at the wall. Thank God Lawrence only had one neighbour. The last thing he wanted was to be around people. There were eight beds on the ward, but only four patients and Lawrence was mercifully at the far end and away from most of the other men.

"Here you are." The nurse had returned with a tray of something gloopy and a cup of brown liquid bearing a passing resemblance to tea.

"I told you, I don't want it."

She removed a jug of water from his bedside table and put it on a wooden chair, before replacing it with the breakfast tray.

"And I said I'll leave your food here. You might feel hungry later, but you must be quick. You've got a visitor."

"Who?"

"I don't know. I'm just the messenger."

"I don't want to see anyone."

"That's not up to you. Matron thinks it would be a good idea, and I agree. Consider putting your robe on first, and I'll see to your bandages shortly."

Lawrence glanced at his chest and the stained dressing where he had knocked his wound the previous evening.

"Tell them to go away," he said, but she turned her back and walked down the ward.

Sighing and resigned to his unwanted visitor, Lawrence reached for his dressing gown, wincing as he stretched towards the chair. He grabbed it by the sleeve and struggled into it, hearing the squeal of a child at play beneath his window. "Shouldn't let them near a hospital," he muttered.

"Come on then." The nurse had returned with a wheelchair. "Hop in."

"I can walk," said Lawrence.

"I'll fetch matron."

Lawrence removed the bedcover and limped to the chair.

"Where are we going?"

"To the visitors' room. It's just off the ward."

"Why couldn't my visitor come here?"

"She's a lady. It wouldn't be proper."

Lawrence raised his eyes, about to give his views on propriety and what matron could do about it, but gloom enveloped him, and he couldn't raise the energy.

He shook his head, and passively sat as she pushed him into a small, sparsely decorated room.

"Hello, Lawrence. How are you?" said Violet, gazing at him with an uncertain smile.

"As good as any man who finds out his life was a lie," he said with a lump in his throat. His heart ached as he regarded Violet.

Under different circumstances, the sight of her would brighten his day. But not this time. He felt numb, bereft. She was another reminder of that painful night.

"Don't believe everything Francis told you," said Violet, as if she had read his mind. Her eyes were tear-filled, expressing the same compassion as when he'd last seen her. But then, of course, she must have known what Francis was going to say. He'd held her captive for the best part of a week, and they must have talked about something during that time.

"It's true, though."

"You don't know that."

"I do with hindsight. At least about Lily. I loved her so much, and she wasn't even mine. She didn't look like me."

"She was yours in every way that mattered."

"What happened to him? Is he in jail?"

Violet shook her head.

"Where then?"

"He got away," she whispered.

Lawrence put his head in his hands. "Great. So, they've carted me back to Bury, and that lunatic is close by."

"No. Michael checked. Francis must have briefly returned to Netherwood. All his valuables, including his latest car and trunk, have disappeared, but Francis is long gone. He has escaped justice, Lawrence."

"Damn it. I'll find him and when I do..."

"I'm so sorry."

"What about you, Violet? You're not safe in Swaffham."

"I know. I've put my cottage up for sale, and I'm moving back here."

"To Bury?"

"Yes."

"For good?" His heart fluttered with a faint ember of hope which died just as quickly as unbidden thoughts of Lily doused the flame.

Violet nodded.

"That's good," he said.

"Perhaps I can help you with the business?"

"I'm not interested in the business. It can go to hell and back, for all I care."

"I need to tell you something."

"What?"

"The reason I left."

"You've already explained it. I thought you left because of me, but it was Francis' behaviour that worried you."

"Yes. But there was more to it."

"I didn't marry Loveday, you know."

"I know now, but only since Michael told me last week. It's changed everything."

"I don't see why. Loveday and I parted ways over three years ago, and she married Tom Melcham. The fact that you've just found out is neither here nor there."

"Oh, but it is. There is something I would have told you many years ago had our circumstances been different."

"Violet. I'm more pleased to see you than I can say, but you're speaking in riddles, and it's exhausting."

"When I left to visit my aunt, it wasn't just to spend time with her. I went away for a long time if you remember."

"An exceptionally long time, and on two separate occasions. I missed you, Violet. More than you can imagine. If you'd been with me, I would never have – well, you know."

Violet nodded. "I know. It was unavoidable. Too many secrets. If I'd told you when I first suspected, it could have been very different."

"Suspected what?"

"I fully understand the depth of your grief, and this may be the wrong time to tell you. It's risky. But there may never be a better opportunity. I don't know, and all I can do is take a chance. You think you're childless..."

"I don't think I'm childless – I know it. I had a daughter, and now I don't."

"But you do, Lawrence. You do."

Violet stood and walked to the door, opened it, and beckoned beyond. Then taking a deep breath, she turned to face Lawrence, her fingers entwined in the pale hand of a little girl, clad in a pretty pink dress. Dark-haired and elfin-faced, the child looked nothing like her mother. But the resemblance to her father was unmistakable.

"This is Daisy," said Violet pushing her forward. The child reached out and touched Lawrence's arm.

His eyes filled with tears and his heart swelled as he clasped her little hand. Then he reached for Violet, and they clung together, heads bowed and united, at last.

## THE END

# AFTERWORD

## *Afterword*

I based the Moving Stone on a strange tale initially reported in the *East Anglian Daily Press* in June 1981. It concerned the unusual alignment of a stone cross belonging to Ella Morse. The stone, now broken, still lies in St Peter and St Paul's churchyard in Swaffham. At some stage, members of the clergy reorganised the churchyard, moving the older stones into straight lines. One day, the church sexton, Mr Frank Sandell, noticed the misalignment of Ella's stone during his walk from his house to the church. Seizing the initiative, he took measurements from the cross to a fixed point, proving that the stone had changed position. It continued to move for another seven years. The newspaper report described the grass around the base of the cross as flattened and bearing evidence of a twisting action. The cross itself had turned a full ninety degrees and faced north to south, contrary to every other stone in the churchyard.

Once reports of the unusual activity hit the press, theories about Ella Morse abounded. The church contains a glass window dedicated to Ella Morse. Some suggested that her family purchased it to ease their conscience about their ill-treatment of her as no other family member had received such a tribute. Other theories touched on witchcraft or whether Ella might be mad. Ideas ranged from the sublime to the ridiculous, the most outlandish being that someone else occupied her grave and was trying to get out.

The truth, of course, is more prosaic. Ella Morse died on 14th September 1852 from an ovarian tumour. It's easy to trace her family history, which reveals that she was the daughter of John Morse and Ann Howes who died within six weeks of each other in 1830. John Morse was a well-regarded brewer and left his business to Ella's brother Arthur when he died. Ella and Arthur appear on the 1851 census records and lived together at 2 London Street, Swaffham, Arthur employing twenty-two men at the brewery.

Sadly, all but two of the Morse children did not make old bones. Anne and Philip died as children and Caroline and Marian as young adults. Henry Porson Morse died off Dungeness on a voyage from Melbourne, and Herbert Morse drowned in Emsworth harbour while trying to rescue his friends. They were twenty-eight and thirty-one years old, respectively. Ella and her brother Arthur died within four years of each other, followed by their sisters Jane Edwards in 1860 and Isabella Rose in 1880. Only Margaret Morse lived a full life span, dying in the Lake District in 1903 aged eighty-two. So, it's fair to say that the Morse family did not have an easy time of it.

But, if nothing else, establishing the provenance of the glass window dedicated to Ella Morse was relatively simple. Ella left a will – a very difficult to read will, as it happens, but presented well enough to see that she paid for the window herself. She also provided bequests to the church to move the organ to a superior position and increase the salary of the church organist. God-fearing and generous, Ella Morse left money to the poor of the parish and funded societies to spread the gospel abroad. However, her will was not straightforward and contained a statement at the end from her brothers, Arthur and Herbert. They jointly made an oath about a section of the will in which Ella used pencil for some names leaving gaps in the document. The brothers could not explain the missing words, but they identified the pencil marks as Ella's writing, and they proved the will in the normal way.

Swaffham has been the focus of several hauntings over the years. One concerns a ghostly woman seen walking in the churchyard as if looking for a headstone. Another reports a figure who appears in the back garden of a cottage near Northwell Poll. There were many tragedies in Ella's life, but none of sufficient magnitude to bind her to this earth as an apparition – unless you know better. If you have any theories on Ella's stone or the West Ham disappearances, I would love to hear them. You can contact me or find out more about my books on the website below.

Join my mailing list or visit my website
https://jacquelinebeardwriter.com/

Like my Facebook page
https://www.facebook.com/LawrenceHarpham/

If you have a moment, I would be grateful if you could leave a quick review of The Moving Stone online. Honest reviews are very much appreciated and are useful to other readers.

Also, by this author:

Lawrence Harpham Murder Mysteries:

The Fressingfield Witch
The Ripper Deception
The Scole Confession
The Felsham Affair

Short Stories featuring Lawrence Harpham:

The Montpellier Mystery

E-book Box Set containing
The Fressingfield Witch, The Ripper Deception & The Scole
Confession

Novels:

Vote for Murder

Printed in Great Britain
by Amazon

79841729R00142